THE HARBINGER

WENDY WANG

Copy right

Copyright © 2018 by Wendy Wang

All rights reserved.

No part of this book may be reproduced in any form or by any electronic or mechanical means, including information storage and retrieval systems, without written permission from the author, except for the use of brief quotations in a book review.

v1.2

❋ Created with Vellum

For my own little Coven who supports me through thick and thin and preorder deadlines - Paula, Helen, Gwen, Vicki, RA and MK. Love you all, Witches!

CHAPTER 1

There wasn't a cloud in the bright, blue sky when Charlie Payne shifted in her lounge chair. The strong June sun shone down, burning the tops of her feet, so she curled her legs up, drawing her pink painted toes beneath the shade of the large red umbrella towering over her chair. She dropped her book onto her lap and took a deep breath of warm sea air. She loved beach days. They were a rare treat lately with her busy work schedule, making time for Evan, her psychic readings and helping Lieutenant Jason Tate on missing person cases.

A high-pitched half-scream, half-laugh pierced the roar of the ocean, and a smile tugged at Charlie's lips as she watched her eleven-year-old boy boogie boarding in the surf with their six-year-old cousin Ruby. A prickle of intuition in her stomach caught her off guard as Evan flipped off his board and stood up in the surf. A wave broke around the backs of his legs but he didn't buckle against its force. The grin he'd been wearing since they'd arrived a couple of hours ago morphed into a grimace. Charlie sat up straight in her chair.

"Evan," she called over the rumbling of the waves and wind. Maybe the boy had been stung by a jelly-fish. The cloudy pink and brown floating blobs tended to wash up on shore this time of year. She'd been stung many times as a child just playing in the surf. "Evan, are you all right?"

Her cousin Jen stirred on a lounge chair just out of the umbrella's shadow. Jen pushed up on her elbows and then lay flat again as if remembering she'd untied the strings of her bikini to avoid tan lines. Quickly she retied the strings and pushed up from her stomach to sitting.

"What's going on?" she asked in a groggy voice, rearranging the triangles of black and white fabric to make sure her small breasts were fully covered.

"Not sure." Charlie hopped to her feet. Every hair on the back of her neck stood at attention when she stepped out of the shadow of the umbrella and into the hot sunlight. She waved her arm to get her son's attention but he didn't seem to see her. His unbroken gaze was centered on something else on shore. Charlie followed his line of sight. A trickle of sweat traced its way down her spine and she shivered despite the eighty-five-degree heat.

A dark shadowy form moved along the edge of the water. It had no shape but flickered in and out, the way a bad television signal did. Charlie's feet started to move before she could even engage her brain. By the time she was halfway between their spot on the beach and the water the spirit had taken form.

"Jen," Charlie called over her shoulder, her voice strident. "Do you see it?" She didn't wait for her cousin's response. Instead she picked up her pace and used her long legs to their full advantage. Evan stood frozen in the water, a look of terror in his blue eyes. Charlie walked past the apparition of the woman, pretending not to see her, waving her arm.

"Evan! Ruby! It's time to get out of the water."

Ruby ignored Charlie and tried to ride another wave. The spirit floated over the water, moving closer to the children. Her body was almost opaque and she no longer had a shadowy quality. If the spirit hadn't been hovering, Charlie might have mistaken it as a strangely dressed beach goer on a hot Saturday afternoon in June, but the dark energy emanating from the spirit galvanized Charlie from the inside out.

Every nerve in her body cried out, "Danger! Danger! Danger!"

Charlie waded into the water, slogging through the

fast-coming waves that splashed against her shins. "Evan Lucas Carver! Get out of the water right this minute."

The sound of his full name shook him from his stupor and Evan turned his gaze to his mother. Confusion filled his tanned face. He started out of the water, stopping only to gather Ruby, kicking in protest, and her boogie board.

"Mom?" Panic fluttered in his voice.

"It's okay." Charlie called up a soothing smile. "Don't worry, I'll make it go away." Evan's gaze flitted toward the spirit and a storm of fear crossed his handsome features.

"It's okay, sweetie." Charlie brushed her knuckles over his cheek and he locked eyes on her face.

Evan set Ruby down and grabbed her free hand. His gaze flitted to the spirit and back to his cousin. "Come on, Ruby, let's go."

Ruby jerked her little hand out of his and gave him a pouty stare. She whined, "I don't wanna go. Please Charlie?"

Charlie opened her mouth, trying to find the right words. Ruby's innate magical talent had shown itself early, but to Charlie's knowledge, she'd never been one to see spirits. She didn't want to scare the girl. Jen's voice carried over the roar of the waves and wind, calling the children out of the water.

Charlie raised her eyebrows and gave Ruby a pointed look. "Your mama's calling. You better go on now."

Ruby pressed her lips together and narrowed her wide, blue eyes into a death stare. The image of Ruby as a teenager, full of defiance flashed through Charlie's head while she watched the little girl wade forward, sullen and dragging one corner of her boogie board across the ripples of water and white foam.

Evan grabbed Charlie's hand, giving it a quick squeeze. "Be careful, Mom."

"I will, baby. Go on now," she said. Evan had shown signs of being sensitive since he was very young but it had intensified in the last year. He'd had dreams that had come true. But seeing spirits? The idea that he'd inherited that particular "gift" made her feel sick. She watched the two children hurry toward Jen who was standing halfway between the lounge chairs and the water, shielding her eyes with her hand. Charlie gave her cousin a reassuring wave, took a deep breath and headed toward the spirit, taking care to avoid an incoming wave and negotiating the shifting sand beneath her feet.

As Charlie approached, the spirit sank into the water up to her ghostly knees. Her long, flowing blue dress floated in the shallow surf. In her hands she held a large square of lace and her ghostly fingers worried over one frayed corner. Charlie pressed her hand against her belly, quelling her nerves.

"Hello there."

The spirit turned to face her. In life she must've been

stunning. The spirit's pale blonde hair was swept up into an elegant bun at the base of her head but tendrils of loose curls blew around her shoulders. Sharp green eyes stared at Charlie and she had a quizzical look on her face. The way the spirit held her bow-like mouth, Charlie could tell this was a woman used to getting her way. Even in death.

"Hello," the spirit said with caution. "I didn't see anyone else on the beach today. I'm looking for a ship. Have you seen a ship in the distance?"

"No." Charlie shook her head. "I haven't seen any ships today."

The spirit's skin shimmered and her forehead wrinkled. A frown tugged at the corners of her mouth and she made a huffing sound in the back of her throat before she shifted her gaze back to the horizon. Charlie drew closer.

"I'm Charlie." She moved directly beside the spirit and turned to face the water too. Thankfully it was not too rough of a day for the waves. "What's your name?"

"I'm Vanessa." The spirit's voice whispered across Charlie causing the skin of her arms and back to break into goose bumps. She wasn't sure which was more dangerous in this case — staring directly at the spirit or not looking at it head on.

"I've been waiting for days and days. Papa says I shouldn't worry, but he doesn't understand."

Charlie shifted her gaze to the horizon but still

watched the spirit from the corner of her eye. It seemed the safest choice.

"Understand what?" Charlie prodded lightly.

"I see things. Know things that others don't." Vanessa wrung the lace in her hands. "Do you know what I mean?"

An icy finger touched Charlie's heart and she nodded. "Yes, I do know."

"It makes it hard not to worry." Vanessa stared out blankly over the water. In the distance thunder rumbled and Charlie noticed gray clouds gathering on the horizon. She fought the urge to run. To scoop up her son, Ruby and her cousin Jen and get the hell out of town for the next week or two. Something inside her wouldn't let her leave, though.

"What did you see?" Charlie asked, but she already knew the answer. It was how the myth surrounding this particular spirit was born.

Vanessa Carnahan had been the daughter of a wealthy merchant in Charleston. She had been beautiful but was known to be eccentric and moody. Charlie had always suspected that the woman had been psychic in life.

"I saw my fiancé's ship tossed on powerful waves." Her high voice sounded distant and other-worldly as she recalled her long ago vision. "He's on a trip for my father you see. France. He's going to bring me back something special. But I just can't get that image out of my head."

The spirit let out a shuddery sigh.

Charlie's stomach tightened into a knot. "Did you see it sink?"

The spirit's head jerked in an odd way and her pale eyes glowed unnaturally, her stare boring into Charlie.

"No!" The ghost shook her head. "I refuse to believe it."

"I know this story." Charlie's voice shook. "My cousins and I used to scare each other with it any time a tropical storm or hurricane came this way."

"I don't know what you're talking about." Vanessa bristled.

"Your fiancé died in a storm over a hundred and sixty years ago," Charlie said.

"No." Vanessa's pale face darkened with anger. She twisted the ring on her left hand. "That's not true. It can't be. He said he'd return to me. He promised."

"I'm so sorry but it's true. And you ... your grief is legendary."

"What?" Vanessa's voice softened, sounding like a scared child. "What do you mean?"

"When you learned he had died, you were overcome. Legend is you walked into the ocean in your wedding dress and drowned yourself," Charlie said. Her heart ached for this spirit who could not let go of this world, or her sadness, even now. "I can help if you let me. I help people like you find peace."

"No. No. No. You're a lying ... witch!" Vanessa gritted her teeth, and her pale, mournful face shimmered. The bright sunny day vanished and the light changed to drab flat, gray. Charlie noticed the clouds had advanced quickly. A cool sprinkle of raindrops fell, their ripples joining the shin-deep water.

"I can see you," Vanessa said. "I can see right through you. You should keep your own house in order before judging mine. Otherwise, it could all disappear in a storm."

The words 'just like mine' hung on the air between them, remaining unsaid but felt. The hair on Charlie's arms rose and thunder rumbled closer.

"Please Vanessa," Charlie said. "Let me help you. Aren't you tired of being stuck here all alone? Waiting?"

Vanessa's face melted into tears and she opened her mouth. A high-pitch shriek surged from her open maw, piercing through the wind. Charlie's bones and teeth ached from the vibration and she covered her ears, trying to block the sound. When the wailing stopped, the spirit charged at Charlie, leaving her no time to react. A sharp, icy pain stabbed through Charlie's chest with enough force to knock her off balance. She fell backwards into an oncoming wave and for a moment she was pulled underwater. The undertow yanked her down, deeper into the surf. Her knuckles scraped over the sandy bottom and she struggled against the vacuum effect of the retreating wave. Unable to breathe, her lungs burned and she kicked her feet, finally breaking through the churning surface. She coughed and spit up the sharp, salty water. Her lungs expanded with several breaths and she headed back to shore, letting the next wave carry her.

"Mom!" Evan splashed into the surf and grabbed her by the arm, dragging her forward. The water receded, leaving her on the sand, coughing. Evan slapped her on the back. Jen knelt in front of her.

"Come on. A wave's coming. Can you walk?" Jen asked.

Charlie nodded and let her son help her to her feet. The three of them headed across the sand to Ruby who was standing next to two folded lounge chairs and the closed umbrella. Charlie's canvas tote was slung over the tiny girl's shoulder. The concern on Ruby's face seemed at odds with the bright pink beach towel wrapped around her shoulders.

"Mom, what happened? Is everything okay?" Evan asked.

"Everything's just fine, baby," Charlie said leaning on him. She looked squarely at her cousin. "We should go, though."

"Absolutely. You sure you're okay?" Jen asked.

"I'm sure." Charlie gave her cousin a reassuring smile

then threw a glance over her shoulder. Darker clouds hung on the horizon. The wind kicked up and the waves churned. Charlie fought the shudder threatening to course through her. "We need to get out of here. There's definitely a storm brewing."

Jen nodded and picked up her chair.

Charlie swallowed back her unease and painted a smile across her face. She grabbed her umbrella and chair. "So who wants ice cream? My treat."

* * *

THE SOUND OF HER SON'S SCREAM PULLED HER OUT OF HER dream and Charlie almost fell out of bed. The hardwood floor felt cold against the bottoms of her bare feet as adrenaline coursed through her bloodstream. She rounded the small space between their two bedrooms and flipped on his wall light. Evan was sitting up and staring at the footboard of his bed.

"What happened, sweetie? Did you have a nightmare?" Charlie asked.

She was plagued with nightmares and did not find it unreasonable that she may also have passed a tendency for bad dreams on to her son. The way she had passed on her blonde hair and, especially after the day's events, her unusual sensitivities to the world around them.

"There was a chicken in here!" he said running his

fingers through his short blond hair. His eyes darted as if he were trying to look everywhere at once. "I know I wasn't dreaming it."

Charlie glanced around the room. "You must've scared it when you screamed."

"Mom, why is there a chicken in the house?"

Charlie sat on the edge of his bed and sighed. "Do you remember a couple months ago when all of Ruby's chickens got killed?"

He nodded. "Yeah."

"Well one of them decided it didn't want to move on. She's been hanging around the cottage ever since."

Evan grimaced. "Mom, that's creepy."

"Yes, it is sometimes. I just can't figure out how to help the poor little thing. It's not exactly like I speak chicken."

"You are so weird," Evan said burying his face in his hands. "Can't you just open the door and shoo her out, like a ..." he paused, his lips twisting with disgust, "like a live chicken?"

"No, it doesn't really work that way. And she's kind've gotten me out of a couple of tight spots so I'm not really in a rush to get rid of her. I figure she'll pass on when she's ready," Charlie said studying her son's worried face. "So you wanna tell me what really woke you up? I don't think it was the chicken."

Evan's shoulders heaved up and down as he took two

deep breaths. "I had a dream about that girl. The one we saw on the beach."

"I'm sorry, sweetie. You know I said we didn't have to talk about it until you were ready but I think maybe we need to. I think that's the only way that you're going to find any sort of comfort or peace." Charlie placed her hands on his leg and gave it a squeeze.

Evan's fingers worried over a loose thread on the quilt. "How old were you? The first time you saw a ghost."

Charlie stilled his hand. She had hoped that they would never have to have this conversation. Wasn't it enough that he had inherited her ability to sometimes sense the future? Did he really have to be plagued with seeing the dead as well? It didn't seem fair. Some part of her wished that he had inherited his father's stubborn ability to ignore things even when they stared him in the face.

"I was a little younger than Ruby," she said.

"And you weren't scared?" He looked up at her and there was something in his face that needed her to tell him ghosts weren't scary. Just like she had been unable to tell him that monsters weren't real when he was little, she wanted more than anything to tell him not to be afraid. That all spirits were lost in their own way and deserved their pity. And most did. But some ... some should be treated with caution. Some were downright dangerous.

"Actually I wasn't scared because it was my sister.

She'd been sick, and I just thought she had come home from the hospital. It wasn't until later that I found out that she had died," Charlie said.

"I knew you had a sister that died but I didn't know she came back," Evan mused.

"Well she did. And it wasn't scary. I think it was her way of saying goodbye to me," Charlie said. "Not every encounter has to be scary. You get to control how you feel when you're around a spirit. The calmer you are the better. They can feed off of your energy. If you're fearful, it can make them more powerful. You understand?"

"I think so," he said. A frown wrinkled his lips.

"What did your mom and dad say when you told them?"

"I never told my mom. She...she wouldn't have understood and somehow I knew that even when I was small."

"What about your dad?"

"I did tell him, and he got very upset. He told me to never tell anybody. It wasn't until after he and mama died and I went to live with my Gramma Bunny that I learned it wasn't something to be scared of or ashamed of," she said. "Although that last part was the hardest thing to learn."

"Yeah." Evan's face became thoughtful. "I can understand that."

"Listen, I don't want anybody to ever make you feel that you are wrong or bad or crazy for seeing and feeling these sorts of things. And that includes your dad."

"We shouldn't tell him." Panic filled his voice and he shook his head. "It would just make him mad."

"Sometimes your dad's first reaction when he's scared is to seem angry, even when he's really not. So he's probably not really mad, just scared. Does that make sense?"

"Yeah, I guess," Evan said.

"You know your dad loves you to the moon and back, right? He'd do anything for you."

"I know," Evan said.

"He hasn't given you a hard time lately, has he?" Charlie asked.

Evan hesitated but his lips curled up into a smile and he shook his head. "No, he's actually been pretty nice to me about this sort of stuff."

"Good. I'm glad to hear that." Charlie smoothed the blanket around Evan's feet. "You think you're ready to go back to sleep now?"

"Yeah. I think so." Evan scooted back down and pulled the sheet and summer quilt up to his chin.

Charlie bent over and kissed him on the forehead. "Sweet dreams, kiddo."

"Night, Mom," Evan said. Charlie made it to the door and started to flip the light switch when Evan called to her. "Hey, Mom."

"Yes, baby?" she said looking at him over her shoulder.

"Please don't tell Dad. I know you say he won't be mad but..."

"I really think he should know, Evan."

"Then I'll tell him. Okay?"

"You promise?" Charlie asked.

"Yeah, I promise," he said.

Charlie waited a beat, feeling out her son. No bells went off in her head indicating he was lying. She gave him a weary smile. "Okay, then that's fine. As long as you tell him."

"Thanks." He closed his eyes.

Charlie gave her son one last look, then surveyed the room to make sure everything was in order. When the copper-colored chicken materialized in the corner of the room sitting on the back of the rocking chair, she brought her index finger to her lips.

"You keep quiet, Penny."

The chicken let out a soft cluck and disappeared again. Charlie turned off the light.

Jason glided along the top of the glassy water, his skis barely bouncing. He hadn't been waterskiing in over five years, but once he'd gotten up on his feet, his muscles remembered what to do. The boat clipped along at a nice pace and he relished the light briny spray in his face.

What a great day to be out on the water. The sun shone in the late morning sky against a nearly solid blue background. A few white puffy clouds gathered out near the horizon but it was nothing to be worried about. A perfect Sunday afternoon.

His lady, Lisa Holloway, looked at home behind the wheel of her father's twenty-four-foot deck boat. Her strawberry blonde ponytail whipped in the wind and the strings of the yellow bikini tied around her delicate neck glowed against her lightly tanned and freckled skin.

Sitting next to her in the passenger seat with a beer in one hand and a small yellow flag in another was his oldest friend Cameron Reed. He and Jason had shared a major of Criminal Justice and been friends since their freshman year of college nearly eighteen years ago now. Both joined the police force after graduation. Somewhere along the way though, they'd each gotten opportunities to grow their careers; Jason joined the Charleston County Sheriff's office as an investigator and Cameron joined the FBI. Still it didn't dampen their friendship. They talked regularly on the phone and spent vacations together sometimes. This year had been hard on Cameron, though. His wife, Caroline, his college sweetheart, had left him six months before. Cameron seemed to be taking it okay, better than he probably should have. It made Jason wonder if his friend believed somewhere deep inside that he deserved to be left because he was never home and when he was, he was consumed by his job. Caroline had gone looking for comfort and love elsewhere.

Jason shifted his gaze from his friend back to Lisa. They'd been doing this "whatever it was" for nearly two and a half months now. She was smart and pretty and they were like-minded in so many ways it scared him a little but not as much as it seemed to scare her.

Her cousin Charlie had warned him that Lisa could be skittish. So he had done everything in his power to keep himself in check. But it was getting harder and harder not to fall in love with her. Not to fall in love with the whole damn coven of them actually. Not only did he love being with her, he loved being with her family and the way they had welcomed him in.

Cameron stood up, chugged back the rest of his beer and tossed it into the paper bag behind Lisa's seat. He moved closer to Lisa and rested his hand on her shoulder. He leaned in as if to tell her something and pointed off toward the right side of the boat. Even at this distance Jason could see Lisa's body stiffen as she nodded. Cameron had said something that had put her on notice. Jason scanned the wide expanse of the inlet looking for the thing that might have alarmed Cameron. In the distance three jet skis driven by what looked like teenagers crisscrossed the inlet, cutting each other off and jumping their own wakes.

Lisa threw a glance over her shoulder at Jason. He waved and her round face lit up with a smile. His chest flooded with warmth. How he'd gotten so lucky, he didn't know.

Cameron looked back too but there was something in his expression that sent off warning bells in Jason's head. It was the look of awareness of imminent danger. He heard Cameron yell but couldn't make out the words. The boat veered sharply to the left and Jason was no longer behind it but headed straight for the side of the boat. His heart leapt into his throat. A long wake of water sent him flying upward. But he landed without his legs splitting or losing his balance.

Lisa stood up in her seat and turned the wheel sharply back to the right, sending another set of waves his way. From the looks of it, she over-corrected and he didn't quite have time to shift his body to compensate. Water rushed over the top of his skis. The rope in his hand tugged forward and he felt himself start to lose his balance. He forced himself to let go of the rope, and continued to sail forward a little ways, the water slowing him down. His skis sank and he fell backward, letting his life vest do most of the work of holding him up.

Lisa threw a glance over her shoulder and turned the boat about, slowing down as she neared him floating in the water. She drove up alongside of him, careful to maintain a good ten feet between him and the boat as she shifted the engine into neutral.

"Are you all right?" Her lightly tanned face was flushed and her green eyes blazed with guilt.

"I'm fine." Jason pushed his wet bangs off his forehead. "What happened?"

"I'm so sorry," she said. "Two kids on jet skis cut right across my path and I had to turn to miss one of them. You sure you're okay?"

"Yeah," Jason said. "I'm good."

"You want to keep skiing?" Lisa asked.

The three jet skiers raced past their boat, and Jason bounced up and down like a buoy. He drifted away from the boat several yards because of the wake and got the brackish water in his nose and his mouth. Lisa pulled the boat closer, presenting the stern to him. She cut the motor and Cameron made his way down to the narrow swim platform on the back of the boat. Cameron bent down and hauled in the ski rope. Once he had the handle he tossed it to Jason.

"Hang on to it and I'll pull you in," Cameron called. Jason took the handle and let Cameron pull him close to the boat, then hopped up onto the platform and removed his skis. Cameron held out a hand for his friend, helping Jason to his feet.

"Damn kids," Cameron said, a smile playing at the corners of his mouth.

"Damn kids," Jason said smirking. It was an old joke between them. Harkening back to when they were in college and serious about their studies when no one else seemed to be.

Jason and Cameron climbed into the rear of the boat. Jason propped his skis up against one of the seats and ran his fingers through his wet hair pushing it off his face.

"You sure you don't want to ski anymore?" Lisa asked. She handed Jason a towel and he began to scrub his hair dry.

"No, I think I'm done for the day." His stomach growled loudly and he pressed his hand to his abdomen. "I think what I really want to do now is eat."

"That sounds like a plan," Cameron said.

"We could find a place close to shore. Jen packed some sandwiches for us," Lisa suggested.

"That sounds good," Jason said, wrapping the towel around his waist and tucking it into the top of his swim trunks. Lisa started the engine and found a spot near a sandy embankment then dropped the anchor. Cameron and Jason made their way to the front deck seats while Lisa opened up one of the many compartments and pulled out a small cooler. She put it on the floor in front of the men and then went back into the driver's area and grabbed a tote bag that had a roll of paper towels, some paper plates and two different bags of chips to choose from. Cameron slipped a beer from the larger cooler on the floor board and offered one to Jason.

"Not with my head still spinning from last night," he said. "I'll just take soda."

Lisa grabbed a diet soda and took a seat next to Jason. She unzipped the small cooler and peered inside the hard plastic compartment. "Looks like I've got ham, turkey and roast beef. Who wants what?"

"I'll take ham if you don't want it, then you can take the roast beef," Jason said to Cameron trying to veer him away from the turkey, which he knew was Lisa's favorite.

"Roast beef sounds great," Cameron said.

"I think you'll really like this," Lisa said, handing Cameron the sandwich wrapped in wax paper. "Jen made it with horseradish mayo and blue cheese crumbles."

She took the ham sandwich and gave it to Jason and put the turkey sandwich on her lap. Jason sorted the paper plates and Lisa pulled out two plastic containers — one with freshly made coleslaw and the other with a mix of berries. She opened the chips so that Jason and Cameron could help themselves then began to unwrap her sandwich.

"This is from the restaurant that we went to the other night?" Cameron asked after finishing his first bite.

"Yep," Jason said. He took a bite of his ham sandwich, savoring the fresh roll, the bite of grainy mustard mixed with mayonnaise, and the tang of the Swiss cheese against the sweetness of the ham.

"This is really good," Cameron said with a nearly full mouth.

Jason nodded and took another bite. In the driver's compartment a familiar ring tone began to sound. Lisa gave Jason an irritated look.

"Don't worry," Jason said. "I'll get rid of him." He put his plate down on the seat next to him and grabbed his phone from Lisa's canvas bag behind the driver's seat. He scowled at the picture of his partner displaying on his small phone screen and pressed the green answer button.

"I know you're not calling me on my vacation," Jason said.

Beck sighed. "Well since I couldn't get to you telepathically like your girlfriend there, I didn't have much choice."

"There's only one choice which is not to call. So bye," Jason quipped.

"Wait! Don't hang up! He's back." The urgency of Beck's tone and his words sent a chill skittering across Jason's shoulders.

"That ain't funny," Jason said in a low growl.

"Good. I wasn't trying to be. We have another angel," Beck said in a low serious voice.

The damp hair on Jason's neck stood at attention and

he straightened up. His smile faded, weighed down by the heaviness that filled his cheeks.

"Shit," Jason muttered. "You sure?"

"I'm staring right at her. So yeah I'm pretty sure. I know you have your buddy visiting but I need you on this."

Jason nodded as he spoke, "We're out on the water. It'll take at least an hour to get back to the dock and then ... where are you?"

"I'm out near Ravenel."

"That'll be another forty-five minutes so we're looking at least two hours."

"I'm not going anywhere."

"Yep," Jason said. The line clicked and Jason tucked the phone back into Lisa's bag. He took a deep breath. He dreaded looking into Lisa's beautiful face and asking her to hang out with Cameron. The guy was his oldest friend and he trusted him not to do anything untoward with Lisa. But he knew Lisa wouldn't want to babysit either.

"What did Beck say?" Lisa asked, sitting up straight. There was a wariness in her face and voice. They'd only been together a couple of months but he recognized the concern.

"One of our cases has gotten intense. It looks like we have another victim," Jason said.

"And Beck can't handle it without you," Lisa said flatly.

"Yeah," he said. "I'll just go to the crime scene and check it out. I promise I'm not gonna get embroiled in this thing, at least not until I get back. Would you mind hanging out with Cameron for the rest of the day?"

"Wait," Cameron interjected. "This is the second victim?"

Jason shook his head. "Third. Assuming it's tied to the other two. Beck seems convinced but —"

"Do you want me to help? I mean this is my area." Cameron sat up on the edge of his seat balancing his plate precariously on one knee.

"How many beers have you had?" Jason asked.

"One and a sip."

"I don't know," Jason said. "Last thing I want is anybody questioning the sheriff's department and their professionalism."

"Well I don't work for the sheriff's department. Need I remind you that I work for the FBI and serial killers are in my wheelhouse? So I wouldn't reflect poorly on you at all. We consult on cases like this all the time," Cameron said sounding almost excited.

"Okay," Jason said. "But that's the last of that beer."

"Do we at least get to finish our sandwiches?" Lisa asked.

"Can we drive and eat?" Jason said warily.

Lisa's mouth pressed into a flat line. "Fine."

She took another bite of her sandwich before wrapping it back up and putting it into the cooler. Her shoulders slumped a little as she rose and got behind the wheel. The engine cranked to life and she maneuvered them back onto the main thoroughfare of river traffic.

Jason gave her a smile and continued to eat his sandwich. He would make it up to her. Take her someplace fancy in Charleston for dinner one night. Just the two of them. Jason pointed to Cameron's plate. "Better eat up. I don't know how long this is going to take."

CHAPTER 2

Jason pulled his Dodge Charger behind one of the parked sheriff's cruisers. He and Cameron hopped out and were met by a deputy that seemed to be waiting for them.

Jason acknowledged him. "McCleary, this is a friend of mine from the FBI. What have we got?"

"Two boys out squirrel hunting noticed some buzzards flying up above. They thought it might be cool." McCleary made air quotes with his fingers. "To go shoot at the buzzards, sir."

"What happened?" Cameron asked.

"They found a body, sir," McCleary said. "I'm afraid the sight of it made them wet themselves. They ran all the way home and called the sheriff's department."

"Whose property is this?" Jason asked. McCleary led them across a ditch and into the dense grove of pine trees.

"The owner's Carl Harper," McCleary said. Pine needles crunched beneath their feet as they walked through the pine forest. "He owns about twenty-five acres out here for hunting and recreation. His son Jordan is the one that found the body."

"How old's Jordan?" Jason asked.

"He and his friend Neil Bellows are both fourteen. They got quite a scare I'm afraid."

"I'll bet they did. They've probably never seen a dead body before," Jason said.

"Yes sir. Especially not one like this," McCleary said.

Cameron scowled and lightly punched Jason in the arm making him look at him. He mouthed, "What's he talking about?"

"You'll see," Jason said softly. "Is the coroner here yet?"

"Yes sir," McCleary nodded. "They're working the scene now and we've got a forensics team combing the area for evidence."

The woods opened into a clearing and in the center was a large fire ring made of rocks. Thin, evenly spaced lines led away from the body, toward the ring of rocks, spreading ash and charred wood across the sandy dirt. The coroner knelt next to the naked body of a young woman. Jason drew closer and stepped into the ring. A sour taste bubbled in the back of his throat and he stopped at her feet, peering down at her. No wonder the boys had wet themselves. Her corpse had been laid out in the center of the ring. Her arms had been tied together at the wrists with gold ribbon and folded across her chest like an Egyptian pharaoh. Purple marbling spread across her gray skin and there were chunks of tissue missing. Some of the gashes were so deep he could see the yellow-white bone. Stretched behind her was a pair of meticulously crafted black wings. Her long reddish blonde hair had been braided and coiled around her head, making a halo. Two gaping black holes in her face where her eyes used to be, stared up at Jason.

"Fuck," Jason said under his breath. His lips twisted with disgust. "Where are her eyes?"

The coroner pulled a yellow tarp over her body and the thin balding man stood up and put his hands on his hips. "Buzzards got to them."

Jason focused on the coroner's skinny, sallow face. Cameron sidled up next to Jason and said nothing. The expression on his face said it all. He was as disgusted as Jason felt.

"So what've we got?" Jason said.

"She's out of rigor. Been here at least thirty-six hours or so and you can see, she's been picked over by the critters," the coroner said.

"Great," Jason scowled.

Jason's partner, Marshall Beck stalked over from outside the fire ring. "Well it took you long enough."

"Really? You're bitching 'cause I'm late when I'm on vacation? I told you we were out on the water," Jason said.

"I don't have anything else to bitch at you about at the moment," Beck said. He glanced down at the tarp-covered body. "Come on, let's go someplace we can talk."

Jason nodded and followed Beck to the outer ring. "So it looks like the others. Body brought in and posed."

Jason pointed to the pattern in the sandy dirt. "The raking is new."

"Yep but it's about the only new thing. I've had these guys combing through every pine needle and rock within a 500-yard radius and they haven't found shit," Beck said.

"You mentioned others. How many?" Cameron asked.

"You must be the FBI friend," Beck said eyeing Cameron with caution. "I'm assuming you're here in some sort of official capacity?"

"If you need my help you have it," Cameron said. "This just happens to be my area of expertise."

"Well, that's convenient," Beck said his tone full of sarcasm.

"Actually it's fucking lucky," Jason said. "Saves me from having to make a call."

"Did he set up the fire ring?" Cameron asked.

"Nawp. According to the boys that found her, the fire ring has been here for years. They come out on holidays and have a big cookout and a bonfire. The boys said they haven't been out here since New Year's Day," Beck said.

"Who has access to the property?" Jason asked.

"We're waiting on the owner to come down to find out more," Beck said.

"I'd like to be in on that interview," Jason said.

"You got it," Beck said.

"I'm not paying you overtime for this," the sheriff said sidling up next to Jason.

"Yes sir," Jason said chuckling. He knew what the sheriff said and what he meant were two different things sometimes. "Sheriff Bedford, I'd like you to meet Special Agent Cameron Reed. He's a friend of mine from way back and he's agreed to help us with the case."

"Well we really appreciate that," the sheriff said extending his hand out to Cameron. The two men shook hands, and the sheriff cracked a half-smile that Jason had seen only on a few occasions.

"Well I'm here to help sir," Cameron said.

"We appreciate that," the sheriff said. "Whatever y'all need you let me know."

"Thank you sir," Jason and Beck said in unison. The sheriff tipped his hat and headed back to speak with the coroner.

"Well, he seems like a nice guy," Cameron said.

"Yes, he is unless his dander's up," Beck said. "I hate to pull you off vacation but I could really use you on this."

Jason put his hands on his hips and sighed. There was no way he was going to just go back to his vacation. "Hopefully, Lisa will be able to forgive me."

"You're on your own there, buddy." Beck clapped him on the shoulder. "Come on, let's do this."

* * *

THE CLOCK ON THE WALL READ 8:30 P.M. WHEN JASON taped the picture of Bethany McCabe to the oversized whiteboard and wrote her name beneath it. He did the same with pictures of Ruthanne Coker and Ginny Garrity.

"Our third vic's name is Bethany McCabe," he said.

"She was a thirty-year old nurse at St. Frances Medical center in West Ashley. Family reported her missing six days ago." Jason pointed to the picture of the slim strawberry blonde, standing on the edge of a precipice, wearing climbing gear, glowing, her arms in the air celebrating her accomplishment of scaling the rock face below.

Jason fought the churning in his stomach as he looked into these women's faces, and knowing their fates. Beneath the photos he wrote the words, No crime scene.

"The only physical evidence we have is what we found on the bodies, which isn't much of anything. He thought of everything. Each body was washed thoroughly before being dressed and posed."

"So he's organized," Cameron said. "And he obviously has someplace private to take them."

"Yep," Jason said.

"What's the timeline?" Cameron asked.

"Three months ago, Virginia 'Ginny' Garrity disappeared from the parking lot of Palmetto Beach after an argument with her boyfriend. She turned up two days later – same as our latest victim – posed."

"As an angel," Beck added. He sat at the end of the conference table with three accordion file folders in front of him. Each folder held all the pictures from the discovery scene, and the pertinent reports.

Beck looked frustrated as he paged through the photographs. Cameron half-leaned, half-sat against the edge of the conference table staring at the whiteboard. "Go on."

"Six weeks later, Ruthanne Coker disappeared after leaving her job as a waitress. She turned up the same way our first vic did. Posed as an angel."

"And now Bethany." Cameron scrubbed the stubble on his chin. "Well he definitely has a physical type. Anything else they have in common?"

"None of them were high-risk," Jason said. He pointed to the first photograph. "Ginny Garrity was a grad student at Charleston College. Ruthanne Coker was a single mom, putting herself through culinary classes at the local tech school and working as a waitress downtown at night."

"You said the first victim disappeared after a fight with her boyfriend?" Cameron asked.

"Yep," Jason said.

"And he wasn't good for it?" Cameron asked.

"Nope," Beck said. "We looked at him pretty hard, but it ended up they were fighting because he was drunk. She left him on the beach where he promptly passed out. We have a report from a sheriff's deputy that he found him and ticketed him for unlawful camping."

"What about the second victim?" Cameron asked.

"We have a witness that has her leaving her job around eleven PM on a Thursday night headed for home but she never got there. Her mom took care of her son while Ruthanne worked. It wasn't until the next morning that her mom discovered that Ruthanne never came home. Her mom thought maybe she'd gone to see a boyfriend and didn't think much about it."

"It had happened before?" Cameron asked. "Did you ever find a boyfriend?"

"No we didn't. It wasn't till late the next day when the boy's daycare called asking when someone was going to pick up the boy that she realized something was really wrong."

"So she left work," Cameron said. "What happened to her car?"

"We never found it," Beck said. "It's like she drove off the face of the earth."

"The only theory we had is that she stopped for gas or had a flat tire and was targeted by the suspect. But we have no proof of that."

"Hmm," Cameron continued to stare at the board as if it might suddenly reveal answers none of them had seen before.

"But he still posed her." Cameron mused.

"Yep." Jason glanced up at the board. "What I don't understand is why. Why an angel?"

"Maybe he's a religious nut," Beck said.

"Maybe. Angels are messengers of God. But what's the message he's trying to send?" Jason asked.

"Maybe, or maybe this is his way of preparing them for the afterlife," Beck said.

"Maybe ..." Cameron said. "Did Bethany live out this way, too?"

"No, she lived out near Ravenel, where we found her. It's about thirty-five to forty minutes from here."

"But Ruthanne lived out on John's Island, correct? With her parents?" Cameron said.

"Yes. Lots of people live out past West Ashley 'cause it's cheaper. Quieter," Beck said.

"Yeah and supposedly safer," Cameron said. "So . . . How did she disappear?"

"She had met some friends after work for happy hour. Then she headed home and vanished, until today."

"Were the restaurants of the last two victims close together?" Cameron asked.

"Nope. Ruthanne's restaurant is down on Market Street in the middle of the Charleston hubbub." Jason tapped the map on the wall of the county, pointing to the peninsula "And Bethany met her friends at Mickey O's, a sports bar and restaurant on the way out of West Ashley." He moved his hand down the map, touching the suburb.

"And there's no connection? No overlap in their lives. No common vendors or staff at the restaurants. No ..." Cameron made a gesture with his hand as if to roll things along.

"None the we could find," Jason said.

Cameron blew air out through his lips and scowled. "And another pretty redhead disappears."

"Yep," Beck muttered.

"Was there anything at all in the parking lot where the first victim was snatched?" Cameron asked.

Jason gave Beck a pointed look. "Nope. It's not well lit, and according to the boyfriend, it was deserted."

"All right." Cameron fiddled with a marker, popping the cap on and off a few times. "So this guy has a very specific type and he doesn't seem to be in a hurry. He's controlled and organized and obviously has someplace private where he can hold these women. How long does he keep them again?"

"Two days, then he kills them and poses them," Jason said.

"Not sure. I may see if I can consult with the BAU in Quantico. See if they have any insight to what all this means," Cameron said.

"In the meantime, we just have to keep working it," Beck said. "I just wish we knew where he was taking them."

"My question is why no one saw anything or heard anything when these women disappeared. People pull out their phones for everything these days." Cameron took a seat in one of the chairs and leaned back with his hands behind his head.

"Well if someone recorded it, they didn't report it. We got nothing on the security cameras for the restaurants. Both women left the parking lots in their cars." Jason stretched, and rubbed his neck with one hand. "Once he abducted his target it wouldn't be too hard to disappear with her." He turned to the map of the county hanging on the wall again. "You have a lot of population around Charleston but people thin out the further you go out. And if he has a barn or some sort of workshop."

"Which would make sense," Beck said. "He not only

needs a place to keep her but a place to construct those wings."

"That's a good point. We're talking about somebody who's pretty skilled as a welder," Cameron said. "Have you looked at that angle?"

"Yeah, but it's more than just a welder. The frame is expertly crafted. Along with the leather, there are metal feathers on the wings that have been hammered and polished. I talked to an old blacksmith I know and he was really impressed with the wings. Said it would need somebody who really knew 'smithing," Jason said.

"Okay, that's good information," Cameron said. "We just need to know what goes into that sort of operation."

"Well you need a forge and anvil and some hammers for starters," Beck said. "And a place to do it of course."

"How many manufacturers are there of forges and hammers and anvils?" Cameron asked.

"Too many to narrow things down. And a lot of times anvils are handed down or they're made by the blacksmith," Jason said. "And anybody with a garage could do it. Hell there are YouTube videos that show you how to make an anvil from a block of steel."

"It's just as well. Until we understand what ties all these victims together, we're not going to get a clear picture of this guy or how to find him," Cameron said. "I mean, were they all victims' of circumstance? Or did he target these specific women? There has to be more to it than the way they look. The way he poses them is careful, reverent."

"Almost personal," Jason added.

"Yep. Exactly. Do we have a list of friends and family and ex boyfriends, ex-employers?"

"Yeah, we do," Beck said, sounding tired. He rubbed the back of his neck. "Probably not exactly how you wanted to spend your vacation is it?"

Jason rolled his eyes. "Well hopefully Lisa will forgive me. She took off this week, too."

"I'm sure she will," Beck said. "She's one of the good ones."

"You know I've been thinking ..." Jason began.

"Oh hell ... that can't be good," Beck chided.

"Maybe I should talk to Charlie," Jason said. "She's really good at ferreting out information."

"Good God man, there's nothing hinky going on here, other than your run of the mill psychopathic behavior." Beck scowled. "Can't we just treat this like a normal case?"

"Fine." Jason twisted his lips with disdain. "If you're that opposed."

"Who's Charlie?" Cameron asked.

"She's Lisa's cousin," Jason said. "You'll meet her Friday."

"Lisa's psychic cousin," Beck interjected. "You ask me, there's something weird about that whole family. Except

Lisa. She's the most normal."

"I guess it's a good thing nobody asked you," Jason sniped.

Cameron rolled his eyes. "A psychic? Really? Come on. You're kidding me, right?"

"Nope," Beck said.

"Shut the hell up, Beck," Jason's face flushed with heat. "She's helped me close more cases in the last eleven months than you have."

"A psychic." Cameron shook his head.

"What?" Jason snapped.

"I'm just surprised. That's all. It's kinda out there for you."

"Well, she's the real deal. Out there or not, " Jason said. He shrugged. "And I trust her."

"What about you Beck? You trust her?" Cameron asked.

Beck smirked. "Trust? I don't know about that. She's more of a last resort to me, unless you want something fine to look at."

"All right, that's enough," Jason said.

"Yeah? She as pretty as Lisa?" Cameron pushed further.

"Oh yeah. Her ass isn't as tight though. She's got a kid," Beck said.

"Enough! Why don't you do something useful like go

order us some dinner instead of being such a jackass," Jason said.

Beck laughed and pulled his cell phone out of his pocket. "Looks like I hit a nerve."

Jason leveled a glare at Beck and his partner rolled his eyes without apology. Beck turned his attention to his phone and thumbed through his contacts.

"So, what do y'all want? Pizza, Chinese or sandwiches?" Beck asked.

"Pizza," Cameron and Jason said at the same time.

CHAPTER 3

On Sunday evening after Charlie dropped Evan off at his dad's for the week, she stopped at the funeral home as she passed through town on her way to her cottage. She pulled around back of the new modern-looking building and parked next to Tom's black Ford Fusion. Butterflies fluttered in her stomach as she got out of her car and headed for the rear entrance, the one only employees used.

The building was locked but Tom had given her the code and she punched it into the keypad. The door clicked and she pulled on the stainless steel handle, letting herself in. The cool air slapped her in the face and some part of her always thought she expected to smell chemicals but she didn't. Instead, a clean lavender scent hung on the air. It must've been some sort of deodorizer but it wasn't cloying. A strange sense of calm settled over her and she wondered what else might have been in the scented mix. She also wondered if Jen had helped him.

She made her way down the darkened carpeted hallway toward the offices. A beautiful young woman with dark hair rounded the corner with a folder in her hand. She looked up, startled at first, then a smile spread across her face.

"Charlie," she said her voice sounding excited. "What a nice surprise."

"Hi, Joy," Charlie said, offering up a smile. Like Tom, Joy was a reaper. She didn't quite understand the intricacies of their relationship, but Tom always insisted that Joy was his sister. Just like William was his brother. It brought to mind so many questions for Charlie. Like who were their parents? Or did they just band together as supernatural creatures for protection? Maybe working together in groups made it easier to carry out their duties. One day, Charlie would ask Tom these questions. As soon as she worked up the courage.

Joy moved closer, almost gliding across the floor. "Tom didn't say anything about you visiting tonight."

"No," Charlie said, almost regretting her decision to stop by on a whim. "I was just in the area and thought I would pop in. He gave me the code to the door." She stammered and jerked her thumb behind her.

"Yes, I believe he mentioned that," Joy said. She settled

in beside Charlie and hooked her arm into the crook of Charlie's elbow. "He's downstairs working on Margaret Farrington. Why don't you come wait in his office and I'll go get him."

Joy tugged gently on Charlie's arm moving them forward, heading them toward the short hallway of offices.

"Okay, thank you," Charlie said wanly. "How have you been, Joy?"

"Oh, I'm good," Joy said.

"I never see you out and about in town like I do Tom. You don't work all the time, do you?" Charlie asked.

"Sometimes it feels that way. I'm not quite as fond of mingling as Tom is. I find humans a little tedious sometimes. Not you, of course. No offense."

Joy said no offense in a breezy way that made Charlie think that it was more something Joy had learned to say than something she really understood or believed.

"Of course. None taken." Charlie chuckled. "Sometimes we humans are tedious as hell."

Joy flipped on the light to Tom's office and led Charlie inside. She gestured to the leather chair sitting in front of Tom's desk and smiled. "Make yourself comfortable."

"Thanks," Charlie said.

"He'll be up in a jiffy."

Joy tossed her long, perfectly groomed chestnut hair over her shoulder. How long had it taken Joy to master the language of humans in a way that didn't make them question the goose bumps on their skin when speaking with her? Did she choose such a beautiful facade because it disarmed and charmed at the same time? These were the questions swirling in Charlie's brain as she watched Joy give her a smile then disappear down the hallway.

Charlie had never been in Tom's office alone before. She scanned the shelves along the wall beside his desk. There were various books on funeral directing and embalming methods along with a magazine holder filled with magazines about what's new in the industry. There were also little personal mementos that she didn't expect to see. Among them was a small carved angel with no face. Its black polished surface made her pick it up and cradle it in her hands. It felt cool against her skin, like stone but it wasn't heavy. She flipped it over, looking at the bottom to see where it had been made.

"It was a gift," Tom said. "Hand carved ebony wood."

Charlie's heart hammered its way to her throat and she pressed her hand against her chest. She turned and gave him an impish grin. "You caught me red-handed I'm afraid."

He smirked. "I'm surprised you haven't been nosier."

"Ha ha." She threw a glance at the bookshelf and put the figurine back in its place. "Well I see you're not keeping your book of souls on the shelf with your embalming and funerary books."

Tom moved into his office, closing the door behind him but he didn't take his eyes off of her. "This is a lovely if unexpected surprise. Is everything all right?"

"Yes, of course. Everything's fine. I just ..." Charlie swallowed hard, gathering her courage. "I was just wondering if you would like to go on a date with me."

"A date? A real date?" Tom cocked his head and narrowed his dark amber eyes. His voice full of wariness.

"Yes. A real date."

"I don't know what to say," Tom said.

"Yes is usually customary. Unless you aren't really interested and if that's the case ..." Charlie's voice cracked and her cheeks flamed with heat. "Maybe I misjudged things. I ... um ... I should probably just go." She looked away from his face and took a step toward the door.

"I didn't say no." Tom laughed and stopped her in her tracks. He put his hands on the tops of her arms and squared his body with hers.

Charlie gazed into his face and her stomach flip-flopped. She knew he was presenting a façade. A mask for the world. But dammit, he was so beautiful, especially when he smiled. It made her heart hurt just to look at him.

"There's just one thing I want to know before I say yes, though." The wariness in his voice returned.

"Okay." Charlie shifted her weight from one foot to the other and tried to swallow away the dryness in her throat.

"Why all of a sudden you want to take me on a date?"

"It's not really sudden," Charlie protested. "And I guess I'm just tired of waiting for you to ask. You search me out all the time. Want to go for walks or have lunch at the café. It feels like there's this energy between us that's more than just friends but maybe I'm wrong. Maybe ..." She struggled to meet his unwavering gaze..

"You're not wrong. I feel it too," he said in a silky whisper. "I just haven't wanted to rush you. So ... what would you like to do?" His brows knitted together framing the quizzical look on his face. "Dinner? A movie?"

"Picnic," Charlie said.

"Picnic?" he asked.

"Yes." Charlie gave him a resolute nod.

"A picnic is perfect. I can't even remember the last time I went to a picnic. Maybe half a century ago?"

"Well my dear, that's kinda sad," she teased.

"Indeed it is." His mouth curled into a grin. "When shall we go on this picnic?"

"How 'bout Tuesday? I don't have to work. And I noticed there weren't any obituaries for a Tuesday service." She smiled at him.

"You did your homework. I'm impressed." He moved closer. "Do you have Evan this week?"

"No, he's at his dad's." Charlie inched forward until the toes of her shoes touched the toes of Tom's boots. His breath was warm on her face and it smelled sweet and sharp like spearmint. Would his lips taste like Wrigley's gum? Her cheeks blazed with heat at the thought.

"Tuesday it is then." His gaze darted to her lips and she thought for sure he would lean in and press them to hers.

Charlie's purse began to ring and buzz at the same time, breaking the spell. She stepped back and gave him an apologetic look. "Sorry, I have to take this. It could be Evan."

"Of course," Tom said.

Charlie reached into her bag for her phone. A photo of Jen holding a piece of pie in one hand and a fork in the other filled her screen. Her cousin wore a mischievous grin on her face. Charlie pressed the green phone icon.

"Come eat ice cream," Jen yelled into the phone.

A chorus of other voices echoed behind her. "Yes, come eat ice cream."

"Hello to you too," Charlie said. "Sounds like y'all are having a party."

"Evangeline's been testing ice cream recipes all afternoon and brought over the results. This strawberry lavender ice cream is to die for." It sounded like Jen had taken a bite of the frozen treat. The rest of her words were a little garbled. "Why don't you come over and join us on the back porch."

"I would," Charlie laughed and glanced at Tom a little embarrassed. "But, I'm not at home."

"Hang on," Jen said. Charlie heard her swallow the rest of her ice cream. "Sorry about that. I figured you were on your way home from dropping off Evan," Jen said.

"Yeah, I am," Charlie said.

"What's wrong with your voice?" Jen asked, her tone full of mischief.

"Nothing. Nothing's wrong with my voice." Charlie cringed at the defensive rise in her tenor.

"You are lying to me," Jen laughed. "Are you with a boy?"

"No ... it's none of your business where I am," Charlie snipped.

"Y'all, Charlie's with a boy."

In the background Lisa and Daphne whooped and shouted things like, Hot to Trot and Safety First - wrap that man up! Charlie squeezed her eyes shut. There was no way that Tom didn't hear them. Charlie gave him a furtive glance and he was politely looking anywhere but at her. The corners of his mouth twitched with a grin. Oh yeah, he heard.

Charlie covered her eyes with her hand and whisper-yelled into the phone, "I swear y'all are so immature sometimes." She cleared her throat and regained her composure. "Um, let me finish up what I'm doing and I'll be there in a little while, okay?"

"Okay," Jen said sweetly but Charlie could hear the amusement in her cousin's voice.

Daphne's voice rang through in the background, "Don't finish up too fast. Where's the fun in that?"

"Tell Tom we said hey," Jen said snickering. A peal of laughter echoed in the background.

"Hush up witches," Charlie said.

Jen snorted into the phone and the line went dead.

Charlie took a deep breath and blew it out then tucked her phone back into her purse. "Sorry about that."

"No worries." Tom's lips curved up.

"Jen says hey by the way."

"Yes," Tom nodded. "I heard."

"They're taste testing recipes, so I think they're a little buzzed on sugar."

"Ah ..." Tom nodded. His gaze settled on hers again and she couldn't look away. "So Tuesday?"

"Tuesday. Twelve PM sharp."

* * *

CHARLIE PARKED HER CAR IN FRONT OF THE SMALL COTTAGE she rented from her uncle on the edge of his property. She tucked her keys in her pocket and walked across the wide green lawn to her uncle's large, white clapboard house. The yellow bulb of the porch light shined, casting her cousins, Jen, Lisa, and Daphne as silhouettes. Their voices and laughter carried across the yard, beckoning her, and she picked up her pace.

The sharp chemical smell of DEET smacked her nose halfway up the stairs. A soft buzzing close to her ear preceded a quick sharp bite to the back of her neck. Charlie slapped at the culprit and pulled her hand back. The bloody corpse of the flattened mosquito clung to the skin of her fingers and she twisted her lips with disgust. She stepped onto the back porch and wiped away the offensive little bug on her jean shorts.

"You better spray yourself down." Jen pointed to the bug spray on the table between the rockers where Daphne and Lisa sat. "Or you might just be eaten alive tonight."

Charlie took the small dark green canister and gave her arms, legs and neck a good dose of the repellent. It may have smelled awful but it did a good job of keeping the bugs away. She would have to take a shower before she went to bed to wash off the oily residue.

"Isn't there a spell to banish mosquitoes?" Charlie asked.

"Probably," Ben Sutton said from the screen door that led to the kitchen. In his hands he held two small bowls of ice cream.

"Hey, Ben, I didn't realize you were you here," Charlie said dropping her purse onto the floor next to an empty rocker. Ben Sutton had come to town to help Charlie find a witch selling illegal curses. But that had been almost two months ago. She thought he would have left as soon as they found her, but he stayed because of Jen.

"In the flesh," Ben said.

"Hey, y'all," Charlie said. Daphne continued to lick a scoop of vanilla ice cream, but she raised her hand in an acknowledging wave. Lisa gave her a perfunctory smile. She held an empty ice cream bowl in one hand. "So why can't we just get rid of the mosquitoes?"

"Well, because even though the spell may seem like it's doing you some good by getting rid of the bugs, they actually serve a purpose in the larger ecosystem. You start with a spell like that you're going to throw things out of balance." Ben pushed open the screen door and let it slam behind him.

"Ben," Jen said stridently. "Ruby's sleeping."

"Sorry." He smiled at her contritely and handed her a fresh bowl of ice cream.

"That looks good," Charlie said pointing to the ice cream in Ben's bowl. "What flavor's that?"

"Something called ..." Ben glanced at Jen with the help me out look.

"It's peach melba ice cream. It is soooo good," Jen said scooping up a little of her own and slipping it into her mouth.

"Okay, great. I'll have some of that. Is it in the freezer?"

"Mmmmhhmmm," Jen nodded.

"Come on, Lisa," Charlie called as she headed inside. "Why don't you come with me?"

"I think I've had my fill," Lisa said.

"So you can come inside and keep me company then," Charlie said.

"Okay." Lisa frowned, confusion wrinkling her brow. She got up from her chair and followed Charlie into the kitchen.

Charlie grabbed a bowl from the stack on the counter and opened the freezer. There were five white plastic containers on the shelves. Charlie pulled the first one she saw and read the strip of masking tape on the plastic top. Mimosa sorbet. It sounded delicious. She took the small container, placed it on the counter and grabbed the ice cream scoop from the drainer. After a quick rinse with a little warm water, Charlie popped open the top of the container and formed one perfect, small scoop of the golden orange-colored ice.

"So what's going on with you and Jason? I thought y'all were spending this week together. How come he's not here?" Charlie asked.

Lisa took her empty bowl to the sink and washed it up. Charlie watched her cousin's slim shoulders draw up slightly with a deep breath and then deflate. "He caught a case."

"How did he catch a case? He's on vacation," Charlie

said. She scooped a little ice cream into her mouth and let it slide down her throat. "Oh my God. Bubbles."

Lisa placed her bowl in the drainer and turned, resting against the counter with her hands behind her back. "Evangeline thought the bubbles would be a nice touch I guess."

"A spell?" Charlie mouthed. She glanced towards the door. Had her Uncle Jack gone to bed?

"He's not here, and yeah I think so," Lisa said.

"So where's Uncle Jack?"

"He's actually out on a date."

Jack's sprawling family of females, daughters, granddaughter, nieces and sister-in-law Evangeline, filled up some of the hole left when he was left a widower many years before. It had never occurred to Charlie he would want for the company of a woman at his age.

"A date with who?" Charlie asked.

"Marva Ackerman," Lisa said. "They don't really date per se as much as they ..." Lisa made a pumping motion with her fist. "You know."

"Ewww ... stop that. I don't need that in my head. Thank you very much."

"Yeah, none of us do," Lisa cracked a smile.

"How long has that been going on?"

"Oh they've been sleeping together for years. But this is the first time I've ever known him to actually take her out." Lisa shrugged. "At least somebody's getting laid tonight."

Charlie took another bite of her ice cream and regarded her prickly cousin with care. Lisa's irritation felt like a poorly done glamour, a spell meant to mask reality. But the edges of Lisa's misery shone like light leaking around the door. If Charlie went too touchy-feely Lisa might scoff and dig in hard behind her anger. But if she didn't apply some sort of pressure, her cousin would slide into nonchalance. Both would be a lie.

"I'm sorry Jason abandoned you. He shouldn't have done that."

"It's all right," Lisa said. "He has a job to do. I know that. And it's important. I don't think he would've given up his vacation for just any old case."

Charlie's senses pricked up. "Really? Do you know what it is?"

"A murder?" A dark shadow crossed Lisa's face. "I don't want to be too gossipy but he asked his friend Cameron to help."

"Right. The FBI guy."

Yep," Lisa nodded. "You know about him?"

"A little."

"They were roommates in college. After seeing them together, I can see how they ended up being friends. Same interests. Same super straight-laced approach to things," Lisa said.

Charlie chuckled. "You know I always think of Jason as having sprung from the head of Zeus as a thirty-four-year-old man. I cannot imagine what he was like when he was a freshman in college."

"I've seen pictures. He was cute. A little nerdy, but he still had those sharp, cynical eyes." Lisa's lips stretched into a thoughtful smile.

"I have no doubt he's had them since he was a toddler," Charlie quipped. "Why do you think he asked the FBI guy to help?"

"Evidently it's an ongoing case. Other girls have been murdered."

"Is that what he said?" Charlie asked. "Did he say how many?"

"Two I think," Lisa said.

"Hmmm," Charlie took another small bite of sorbet.

"You should try this strawberry lavender. It really is delicious," Lisa said.

"I don't know. I was kind of thinking about that peach melba," Charlie said.

"It's really good, too," Lisa said but something in her tone didn't quite convince Charlie.

Charlie walked over and stood next to Lisa, pressing against her cousin's shoulder. "I'm sorry he hasn't called. Are you worried?"

"No," Lisa said. "I'm just disappointed that's all. We

had plans. And now we don't. I'll probably just go back to work myself."

"No, don't do that," Charlie said. "You deserve time off. And goddess love him, you don't need him to have fun. Especially when you've got us. I've got a light schedule this week. We should plan something."

One corner of Lisa's mouth curved up. "Like what?"

"There's a new spa that supposed to be opening up in West Ashley. I heard a commercial for it on the radio today. We should try it out. Go get facials and massages and pedicures. The works," Charlie said, letting her hands animate her excitement.

"That sounds kinda good, I guess. Although I think Daphne has a massage therapist in her salon now."

"She does, but between you and me," Charlie lowered her voice. "She's not that great. Let's just go be pampered."

"Okay. I like that." Lisa nodded. "When do you want to do it?"

"Can't be Tuesday because I'm taking Tom on a picnic. But I've only got a couple of shifts at the call center and aside from a few personal readings, I'm free for the rest of the week after that."

"A picnic? Sounds romantic," Lisa mused.

"No. It sounds corny, but I figured we've been spending all this time together and … well things just haven't progressed much. So I bit the bullet and asked him on a date."

"Good for you." Lisa nudged Charlie with her shoulder. "I think that's great. He's still creeps me out a little, but as long as he makes you happy."

"Thanks." Charlie sighed. "I'm gonna get some more ice cream. You want some?"

"Naw, I'm good. I'm gonna head out. Put on my pajamas, snuggle up with Butterbean and watch some Netflix." Lisa pushed off from the counter and headed out.

Charlie went back to the freezer and perused the other flavors. The screen door creaked. "I don't see the peach melba. You got me all excited about it. You better not have been pulling my leg."

"Hey, Charlie," a familiar voice said.

Charlie looked up to find Jason Tate standing near the door. She smiled. "Lisa just left. Did you pass her on the way in?"

"Yeah, I did. I'm gonna swing by her house later. But that's not why I'm here." He wore a somber expression on his ruggedly handsome face. Dark lavender shadows beneath his eyes spoke volumes about how much sleep he'd gotten last night. "I left you a voice mail. Did you get it?"

Charlie closed the freezer door and turned to face him. "I didn't. I'm sorry. What's going on?"

"I need your help. What's your schedule like tomorrow?"

"Busy. I have to work till three. Are you okay?" Charlie stepped closer.

"Yeah, I'm fine I just —"

"Lisa said that you were going back to work instead of taking your vacation," Charlie said. "I figured it must be bad for that to happen. Especially since you were so excited to be spending the week together."

Jason's shoulders lifted with a heavy breath and then sagged as he blew it out. "Yeah, I'm going to have to make that up to her."

"Yeah, you are," Charlie said. " So, what's going on?"

"I need you to check out a victim's house. Can you meet me tomorrow?" Jason asked.

"Sure. If we can do it after work."

"Yeah, I should be able to swing that," Jason said.

"So you want to tell me about it or —"

"The only thing you need to know is that the victim is dead," Jason said.

"Is this the latest victim?" Charlie asked.

"No, the second victim. Unfortunately the first victim didn't live here and her folks cleared out all of her stuff a couple of months ago," Jason said.

"Okay. Why aren't we starting with the latest victim?"

"Listen, I'll tell you anything you want to know after you see the house," Jason said.

"That's fine. I understand," Charlie lied. She knew he didn't want her to infer anything from him but that's not what this felt like to her. It felt more secretive. She shook off the feeling and smiled.

Jason had a faraway look in his eye for a few seconds and Charlie couldn't tell if he had his mind on the case or his missed time with Lisa. He brought his gaze back to her and said, "I just need a fresh set of eyes."

"Isn't that what your FBI friend is for?" Charlie asked.

"Yeah but he can't do that thing you do," Jason's face softened and he smiled. "We'll see what you find, if anything."

"Okay. You want some ice cream? Evangeline was experimenting with flavors all day and sent home several for us to try."

"No, thank you," Jason said. " I better go smooth things over with my girlfriend."

Charlie cracked a wide smile and chuckled.

"What?" Jason said.

"Nothing," Charlie said. "Go. Get out of here before she gets into her pajamas and snuggles up with the cat. Once she turns on the television I don't think you'll have much of a chance."

Jason's lips curved into a sly half-grin. "Don't you worry about me and my chances."

Charlie snickered. "Oh I never do. Text me tomorrow."

Jason gave her a nod, then turned and disappeared through the screen door.

CHAPTER 4

Charlie sat in traffic on I-526 when her phone rang. She glanced around at the other drivers who looked just as frustrated as she felt and dug her phone out of her purse. Jason's photo greeted her and she pressed the green phone icon.

"I'm on my way," she said. "There must be an accident or something on 526 because I'm sitting in traffic. Seriously, nothing is moving."

"No worries," Jason said. "I'll stall until you get here. Be careful."

"I will," she said. The phone clicked in her ear and the line went dead. She turned on the radio and scanned through the channels, listening for any news about what could be holding up traffic.

"It's gonna be hot, hot, hot the rest of the week, so stay

tuned folks to find out more. Up next, the local weather," a man's smooth, practiced voice said right before a tire commercial began to play.

Charlie stopped drumming her hands against the steering wheel to listen. After two more commercials, one for a new urgent care center and another for a local restaurant, the weatherman resumed.

"It's hurricane season. Are you ready? Because we've got what could become the first tropical storm of the season forming out in the Atlantic, folks. Two tropical depressions pushed off the coast of Africa overnight. We'll be keeping a close eye them as they make their way across the ocean and you can count on us to keep you updated on what they become and the track they take. Here's your friendly reminder to put together your family's hurricane kit and update your evacuation plan for the season. You can get a Hurricane Preparedness Checklist from our website at WROC979.com. Download your copy today and —" Charlie switched off the radio.

Tropical depressions headed into the Atlantic a lot this time of year. She would keep an eye on it, but knew that it was way too early to know if it would even head this way or not. Still the apparition's words rang through her head.

You should keep your own house in order before judging mine. Otherwise, it could all disappear in a storm.

She wished she could shake the feeling that something was coming. Something bigger than anything she had faced before. Something completely out of her control.

Finally, without warning, traffic began to move again. Charlie took her car out of park and rolled forward heading towards West Ashley.

* * *

CHARLIE STARED AT THE LITTLE YELLOW FARMHOUSE WHERE the victim had once lived. The property sat a few miles off of Highway 165 and out here were long stretches of pastures between wooded breaks. There wasn't a neighbor within shouting distance and she closed her eyes trying to gauge the energy of the house, searching for some sign that a spirit might be clinging to this place.

A bead of sweat started at her hairline and traced an itchy path down her cheek. She opened her eyes and swiped away the wetness. Nothing. She sighed and got out of the car. Jason stood up from the top step of the porch and waved. An uneasiness bloomed in her chest when a tall, dark-haired man she had never seen before stood up next to him. The man had large brown eyes and he seemed to observe her with curiosity and something else she couldn't quite put her finger on. Dealing with a new person's energy could be exhausting and she had a job to do. She took a deep breath and touched the black tourmaline stone hanging around her neck.

"Sorry I'm late," Charlie said, the weathered boards creaking under her feet as she climbed up to greet them. "Traffic was a bear."

"No problem," Jason said. "I appreciate you coming out all this way."

The man with dark hair cleared his throat. Jason gave him a quick sideways glance. "Charlie this is Cameron Reed."

"Right, you're the FBI friend." She regarded him with care. Suspicion radiated from him. The uneasiness she'd felt a few moments ago transformed into a cold seed of dread that planted itself in her gut.

"I am." Cameron smiled but it never touched his eyes. His hand jutted forward and he held it there waiting for Charlie to shake it. She forced a smile and her eyebrows rose as she shifted her gaze to Jason. He gave her a short nod and placed his hand on top of Cameron's gently pushing it down.

"Charlie doesn't like to shake hands," Jason said quietly.

"Does that get in the way of her mojo or something?" Cameron's lips twitched at the corners.

"Nope." Charlie kept her face as neutral as she could. Picking a fight with someone who clearly didn't believe in the supernatural was akin to screaming into the wind.

But his smug tone dug into her like a pebble in her shoe. "But it does let me see things about people. Hidden things. And Quite frankly, it's been a long day and I've spent it listening to complaining customers so please forgive me, if I'm not really up for dealing with whatever nasty spirit or wound to your psyche is clinging to you this afternoon. I need to save my energy if I'm going to help Jason with this." She gestured to the house.

"What the fu—" Cameron started.

"Would you excuse us for second, Charlie?" Jason cut him off and pushed Cameron toward the other end of the porch.

"Sure," Charlie said. She toed the top of a nail head that jutted up from the porch and tried not to look at them as they argued in loud whispers. After a few minutes of back and forth, Charlie blew out a breath and walked over to them. "Listen, I've been up since five o'clock this morning and I just sat in traffic for almost forty-five minutes. I'm really not in the mood to listen to y'all snipe at each other like two old biddies. Why don't you call me when y'all have worked out whatever this ..." she waved her hand over them and frowned, "is. Okay?"

"Charlie, please don't leave. I'm sorry," Jason said.

"Yes, Charlie. Don't. Leave." Cameron's mimicry of Jason and the way he inflected Jason's words made Charlie's fingers twitch. Some part of her wanted to reach out, grab him by the arm and pull out whatever secret most haunted him so she could throw it back in his face. Maybe a little shock would put him in his place. It had worked on Jason. But the more rational part of her knew this was never the best way to deal with those who didn't believe. And if she were being honest, it would do nothing but drain her energy and aggravate her if he still acted like a jerk, which she suspected might be his normal modus operandi.

"Stop it Cam. Please Charlie," Jason pleaded.

"Fine," Charlie said. The stress and weariness of the day settled into her body pulling her shoulders down. "But my patience is thin. Don't test it."

"Thank you," Jason said. He knocked on the door and an older woman with a kind, round face answered.

"Hey, Ms. Coker. How you doing?" Jason asked, flashing his best sympathetic smile.

"It's good to see you deputy." She stepped back from the door. "Why don't y'all come in from the heat?"

Jason wiped his feet on the faded plastic Wipe Your Paws doormat and led them inside. He took off his mirrored sunglasses and tucked them inside his breast pocket.

"Is there any news?" Ms. Coker took them through a pair of open French doors into a large and tidy parlor. The carved, tufted sofa looked antique but it fit perfectly atop a faded Persian rug. Two Queen-Anne style chairs with a coordinating fabric sat across from the sofa, facing the large windows that overlooked the small front yard. Two horses roamed the high grass of the pasture beyond the front yard while a third sought shelter beneath a run-in shed near the edge of the fence.

"No, ma'am. I'm afraid not," Jason said.

"Oh," Ms. Coker said. Her round face deflated with disappointment and she bit her bottom lip.

"But just so you know, we're working really hard to find the man that hurt your daughter."

"I know you are," Ms. Coker patted Jason's arm. "I appreciate all you've done for us Lieutenant. "

A pang of admiration squeezed Charlie's heart. Jason could always be counted on. It was one of his best traits. Sure, he could pour on the charm when needed but he shined when dealing with the families of victims. She hoped one day when he retired that he would become some sort of victim's advocate. He would be good at it.

Ms. Coker let out a soft sigh and pressed her hand to her heart. "Can I get y'all some iced tea? I just made some this afternoon."

"Yes ma'am that would be wonderful, thank you," Jason said.

"None for me, thank you," Charlie said, giving her a polite smile.

The wrinkles around her mouth deepened and she gestured to the dainty furniture. "Y'all have a seat. I'll be right back."

Jason and Cameron traded uncertain glances but each took a seat in the delicate chairs facing the couch and windows. Charlie opted to walk around the edges of the room, admiring the Americana artwork, the collection of leather bound books and the bric-a-brac on the floor to ceiling built-in shelves flanking the French doors. She held her hand out, running it above various figurines and music boxes filling the middle shelves, gathering as much information as the energy of this old place would give her. The thing that struck Charlie most was the lack of dust. She reached out and ran a finger across the shelf in front of her and brought back nothing. The poor woman must spend her whole day cleaning.

Charlie moved on to the other side of the door and came to a shelf with various pictures. It appeared that Ms. Coker had built a little shrine to her daughter, complete with a half-burned tea candle and a gold cross on a chain hanging across a framed graduation photo. Charlie could smell the homey scent of vanilla still lingering and she wondered if that was her daughter's favorite scent.

To the right of the frame was a little statue of Jesus holding a lamb and opposite Jesus was a smaller picture frame holding a cross-stitched version of the Lord's prayer. Charlie touched the small gold cross and the image of Mrs. Coker standing in front of this photograph filled her head. Every day the old woman lit the candle, bowed her head, and said a prayer for her daughter's soul right before asking God to cast the man who did this into hell. Charlie understood the woman's feelings. If someone did to Evan what had been done to the woman's daughter, she would hunt that person down and hand him over to the devil himself, if that's what it took.

"Here we are." Mrs. Coker rounded the corner carrying a tray with the pitcher of iced tea and three glasses. She set it down on the marble-topped coffee table and took a seat at the sofa.

"I'm sorry I'm out of lemon." She picked up the first glass and handed it to Cameron, then handed the second glass to Jason. "So what can I do for you?"

Jason took a sip of tea and placed it on one of the coasters on the coffee table. He leaned forward in his chair and rested his elbows on his knees, folding his hands together. "I need to see Ruthanne's room again."

"All right, but y'all have already been through it twice. Last time they left a mess," Ms. Coker said.

"I know and I'm real sorry about that. This time's a little different." Jason glanced up and gestured for Charlie to join them. "See, this is Charlie Payne. She's a consultant that we bring in sometimes to help out. I promise she won't leave the room in a mess."

"And you think it will help find the man who hurt Ruthanne?" Mrs. Coker's voice shook and she regarded Charlie with caution.

The cracks in this woman's carefully constructed

world began to show, starting with the dark shadows beneath her eyes. Her tidy house. The freshly ironed blouse and shorts she wore. Even the perfect curl of her short, silver hair. In her world, there was a place for everything and everything had its place. The only problem? There was no place for ritualistic murder. It didn't fit neatly on a shelf next to family photos or among her collection of cute Hummel figurines.

Words like murder did not have a place in this house and certainly not in Ms. Coker's mind. Charlie could feel her thoughts as they moved around the dark center of her daughter's death, feeling their way along the edges, never getting too close. People lied to themselves all the time. Sometimes it was what made life bearable. Charlie could feel Ms. Coker's lies to herself.

Her daughter was hurt not murdered. She died. She wasn't raped repeatedly then killed and raped again. She was hurt. She wasn't left to the elements and the animals like some sort of sacrifice. Ruthanne was missing. Ruthanne was hurt. Ruthanne had passed away. Simple euphemisms that allowed Ms. Coker to get out of bed in the morning. Those words echoed so loud in the woman's head that Charlie wanted to cover her ears.

"I do." Jason offered up the sympathetic smile.

Ms. Coker's forehead wrinkled with worry and she let out a sigh. "All right then. When you finish your tea I'll be happy to take you up to her bedroom."

"Why don't y'all finish up your tea and I'll go check out her room," Charlie said to Jason. "You can have a good visit with Ms. Coker."

Jason sat up straight in his chair and nodded. "Yes, that's a great idea. Why don't you go on up and take a look around."

"All right," Ms. Coker said, her voice straining.

"I can wait if you would prefer," Charlie said, as gently as she could.

"No," Ms. Coker said. "It's fine. Come with me dear."

Charlie traded a look with Jason then followed Ms. Coker into the foyer and up the staircase that wound its way through the three-story farmhouse. They walked together side-by-side on the wide steps until they got to the landing for the second floor. Ms. Coker rounded the walnut banister and walked along the balcony that overlooked the first floor. The very last room on the right was closed. Ms. Coker pulled a key from her pocket and unlocked the door.

"We don't really go in here anymore," she said apologetically. " Just to clean. My husband would come in and stay for a little while but he'd just get mad. So I asked him to stop."

"And he did?" Charlie asked.

"Yes, he did. Losing Ruthanne has been very difficult for both of us."

"I imagine so. I can't even begin to understand how

profound your loss is. I have a son and if anything ever happened to him ..." Charlie paused and patted Ms. Coker's shoulder and the woman stiffened at her touch. A zap of pain shot up Charlie's arm and she pulled her hand back as if she'd been stung by a bee. The sting of the woman's raw grief was worse than any bee sting that Charlie'd ever felt. Her fingertips pulsed with the sensation and Charlie massaged the fingers and palm. "I'm so sorry."

Ms. Coker smiled but it seemed perfunctory. Charlie recognized the universal politeness of someone who was sick and tired of people telling them how sorry they were. But Ms. Coker couldn't very well say that. What would people think?

Charlie wished there were words or even a spell that could ease the woman's pain. But nothing she could think of would soothe the hole that had been ripped into the poor woman's heart. The only true balm was time and maybe justice, if they caught the man who tortured her daughter. The lock clicked and the older woman turned the knob and pushed open the door. Charlie walked inside the room but Ms. Coker stopped at threshold.

"I'll be right downstairs," Ms. Coker said. "I'd appreciate it if you would put things back the way you find them."

"Yes, ma'am," Charlie said. "I will."

Ms. Coker let her cloudy brown eyes scan across the

room for a second then she let out a sigh, turned and headed quickly down the stairs.

The stale air coated the back of Charlie's throat, but even this room that had been closed up for months was as clean and tidy as the parlor. No dust motes dared to dance in the light streaming through the windows.

Charlie walked around the room with her arm out and hand splayed. She let her palm hover over the furniture, across the pillows and stuffed animals. Over the books on the bookshelves. But there was not one tingle. Not one twitch. Not one sign that Ruthanne had been here physically or as a spirit.

"Come on Ruthanne. Talk to me," Charlie muttered. She paused, hoping for a whisper. For any sort of sign. She faced the wall behind the bed. A framed poster of van Gogh's irises hung above the old spindle headboard. One white iris among a sea of purple. Why had Ruthanne chosen this one? Why not the starry night? Or sunflowers?

This particular painting always left Charlie feeling lonely. Maybe that's how Ruthanne had felt. Something dropped to the floor behind her, drawing her attention. Charlie approached the blue glass marble with caution.

"Ruthanne?" Charlie whispered. A milky green glass marble hopped out of a shallow bowl on one of the shelves and rolled to the edge and stopped. Charlie picked it up from the shelf and held it in the palm of her hand. She closed her eyes for a second and the screams started. Far off at first, the sound reverberated through her head. Then beneath the screams she heard the words my angel, my angel. Born of pain. Be my angel.

A warm, heavy hand touched her shoulder and Charlie screamed. Her eyes flew open and she rounded on the hand's owner with a gasp.

Cameron stood beside her, a concerned look on his face. "Are you all right?"

Charlie shook him off and took a step back. "I'm fine. Why did you do that? I was just starting to make contact."

"I'm sorry. I was passing by on my way to the bathroom and you were making a strange noise and your eyes rolled back in your head. I thought maybe you were having some sort of seizure or something," he said.

Liar. She'd had her eyes closed. Charlie silently counted to ten to contain the anger she felt bubbling close to the surface. She took a deep breath and blew it out before speaking. "Listen. I know you don't like me."

"I never said..." he started.

Charlie held up her hand and cut him off. "You never had to. I can feel your doubt rolling off of you in waves. I get it. It's normal. But don't ever touch me again while I'm working. Do you understand me?"

Cameron held his hands up in surrender. "Sorry, I really did think that you needed help."

"Believe me, if I need help I will ask for it." Charlie

folded her arms across her chest. "Now if you don't mind, I'd like to continue working. Alone."

"Sure. No problem. I'm sorry I upset you," he said but somehow Charlie didn't believe him.

She waited until he left the room and then closed the door behind him. The glass marble pressed into her palm, cool and hard. She opened her fingers and stared down at it.

What are you trying to tell me Ruthanne?

A pink, floral-themed quilt covered the full-sized mattress. It looked as if it had been hand quilted. Charlie ran her hand over the top of it and her eyelids grew heavy. She distinctly got the feeling she should lie down and rest her eyes for just a minute. It had been such a long day. The mattress squeaked when she stretched out on top of it. Her fingers tightened around the marble again and she held it close to her heart. Her eyes drifted closed and a whisper echoed through her mind.

My angel, my angel, my angel. I will make you into my angel.

When Charlie opened her eyes she was no longer in Ruthanne's bedroom. She was lying on her back, and her arms and legs wouldn't move. She jerked against the restraints holding her down. Cold seeped through the back of her clothes, chilling her. The table must be metal. Panic squeezed her chest making it hard to breathe. Her heart clamored into her throat, beating so loudly it almost drowned out the sound of him talking.

You're safe Charlie. He can't hurt you. She's trying to tell you something. Just listen.

Charlie tried to turn her head but found it locked in place. Panic threatened to choke the breath from her again and she closed her eyes. He had thought of everything.

She looked as far left as she could and saw rusty metal walls. She fought the urge to shiver when all of a sudden she heard the scrape and rattle of a metal door. And she looked as best she could toward that sound. His heavy boots echoed on the floor, reminding her of a childhood memory. An abandoned boxcar that had been left in a field near the train tracks behind Bunny's house. Charlie and Lisa and Jen had explored it one Saturday afternoon when they were ten and eleven.

"Good morning, Selene," he said. Charlie tried to memorize the sound of his voice. It struck her as odd that it had a pleasing tenor and not a trace of creepiness or anything scary about it. Maybe how normal he sounded should have scared her more. "Hopefully you were able to rest. We have a big day today."

His boots scraped against the metal floor as if one of his legs was dragging a little. Like he had a limp. A heavy hand wrapped around her ankle. She tried to tip her chin down so she could get a better look at him, but he was just a silhouette and it made her eyes ache after a minute. He ran his hand from her ankle across the top of her foot and moved to the end of the table so that the bottom of her foot was perpendicular to him. He ran his thumb along the center of her arch until he got to the heel.

"I'm sorry that I have to do this but I can't have you running away again, Selene."

The thin sound of metal clinking sent an electric shock through her body. She struggled against the strap holding her head in place trying to find that sound. A flash of silver drew her attention and she saw the long thin sharp rod he held. "Don't you want to be an angel?"

"No," she said and found her words garbled as if behind tape. Adrenaline coursed through her body and she fought against the restraints holding her.

Just a dream Charlie. Calm down.

Her heart didn't listen. It beat harder and her breath felt short and rushed. "No, no, no."

"It will hurt less if you don't fight it, Selene."

Tears seeped from the corners of her eyes, burning a path along the side of her face to her ears. He grabbed her right foot and jerked it hard. Sharp white-hot pain drilled into the bottom of her heel.

Charlie flew up from the bed, choking on a scream. In less than a minute Jason was in the room. Charlie blinked away the tears and the pale yellow walls of Ruthanne's room appeared. Jason reached for her and she stepped back. A searing pain in her heel made her scream again. Jason took a step forward and she held her hand up to stop him. "No. Not yet."

She hobbled over to the edge of the bed and sat down. She slipped off her tennis shoe and the white footie sock she wore was soaked in blood.

"What the hell?" Jason muttered he knelt beside her. "What happened?"

Charlie peeled the sock off. A small wound in the center of her heel dripped with blood. She pressed the sock against it applying as much pressure she could stand.

"Holy crap, we've got to get you to the hospital."

"It'll stop in just a minute, Jason. I'm sure."

"Charlie that looks deep," Jason said.

"How are you going to explain it? To the doctor?" She looked at him with confusion blurring her eyes.

"I don't know. We'll tell them you stepped on a nail or something. But you're going to the hospital, no arguments."

"Oh my Lord." Ms. Coker's voice came from the doorway. All the blood had drained out of her face making her look tired and a little dead.

"I'm so sorry, Ms. Coker."

"What happened?" she asked.

"I ..." Charlie traded looks with Jason. "I think I must've stepped on a nail or something."

"A nail?" Ms. Coker walked in and looked around at her impeccably clean floor. "Where?"

"I'm not sure."

"It doesn't matter. I'm taking her to the hospital."

Ms. Coker wrapped her arms around her waist. "Yes. That's a good idea."

"I'll be in touch Ms. Coker, okay?" Jason said. "If I have any new information."

"Thank you, Lieutenant. I appreciate that."

"Do you think you can walk?" Jason asked Charlie.

"I don't know. Y'all may need to help me," Charlie said.

"Let me get my first-aid kit. I will wrap that up so that you can get her out of here without too much bloodshed," Ms. Coker said, then disappeared down the hallway.

Charlie glanced up at the door and saw Cameron standing in the middle of the hallway watching this scene unfold wearing a critical expression on his face. She didn't have the energy to deal with his negativity. Ms. Coker reappeared with a white plastic box with the Red Cross logo on the top. She popped it open and took two large gauze pads and ripped open their paper wrapping. Gently she pressed one against the bottom of Charlie's heel.

"Lieutenant, there's some tape in the box there." Ms. Coker tilted her head towards the first-aid kit.

"Of course," Jason said. He rummaged through it until

he found a roll of tape and a small pair of blunt-ended scissors. He popped the tape out of the metal ring that protected it and pulled several inches from the roll. Ms. Coker wrapped the tape around Charlie's foot. Then she took the scissors out of Jason's hands and cut it. She peeled another long piece and wrapped the other side of the gauze around Charlie's ankle, taping it as well so that it would stay in place.

"Now do you think you can walk?" Jason asked. Charlie grabbed her shoe and stuffed the bloody sock inside. "Take my elbow and help me up."

She put most of her weight on her uninjured leg and with Jason's help was able to get to her feet. Charlie limped forward on the ball of her foot. Jason kept one hand wrapped around her upper arm for balance.

When they got to the top of the steps Jason scooped her up as if she weighed nothing. Charlie yelped and started to protest.

"I don't want to hear it," he said cutting her off. He slowly took the steps and Charlie wrapped her arms around his neck. She glanced at Cameron coming down behind them. He stared at her with his hard brown eyes as if she were some sort of traitor. She could feel his dislike for her growing with every step they took. Jason carried Charlie out of the house and down to his Dodge Charger. He managed to fish his keys out of his pocket without dropping her and unlocked the doors with his thumb. "Cam, can you open the door for me?"

Cameron didn't say a word but did as he was asked. Jason eased Charlie to her feet and helped her slide into the bucket seat.

"What about my car?" Charlie tucked her purse in the floorboard behind her calf so it would help elevate her heel off the carpet.

"Cameron will drive it to my apartment and park it. Once the doctor fixes you up I'll have him follow me to your house and we'll drop off your car. Okay?"

"Fine," Charlie said in a sulky voice. She fished her keys out of her purse and handed them to Jason.

"Good. Now watch your hands. " Jason said, closing the door on her.

Jason gave the keys to Cameron and the two of them exchanged a few more words that Charlie couldn't hear. The look on Cameron's face told her he was not happy about the situation.

Charlie pulled her phone from her purse and quickly jotted off a text.

I had an accident. I'm not ready to cancel our picnic yet. Heading to the ER now. I am okay. Jason is being overly cautious.

Tom responded to her text almost immediately.

What happened?"

Not sure exactly. Weird encounter.

What kind of encounter?

I had a vision. It got kind of physical.

You sure you're okay?"

Yes.

Which hospital?

You don't have to come.

Yes I do. Which hospital?

Charlie smiled. And for a brief second her heart felt like it might burst. She would never admit it to his face but she was glad that Tom worried about her and that he wanted to be there with her.

St. Frances in West Ashley.

I'll be waiting for you when you get there.

Charlie stared at the screen, grinning.

Jason climbed into the driver side and buckled up. "Did you text Jen and Lisa?"

"Not yet," Charlie said, letting out a sigh and buckling her seatbelt. "I'll do that now."

Jason turned his car around and sped down the long driveway, heading back towards West Ashley.

CHAPTER 5

"What is he doing here?" Jason grumbled as he carried Charlie toward the automatic doors of the ER.

"I texted him. You be nice," Charlie scolded as they approached the building.

"I've already talked to the nurse inside. She's expecting you. There's about a thirty-minute wait unless you're having a heart attack or are bleeding so profusely that it could endanger your life. Are you bleeding that badly?" Tom asked.

"No," Charlie said.

"Do you need some help, Lieutenant?" Tom asked.

Jason narrowed his eyes and tightened his grip on Charlie, hiking her legs a little higher in the crook of his arms and swinging her away from Tom as he hurried along. "I got her. Thanks."

"Wonderful." Tom offered up a confidant smile, and it only seemed to irritate Jason more. Charlie bit the inside of her lip to keep from laughing as the three of them walked through the ER doors. The nurse behind the reception counter looked up, her gaze shifting to Charlie's bloody foot. She directed a nearby orderly and he met them with a wheelchair. Jason set her down gently and Charlie shifted in the seat until she found a comfortable spot.

"So, what happened here?" the nurse behind the counter asked.

"I had an encounter with something sharp. I'm not sure exactly what but it went pretty deep," Charlie said. She dug through her purse until she found her wallet then pulled her insurance card and driver's license from the see through ID slot and handed them to the nurse.

"A nail?" The nurse glanced at the cards and attached them to a clipboard with a form and gave it back to Charlie.

"I don't …" Charlie started.

"Yeah, it was probably a nail," the nurse muttered. Her pinched expression didn't change. It was as if she'd seen this sort of thing a thousand times today. "Fill this out."

"Elaine, she's bleeding," the round-faced orderly said,

pointing to the drops of blood pooling beneath Charlie's foot and dripping onto the floor. He seemed as unruffled as the nurse.

"All right," the nurse said. They exchanged a glance and the orderly nodded.

"Y'all come on back," the orderly said with an easy smile. The only thing that made him look older than twelve was the hint of a five-o'clock shadow. He swiped his badge over a sensor and pushed through the heavy door leading to the emergency exam rooms.

Tom slid behind Charlie's wheel chair and followed the orderly. He leaned over and whispered into her ear, "I guess it won't be too long of a wait after all."

The orderly hummed to himself and led them down the corridor to room number eleven. Tom pushed her into the small room with a large glass window and equipment lining the walls. He fiddled with the narrow emergency room bed until it reached the lowest height and helped Charlie transfer from the chair.

"This controls the bed. Do you need more pillows?" The orderly handed her a large controller attached to a cord.

"I think I'm good. This isn't my first rodeo," Charlie said as she scanned the remote looking for a button to raise the head of the bed to a 45-degree angle. When she found it, she pressed it and the bed whirred to life, moving into the upright position. Tom fluffed a pillow and placed it behind her. Charlie lay back and let out a deep sigh, then started looking over the clipboard.

A tiny, chipper nurse wearing pink scrubs and a friendly smile appeared in the door. "Hi, how are y'all today?" Her long dark hair reached the middle of her back in a neat French braid. She grabbed a pair of latex gloves from a box on a wall and pulled them on. "I'm Jolie and I'll be your nurse today. So what happened here?"

"She stepped on a nail," Jason piped up quickly.

Jolie gave him a side-eyed glance. "Are you her husband?"

"Uh, no," he said.

"Okay then, I really need her to answer my questions. Okay?" The smile never left the nurses lips. Jolie the nurse was barely been five feet tall and might have weighed eighty pounds soaking wet, but the firmness in her cordial tone made it very clear she was in charge here. Charlie stifled a laugh.

Jason's face reddened and he mumbled, "Okay."

"You wouldn't believe me if I told you." Charlie waved her off in the most nonchalant way she could muster. "I stepped on something but I'm not sure what. It was sharp though and it felt like my heel was on fire."

"Sounds painful," the nurse said. She pulled a disposable, clean under pad from one of the cabinets and gently lifted Charlie's calf and deftly slid it beneath her bleeding foot. "I'm just gonna pull this bandage off so the doctor can get a good look at what's going on."

Tom took the chair on the right side of the bed. He slipped his hand over Charlie's, giving it a supportive squeeze, while the nurse peeled the bandage Ruthanne's mother had improvised from Charlie's wound. Jolie frowned and went to the cabinet again, bringing back a large gauze pad. She pressed it against the bottom of Charlie's foot to stop the bleeding. Charlie jerked her foot and for a moment the world grayed at the edges.

"I'm sorry, hon. I know it hurts," the nurse said, reapplying pressure to the foot. "But we need to get this bleeding stopped."

Charlie squeezed Tom's hand. A tear slipped from the corner of her eye and she swiped it away and took a breath through her nose and blew it out through her mouth.

"So what have we got?" the doctor said as he rounded the corner into the small room. He stopped beside the nurse and his sharp blue eyes surveyed the situation before settling on Charlie. A familiar grin spread across his face. "Charlie? Charlie Carver, is that you?"

Charlie found herself staring into the face of Dr. Matthew Skerrit, her husband's best friend.

Charlie mustered a smile. "Hey Matt. I was kinda hoping you weren't working today."

"Come on Charlie, you know me better than that. I'm

always working." His grin widened. He was classically handsome, with short, dark hair, perfectly groomed dark brows to match that framed his large blue eyes.

"Charlie Carver," he said again, sliding the wheeled stool up to the foot of the bed. He donned a pair of latex gloves from the box on the wall and took a seat.

"It's Payne now. You know I dropped Scott's name."

"Oh yeah, that's right," he mused. His smile faded. "So what's going on? What's brought you to my ER?"

Charlie bristled. Matt's way of making the world sound as if it belonged to him had always rubbed her the wrong way. "I stepped on something sharp."

"Well, let's take a look and see what we've got, shall we?"

The nurse peeled away the bloody gauze and Matt leaned in close, examining her wound, pressing gently on the tissue around it. Charlie squeezed her eyes shut and kept her breathing as steady as she could.

Matt gave the nurse some instructions on irrigating the wound and ordering an x-ray. When he was done, he glanced back at Charlie. "So, should I give Scott a call, let him know what's going on?"

Charlie's eyes flew open and she gave him a pointed look. "Don't you dare," she said, her voice full of aggravation. "Scott is not my husband anymore and you know it."

Matt smirked. "I know. I just always thought it was a shame you two split up."

"I'm sure you do." Charlie's lips twisted into a disdainful scowl at Matt's boldfaced lie. If she'd had something solid in her hands, she would've thrown it at him. She'd known Matthew Skerrit as long as she'd known Scott. Once when she and Scott had broken up for a month, Matt had chased her, trying to keep them from getting back together. But he failed. If there was one thing she knew about Matt, it was that he didn't like to fail. "

"So when was your last tetanus shot?" Matt asked.

"I don't know. A while I guess," Charlie said.

"Well, it's your lucky day." His blue eyes glinted with mischief as he grinned. "Let's give her a booster," Matt said to the nurse.

"Yes, sir," Nurse Jolie said and typed it into her computer.

"Great" Charlie laid back against the pillow and stared at the crisscross pattern of the drop ceiling tiles.

"Are you allergic to penicillin, Charlie?" Matt asked.

"No," Charlie said.

"Great, we'll give you a shot and then send you home with some oral antibiotics, okay?"

"Whatever you think is best, Matt," Charlie said not taking her eyes off the ceiling.

"Great." Matt peeled his gloves off. "It was great to see you, Charlie. How's that cousin of yours, Lisa?"

Charlie gave Jason a furtive glance. He'd moved closer

to her bed and his lips puckered as if he'd been sucking on lemons.

"She's great." Charlie reached out and touched Jason's arm.

"Maybe I should give her a call," Matt mused.

"Awww, maybe you shouldn't," Charlie quipped. "She's got a boyfriend."

"Well you know what they say," Matt said. "Unless he's put a ring on it. She's fair game."

Jason took a half-step forward and Charlie tightened her grip on his arm. "That's not what they say at all."

"Charlie's right. That's not what they say at all, Matthew Skerrit," Lisa said from the doorway. "

Matt chuckled and turned. "Lisa Holloway, as I live and breathe. Dang girl, you look good."

"Uh-huh," Lisa put her hands on her slim hips and narrowed her eyes. "How's Charlie?"

"She's gonna be fine. We're gonna take good care of her."

"Good," she said, seeming to ignore the way he looked her up and down. "Well, I wouldn't want to keep you from your patients." Lisa took a step back and raised her hand in a dismissive gesture.

"Looks like some things never change." Matt's smile disappeared and his expression hardened. "Take care, Charlie. Make sure you follow all the instructions the nurse gives you, okay?"

"I will. Thanks, Matt," Charlie said. She sank into her pillow and closed her eyes as the nurse began the painful process of debriding and irrigating her wound. Hopefully, Matt wouldn't be the jerk she knew he could be and call Scott against her wishes. That was the last thing she needed today because she could lie to Matthew Skerrit's face and wear a smile as she did it, but Scott would want the truth.

They'd come a long way over the last year but there was no way he'd believe her. Hell, she barely believed it. She couldn't wait to get Lisa alone to talk about what had happened and try to make some sense of all this. Charlie looked to Jason and Tom. "Listen, this may take a while. Y'all don't have to stay."

"Charlie's right," Lisa said. "I'm here now. I know y'all have other things to do. I'm her family. I'll take care of her now."

Jason's mouth drew up into a sour pucker. "Fine. I need to go back to work anyway. Will you text me later? Let me know you're okay?"

"Of course," Charlie said. "If y'all would just drop my car off and leave the keys with my uncle, that'd be great."

"Sure thing," Jason said. He shifted his gaze to Lisa. "Can I speak with you a minute?"

Lisa jutted her chin. "All right."

Charlie watched the two of them disappear from view.

"Do you want me to stay?" Tom asked. He rubbed his thumb over the back of Charlie's. "I don't mind."

"I could be here for hours. I don't want you to have to wait," she said.

"I don't mind."

Charlie slipped her hand out of his and cupped his cheek. "You are sweet to me. Why don't I call you when I'm on my way home."

Tom took her hand in his and pressed his lips to her palm. "Whatever you wish."

Charlie watched as Tom left the room, heading in the opposite direction of Lisa and Jason. Didn't he know the exit was the other way? Maybe he has business here. The skin on her arms broke into goose flesh and she shivered.

"Are you cold?" the nurse asked. "Do you need a blanket?"

Charlie cracked an automatic smile. "No, I'm fine, thank you."

"Okay, Charlie, I'm just going to irrigate your wound and make sure it's good and clean. Then we're gonna send you off for a quick x-ray."

The nurse settled on the stool at the foot of the bed and held a plastic kidney shaped basin in one hand.

"Great," Charlie muttered.

She lay back on the pillow and stared up at the ceiling again and waited for the pain to be over.

* * *

LISA'S SHOES CLICKED ON THE LINOLEUM FLOOR AS SHE walked away from Charlie's room with Jason trailing behind her.

She'd gotten a text from Charlie. I'm at St. Frances. Had an accident. I'm okay. Don't come. Heart heart heart. Your boyfriend is here with me.

My boyfriend?

You know. Cop. Average height, light brown hair, intense demeanor. Your boyfriend Jason.

Who said he was my boyfriend?

He did. Well. Said you were his girlfriend so...

When?

Last night. So, I just wanted to tell you not to worry and not to come. Okay?

What the hell was she supposed to do with that? It was information overload. How on earth could Charlie expect her not to come? She totally didn't want to deal with the other little bomb Charlie dropped. Sometimes her cousin could be infuriating. After a quick call to her sister Jen, they had decided that it was best if Lisa went to the hospital, since Jen had to pick up Ruby from tap dance class.

Her heart beat hard in her throat matching the click-clack of her shoes on the tile flooring outside Charlie's room as she replayed last night in her head. Jason had swung by after she'd left her father's. He'd been sweet, hopeful, penitent and she'd picked a fight. Could feel herself doing it. Words had been thrown like daggers. Mean words meant to wound. Words she regretted in the harsh light of this place. She stepped back against the wall as a nurse rushed by carrying a small child in her arms.

She should have known he'd be here, that Charlie's injury would somehow of course be connected to him. Seeing skeezy Matt Skerrit didn't help matters much either. She saw the way that Jason looked at her. Why were men so damned territorial?

"Hey," Jason sidled up next to her.

"Hey," she said trying to keep her voice under control. She wanted to say she didn't mean anything she'd said last night, but the words wouldn't come. They flowed so easily when she was angry, but froze in her throat as soon as she wanted forgiveness. Why was sorry so hard to say?

"I'm glad you're here," he said. He pressed his arm against hers. Maybe he'd forgiven her. Maybe.

"You are?"

"Yeah, she needs her family," he said.

"Yeah, she does." Lisa nodded. It wasn't what she'd hoped he'd say.

"Listen, I've gotta go back to work. I need to finish up a few things," he said. His gaze felt heavy on her.

"Sure." She stepped away from the wall and crossed her arms. "Don't let me stop you."

Jason blew out a breath and looked away. "You're still mad at me."

It wasn't a question. Lisa blinked, not sure how to respond. A pang of guilt filled her chest. She'd hurt him. Her cheeks and chest burned with shame. "I'm not mad."

"You're not?" He narrowed his eyes.

"No," she sighed. "I was. But I'm not anymore."

"Really?" He cocked his head like he didn't believe her, but a smile played at the corners of his mouth. "I don't want you to be mad at me."

"That's good because I don't want to be mad at you," she said, her eyes casting about, not able to land on him.

"You forgive me for working on our vacation?" He took a step, closing the gap between them.

"You forgive me for being mean to you last night?" Now she could look up.

"Maybe," he said. "Did you really date that doctor guy?"

"So what if I did? I don't harass you about the girls you've dated," she huffed.

"It's just he doesn't really seem your type."

"He's not. That's why we're not still dating," Lisa said. She tightened her arms across her chest. "Did you tell Charlie I was your girlfriend?"

"Maybe," he said grinning. "Does that make you mad too?"

"No. Not exactly mad. It would've been nice if maybe you would have asked me. Instead of declaring it to my cousin."

Jason's lips twitched at the corners and he moved closer, putting a tentative hand on the top of her hip. "Lisa Marie Holloway, will you officially be my girlfriend?"

"I don't know," she said, trying to keep her own smile under control. "You seem like you could be more trouble than you're worth."

"I think you like trouble," he grinned, putting his other hand on her hip. "I need to go back to work for two hours tops. After that, I'm all yours. How about I take you someplace nice. We'll eat some dinner, watch the sunset."

"What about Cameron?" Lisa said.

"He's a big boy. He can take care of himself," Jason said.

"I don't know. I need to get Charlie home after this and she may need me."

"She's not gonna need you," Jason said.

"Oh yeah? How do you know that?"

"Two reasons. Tom and Jen. You know once you get her home the two of them will be mother-henning her all night," he chuckled.

"Yeah, you're probably right." Lisa wrapped one arm

around his neck. "Okay. You've got yourself a date. But I want to go someplace nice."

"It's too late for reservations," Jason said, looking at his watch.

"Well I don't want to go to the café, if that's what you're about to suggest."

"Fine. How about we go to Margie's Crab House."

"Okay. Fine. Meet you at 7:30. Don't be late," she scolded.

He smirked. "When am I ever late?"

She quirked one eyebrow and opened her mouth to answer but he pressed his mouth to hers making, her forget the question.

CHAPTER 6

Ben Sutton sat on the porch swing in the rear of the Holloway house with his arms stretched across the back. Twilight cast a murky blanket across the yard and sky. The sharp piney scent of bug spray still hung in the air from where Jen had sprayed them both down. But it was giving way to the smells of cooler air. A flash of lightning streaked across the sky and, as if on cue, a rumble of thunder answered. A promise of rain. Jen emerged from the house, letting the screen door slam with a flat thud behind her. She had two cold beers in her hand and held one of the sweaty bottles out for him. He took it and smiled at her.

"Thank you," he said. She sat down next to him, rocking the swing a little bit.

"So how much longer do you think you're going to be in town?"

She asked the question that had been hanging between them for the last month. When he hadn't received a new assignment, instead of resorting to his nomadic ways he had stayed put, something he rarely did. But it was the pull of this woman that had kept him here. Her vivacious and loving spirit, and it didn't hurt that she was adorable. With her heart-shaped face and elfin features. And her pink full lips. That beckoned to be kissed. He leaned in and brushed his lips across hers.

"Until I get a call," he whispered. He felt her shiver next to him despite the 75-degree heat. She nodded and sat back, taking a long draw from the bottle of beer.

"So that could be any time then?" she asked.

"Yes," he said, sitting back. The chains squealed in protest as he pushed the swing with his legs back and forth. Back and forth. Measuring the moments of silence between them. He could feel her next to him, her body thrumming with questions that she didn't really want the answers to. He reached over and put his hand on top of hers. And pulled it to his mouth, kissing her knuckles. "You know I don't stay in one place for very long."

Jen didn't look at him. She stared down at the bottle in her hand. Her thumb traced a line through the condensation on the bottle's neck.

"Just because I leave a place, you know," he said. He

leaned forward letting the swing settle and resting his elbows on his knees. "It doesn't mean I can't come back."

"Right," she said. "Do you like it? Just sort of drifting around with no home?"

He shrugged one shoulder. "You know I used to. But as I've gotten older ..." He blew out a heavy breath. "It's not like I haven't thought about finding a place to live. You know, settling down. But what I do for a living ..."

"Yeah," Jen said. "It's kind of unusual. I don't think I would know how to explain it to somebody. Hi, this is my friend Ben. He hunts down witches who break the rules and exacts justice. It doesn't really roll off the tongue like police officer or doctor or dogcatcher," she chuckled.

He was glad of the sound. Maybe it meant that she could accept it if he wanted to come back.

"Hotel living gets old," he said. "That's for sure. I mean being able to spend time with you and your family here. It's meant a lot to me." He wanted to say it showed him a different world. A world that he'd never really known before. But he didn't. She didn't need to know that much about how he grew up. Not yet. Why infect her with that darkness?

"Well you know you're welcome here. Any time. Even my daddy likes you. And he doesn't like anybody that I bring home," Jen said.

"So he didn't like Ruby's father?" Ben asked.

"No. My father hated Mark Goldberg with a passion.

Especially after he ... well, especially after ..." She paused and her face became thoughtful.

He could feel her searching for the most delicate way to say, Before he knocked me up and left me. One thing he'd learned about her is that no matter how bad something might be, she always found that silver lining. It was one of the things that endeared her to him. He'd never known anyone who could see the light in a dark situation quite as easily as Jen.

"Well after things didn't work out and Ruby came along."

"I can imagine he did. I would've felt the same way if you had been my daughter," Ben said.

"Well," Jen said, straightening her shoulders. She tipped her chin and smiled. "I can't complain. I've had you for a month and a half now. And I've enjoyed every minute of it."

He shifted again, putting his arm around her. The swing rocked back and forth a little. "I have, too. And I want to keep enjoying every minute as long as I'm here. Are you okay with that?"

She looked up at him, her blue eyes wide. "Yes," she said. "I am if you are."

"Good," he said. He leaned in and kissed her, this time lingering for a moment. His empty hand found her cheek and cupped it. There was so much he wanted to say, wanted to admit but couldn't quite bring himself to do it.

THE HARBINGER

The phone in his pocket buzzed against the front of his thigh. He broke the kiss and smiled. He pulled his phone from his pocket and stared down at the face of Lauren Coldwater. His boss at the Defenders of Light. He'd almost hoped she'd lost his number. Being a rogue witch hunter had become more tedious and less exciting since meeting Jen. "Sorry. I need to take this."

"No problem," she said. She pushed to her feet. "I'm gonna go kiss Ruby good night. You take your phone call. I'll be back in a few minutes."

He nodded and pressed the green answer icon. "Lauren, what have you got?"

"We have a problem," Lauren said. There were no niceties between them now. No, how are you? Lauren always got straight to the point and perpetually sounded like she was gritting her teeth.

"We always do," he said. "What's going on?"

"There's a demon on the loose in a place called Arcadia, Georgia. He's been picking off livestock and it appears that he's moved on to humans. We believe he was called by a solitary practitioner in that area." She meant a witch not affiliated with a coven like Evangeline's and the cousins, sworn to only practice white magic. "We need you to pick her up and slay that demon. Or send him back to hell, whichever one is easiest for you," Lauren said nonchalantly.

"I'll pick up the witch but I don't usually slay demons,

Lauren. Don't you have a cleanup crew for that?" Ben asked.

"Well, I have a problem with that," Lauren said. "Unfortunately, my last cleanup crew ... well," she sighed. He wasn't sure if it was for dramatic effect or if she was really emoting. She made it hard to know the difference sometimes. "They failed their last mission."

A failed mission meant only one thing. The crew had died. There was no in between. Succeed or die. Those were pretty much the choices.

"... and we haven't had a chance to hire anyone new yet, so we need you to do it. You absolutely have a budget and can hire whomever you need to help you. But we just need it done as soon as possible. All right?"

"All of them? How? How did that happen?"

"Well," Lauren said, drawing out the word. "They were evidently led by a less experienced team leader and the witch they encountered had aligned herself to some very dark forces."

"This is the demon they were after, isn't it?" Ben said. "Your cleanup crew went in and they couldn't slay this demon."

"Not exactly ..." Lauren started.

Ben cut her off. "And now you want me to go in and risk my life."

"Would it help if I told you that it killed a young

couple and snatched their baby?" Her flippant tone sent a surge of electric anger through him.

"No, Lauren, it wouldn't." He gritted his teeth. From the corner of his eye he saw Jen's silhouette standing in the screen door. She was everything warm and light. All Lauren offered was the odious bloody darkness that came with dealing with demons.

"Damn you, Lauren. How many people were on your crew?"

"Four," Lauren said. "I'll pay expenses for ..." He heard her cluck her tongue. "You and two other people. I've already expended too much on the situation."

He lowered his voice, hoping Jen wouldn't hear him. "You are such a coldhearted bitch sometimes, you know that, Lauren?"

"I'm going to ignore that. You need to be there by tomorrow, end of day. I will text you the address," she said sounding irritated.

Ben pulled his phone from his ear and pressed the red icon to end the call without saying yes or no. Because when it came down to it, he didn't have a choice. The answer was always yes.

He placed his phone on the arm of the swing and looked up at Jen's silhouette. He couldn't see her face but he could feel her anxiety and uncertainty. His wide smile answered her uneasiness as he held up his hand, gesturing for her to come out onto the porch. She took a deep breath and pushed open the screen door. It squeaked at the hinges and she closed it carefully so it wouldn't slam this time. Because Ruby was in bed.

She carefully sat down on the swing, keeping her hands on either side of her knees. He placed his palm flat in the center of her back with his fingers splayed.

"So you're going," she said. It wasn't a question this time.

"Yeah," he said. "That was my boss. She has a job for me. A witch evidently summoned a demon and now a baby is missing."

"Will you be back?" Her voice quivered on the last word and she leaned forward, staring at her feet.

"I..."

Jen finally looked up at him. Her blue eyes searched his face and her lips pinched into a bow.

"Even as a kid I traveled around with another witch from the Defenders of Light working as an apprentice. So I've never stayed in one place before," Ben said.

"I can't imagine what that's like," Jen said. "I mean I've lived here my whole life. With the exception of the time that I went to school and lived in San Francisco, I've always had a home. Roots. People who love me."

"You're one of the lucky ones, Jen. The whole lot of you, actually. It makes me envy you."

He felt her defenses draw up, like a flower that closed

when the sun went down. She shut her eyes. "We're always here if you need us."

"Thank you," he said. He wanted to say he'd be back as quickly as he could, but he knew he couldn't. Lauren's cleanup crew had died dealing with this demon. He wouldn't get her hopes up. Or his.

"I should go inside now," she said. "I've got a few things to do before I get ready for bed. Four o'clock comes really early you know?"

"Yeah, I know."

The chains of the swing squeaked as she rose to her feet. "Be careful," she said. "Whatever it is you need to do. Just be careful." She pecked him on the cheek and was through the back door in a minute, closing it with care behind her. He watched her through the window pane until she flicked off the light in the kitchen, leaving him in the dark.

CHAPTER 7

Someone knocked on the door, just when Charlie had gotten settled on the couch and turned on channel 5. Walking wasn't excruciating, but it wasn't comfortable either. Lisa had brought her home and offered to stay for a while but Charlie could tell that her mind was elsewhere. So she shooed her cousin away and set about making dinner for herself. After she'd eaten she decided to set up on the couch and catch up on a little television. She pondered staying put, pretending she was sleeping, but it might be Tom. Slowly she rose from her sofa and hobbled across the room.

"Hi Charlie," Ben Sutton said. He lifted his hand and gave her a little wave. "I hope I'm not interrupting anything."

"Not at all," she stepped back and opened the door,

letting him in. "I'm kinda surprised to see you. I thought you were over at Jens."

"I was. But ..." he began. Charlie closed the door behind him and he shuffled his feet, toeing the edge of her welcome mat.

"But?" Charlie prompted.

"I got a call tonight. A job."

"So you're leaving?" Charlie said.

"Yeah," he said.

"I see." Charlie hobbled back over to the couch.

"What happened to your foot?" He followed her to the sofa and took a seat in cushy, overstuffed chair sitting catty corner to the couch. Charlie sat down on the sofa and propped her foot on the pillow she'd placed on top of the old trunk she used as a coffee table.

"Jen didn't tell you?" she asked.

"You weren't exactly the topic of our conversation tonight," he said sheepishly.

"No, I'm sure I wasn't." Charlie chuckled. She met his gaze trying to decide how much to actually tell him. Working for the Defenders of Light put Ben in a special category of witches. He knew more magic than anyone she'd ever met, including Evangeline, her aunt. He'd been generous enough to spend some time with her over the last few weeks teaching her a few things, such as how to pull her magic into her hands so she didn't need a wand to focus her energy. He'd also taught her a couple of tricks for capturing ghosts and forcing them to move on without having to call a reaper. He had similar talents to hers and talents that she hadn't even seen yet. She was sure of it. She blew out a breath. "I had a vision while helping Jason with a case."

"And you ..." He nodded at her foot. "What? Fell?" His blue eyes glittered with curiosity.

"Not exactly. In the vision I connected with the victim and she was... I don't know the best way to say this but I guess she was mutilated by her captor. He drove this spike into her heel."

"Ouch," Ben leaned forward with his elbows on his knees. Fascination lit up his face.

"When I regained my senses it was because my foot hurt. I thought maybe I had, you know, just some sort of psychic residual pain."

Ben nodded. There was no judgment on his face and thankfully no pity, only understanding. "But you found you had a real wound."

"Yeah. I did." Charlie sighed and rubbed her temples with her fingers. "It's never happened before. So ..."

Ben sat back in the chair and studied her for a minute. "It's rare. But I've heard of it before. An intense psychic connection."

"You have?"

"There was a case that I worked in Houston. A witch seemed to be under psychic attack. She had inadvertently connected with another witch. She ended up with burns and lacerations that almost killed her."

"Oh my gosh, that's terrible. I had no idea that such things even existed."

"Yeah it does," Ben said. "And the doctors can't really do anything for you."

"They bandaged me up and sent me home with oral antibiotics." Charlie shrugged.

"Is it still bleeding?" he asked.

"They kept me at the ER until the bleeding stopped. But it seems to be still seeping. It stops bleeding for a little while and then starts up again. I'm just keeping gauze bandages on it and changing them," she said.

"Do you mind if I take a look?" Ben said.

"Be my guest. I was going to have Evangeline look at it tomorrow and see if there was something she could do," she said.

Ben rose from his chair and knelt next to her foot propped up on the trunk. Carefully he peeled the bandage away. "I see what's going on here."

"You do?" Charlie leaned forward.

"You may still be linked to her," he said.

"How is that possible? She's dead?" Charlie said.

"Maybe she doesn't know she's dead. We've both seen that happen," he said.

"Yeah, I guess, I just... I've never had any sort of physical thing happen before." She sat back against the soft couch cushions and crossed her arms.

"I can fix this. Do you trust me?" he asked.

It was a loaded question. She'd only known Ben for a month and a half and there were moments when their relationship was not exactly cordial. But they'd worked as a team on her last case. "Yeah. I do."

Ben grabbed the leather satchel that he always kept with him and dug through it. A moment later he pulled out a brown bottle with a dropper, a black obsidian stone, which Charlie knew was for healing and a small bottle of herbs.

"I need a bowl and a match. Preferably wooden," he said.

"The match or the bowl?" Charlie asked halfway teasing him. He raised his eyebrows in irritation and got to his feet.

"Check the third cabinet from the right of the stove," she said quickly to smooth over the moment. "I've got some ritual implements in there. There are matches in the drawer next to the stove."

He disappeared into the tiny kitchen at the back of the cottage and Charlie listened to him pilfer around. A few moments later he returned, carrying the things he needed. He sat down on the edge of the chair again, placing the small, carved bowl in front of him. The cork made a popping sound as he opened the bottle of herbs and then sprinkled some into the bowl.

"What is that?" she asked.

"It's a mix of calendula flowers and marshmallow root," Ben said. He gave her a wry smile and looked up at her through his long lashes. "I'm surprised Evangeline hasn't taught you this."

Charlie's cheeks heated. "She's taught me a little about herbs and stuff like that but I haven't had a whole lot of time to spend with her lately."

"Well, you definitely want to have these in your arsenal. They can be used for a lot of things, healing being one of them," he said as he grabbed his satchel again and retrieved a small vial of a clear liquid.

"What is that?" she asked.

"It's castor oil." He unscrewed the little metal cap and poured a few drops over the herbal mixture.

"You wouldn't happen to have a cotton ball would you?" he asked.

"I do. Actually if you look on the floor on the other side of the trunk, there's a first-aid kit. There's some cotton balls in there," she said.

Ben found the kit and opened the blue and white plastic box. He rummaged through the contents and took out three sealed gauze pads, a few cotton balls, and the roll of waterproof first-aid tape. He ripped open one of the gauze pads and put it in the bowl of herbs, soaking it with more castor oil. When it was good and soaked, he sandwiched it, along with as much of the herbal mix as he could scoop onto it, between the other two gauze pads. With a gentle touch, he pressed the three pads against the heel of her foot. Charlie winced.

"Sorry about that," he said. "I know it hurts."

"You can say that again," Charlie said.

"Psychic wounds are the worst," he said.

"Psychic wounds?"

"Yeah, psychic wounds. From what I know about you and about this phenomenon, it happens when you make a strong psychic connection with someone. It's usually not a spirit. Usually it's another person. But because of your history with spirits, it doesn't surprise me that you'd connect with one. I'm kind of surprised it hasn't happened before," Ben said as he taped the gauze to Charlie's foot.

"How do you break the bond?" Charlie asked.

"Well, first we have to figure out who you're linked to and then it's a matter of a spell."

"Oh," Charlie said suddenly wishing he wasn't leaving town. "You think it's something you could help me with?"

"I'd be happy to help you Charlie, but I have to leave tonight," he said, with a rueful expression. "My boss is expecting me there by the morning."

"Right," Charlie said. "Are you coming back?"

His lips pressed together and a deep line formed between his brows. He didn't look at her. "I don't know."

"Do you want to come back?" she asked.

Ben sat back on his heels. His eyes blinked and his gaze shifted, meeting her eyes. "I don't know. Not sure Jen would want me to come back."

"Well that's ridiculous," Charlie said. "Jen's crazy about you."

"I know," he said. "I'm crazy about her too."

"So what's the problem?" Charlie asked.

"I don't stay in one place, Charlie. I can't. Not with my job."

"I am sorry but I'm gonna call BS on that," Charlie said. "If you want to be together. Then you find a way to be together. Even if it means that this is your home base and you travel all the time. There are people who do that every day and have wonderful, happy, healthy relationships."

"Really?" Ben said sounding unconvinced. "Name one."

Charlie sat back, aggravated at him questioning her. "I can't think of anybody off the top of my head right this second but I know it exists. Where there's a will there's a way."

His lips curved into a half smile. "I guess we'll just have to see what happens. I'm not holding my breath right now. I've got bigger fish to fry."

"The job," she said, curious now.

He nodded as an answer. "Let's get you healed up all right. And then maybe we can talk about why I actually came here."

"Sure. What do we need to do?"

"Well." He settled in front of her again, down on the floor on his knees, gently placing his hands on either side of her foot. "I want you to think about a light burning at the center of your chest."

"Okay. A light," Charlie said.

"Yes. Close your eyes. Picture it. It starts as a pinprick at first, barely visible like a star you can barely see on a foggy night."

Charlie imagined the light as he spoke about it and felt herself lulled by the gentle tone of his voice. It was almost meditative. Listening to him speak in measured instructions

"Do you see the light?" he asked.

"Yes," Charlie said, her voice sounding distant to her own ears.

"Good. That's very good, Charlie. Now I want you to picture that light growing brighter, burning away the fog, becoming so bright it's almost blinding."

"Do you see that?"

"Yes," she said.

"Wonderful. Now I want you to imagine that light traveling from your heart into the floor of your pelvis, down your leg, all the way to your foot, burning a straight white-hot line through your body. Can you see that?" His voice was soft and encouraging.

"Yes," Charlie whispered.

"That's great, Charlie, you're doing just great."

She heard him strike the match across the rough paper on the side of the box.

"Keep concentrating on that light, Charlie, burning a line from your heart to your heel."

"I am," she said softly.

"Great," he said. She felt him press the flat, oblong piece of obsidian against her arch. Just above the wound.

"Keep thinking about that light, Charlie, okay?"

"Okay," she said.

"Mother Goddess hear my prayer, heal this wound for this witch fair. Draw the wound closed indeed. So it will not continue to bleed."

Ben whispered the prayer over and over again.

The stone pulsed against the bottom of her foot and the acrid smell of the match tip burning stung her nose. The stone warmed to an uncomfortable level against the bare skin of her arch and she had to force herself not to pull her foot away.

Ben said his prayer one last time and finished with, "So mote it be."

The light in Charlie's mind dissipated, spreading like

an explosion. Ben pulled the stone away from the center of her foot. "You can open your eyes now."

Charlie took a deep breath and opened her eyes to find him still sitting by her foot.

"How do you feel?" he asked.

"Okay, I guess? A little light headed maybe," she said, unsure what he meant.

"No, I meant how does your foot feel?" he said, pressing her to be more specific.

Charlie wiggled her toes at first and then pointed her toe. No pain. She pulled her toe back and flexed her foot. Still no pain. She laughed. "It doesn't hurt anymore," she said incredulous. "How did you do that?"

"I healed it. Well, with some help, of course. Now, I want you to put this on the bottom of your heel every day, three times a day until you run out." He placed the small vial of castor oil on the top of the trunk next to the pillow propping up her foot.

Charlie yanked her foot toward her and propped it on the knee of her other leg so she could inspect the heel. She started to peel the bandage tape at the edges.

"Don't," Ben rose to his feet. "Not yet please. Just leave them on for tonight, okay? You can take them off in the morning and then start using the castor oil. In a few days, it will be almost like you never even had a wound."

"That is amazing, Ben. I am constantly in awe of your magical abilities."

"Well I'm constantly in awe of yours, too, so we're even." He smiled and rocked on his feet. "Which leads me to why I'm really here."

"Okay. What is it?" Charlie asked.

"I need your help." He scrubbed his chin and began to clean up the small mess he'd made, picking up the herbs, stone and bottles and placing them back into his bag.

"What can I do?" Charlie asked.

Ben took a seat on the chair again. "Like I said I've got a job and it's more dangerous that I've taken in a while. Normally I wouldn't care but …"

"You have Jen now," Charlie said.

Ben leaned forward and put his elbows on the tops of his thighs. He looked at her from beneath his long dark eyelashes. Charlie could see why Jen was so attracted to him. Those gorgeous eyes.

"So I was wondering if maybe you'd be interested in helping me."

"Me?" Charlie asked. "Why me?"

"Because you've shown a lot of growth since I started training you."

Charlie paused for a moment, then said, "How dangerous?"

"Let's put it this way. The original crew sent in to take care of the problem died," Ben said matter-of-factly. "I understand if you're not interested, since you've got a kid and all."

"What about you? Are you going alone?" Charlie said, not hiding the alarm in her voice.

"Yeah," he said. "Any chance that boyfriend of yours would be interested? I could pay him."

"Tom? He's not really my boyfriend."

Ben rolled his eyes. "Whatever. If you think he'd be interested I'd love to have him."

"Why? Tom doesn't have any magic other than his glamour," Charlie said.

"He's a reaper, right?"

"Yes he is. But ..."

"Trust me, he has plenty of magic. It's just not the same as ours," Ben said.

Charlie felt her brow furrow. What was that supposed to mean? Tom had specifically told her he didn't have any magic. Had he lied to her? She would have to ask him about it when she saw him tomorrow.

"So what is it that makes this job so dangerous?"

"A hedge witch in a little town in Georgia evidently summoned a demon. The situation seems to have gotten out of control because there's been several deaths," he said.

"You're going demon hunting?" Charlie asked. "Isn't that a little out of your purview?"

"Normally it would be." Ben tipped his head to the side in agreement and pursed his lips.

"Does Jen know?"

"She knows I have a job and that's all. I don't want her to worry."

"I don't think it would make Jen very happy if I went with her ..." It was on the tip of her tongue to say boyfriend but she stopped herself. Charlie finished her sentence with, "You. Plus, I've never done any sort of hunting like that."

"Right," Ben said nodding. He sighed and rose abruptly from his chair. "Right. You haven't. Thanks, anyway." He turned and headed for the door.

"Don't go away mad," Charlie hopped to her feet, noting how easily she could move now. "If you need help I want you to call me. How about that?"

Ben stopped with his hand on the doorknob. "Right, thanks. Take care Charlie. It's been nice knowing you."

"Ben," she called after him but he was already out the door and on her front stoop. "Ben," she called again following him. "Wait."

He stopped and turned. "What?"

"Thank you for healing my foot. I really appreciate it."

"Sure. Anytime," he said. A minute later he was in his restored Toyota FJ50. Charlie watched until his taillights disappeared on the long driveway leading from her uncle's property. She couldn't shake the feeling she might not ever see him again.

CHAPTER 8

The bell jingled overhead as Charlie walked into the Kitchen Witch Café. The breakfast crowd was at its peak and almost every table was taken as well as most of the seats at the lunch counter. Charlie quickly scanned the diners looking for her cousin Jen. She found her milling around the tables with a coffee carafe in one hand. Jen stopped and spoke to a family of four and topped off the coffee mugs of the man and his wife. They looked like tourists. Jen's specialty. She could charm just about anyone into coming back for lunch or dinner or breakfast. Part of it was her manner. The other part was her scrumptious food. Jen looked up, saw Charlie and waved. Charlie waved back and approached her cousin, noting the purple circles beneath her blue eyes. She had not slept from the looks of it.

"Hey," Jen said, her voice full of mild surprise. "I didn't expect to see you today. I figured you'd be laid up with your foot."

"Yeah, funny thing about that," Charlie started. How was she going to tell Jen? She took a deep breath. "I had a visitor last night."

"Who? Did Evangeline come see you?" Jen asked.

"No. Ben did," Charlie said.

The expression on Jen's face deflated at the mere mention of his name. "Oh."

"He stopped by I guess after he left your house. Said he needed to talk to me about something. And he just happened to ..." Charlie looked around. She took a step closer to Jen. "He healed me."

"I figured," Jen said gesturing to Charlie's foot and leg.

"It was really amazing actually. I'd never experienced anything like it."

"I'm not surprised, I guess," Jen said. She glanced sideways at the people around them and seemed to choose her words carefully. "He's an amazing practitioner."

Charlie nodded her head in agreement. "He's taught me a lot in a very short time." Jen didn't respond so she pressed on. "I didn't really come here to talk about him though. I came to meet Lisa for breakfast."

"She's over in the back corner," Jen said. Charlie

glanced toward the booths lining the walls of the café. Lisa sat sipping her coffee in the last booth watching the couple at a nearby table. She wore her long strawberry blonde hair in a French braid. The frown that Charlie had seen on her face yesterday was gone. Maybe she and Jason had made up.

"So do you want your usual order for breakfast?" Jen asked.

"Yes, please," Charlie grinned.

"You are nothing if not predictable Charlie Payne," Jen said. A sly grin tugged at her lips. She pulled an order pad from the front pocket of her apron and scribbled down Charlie's order of banana pecan pancakes and iced tea.

Charlie headed over to Lisa's table.

"Good morning," Charlie said sliding into the booth seat across from Lisa.

Lisa looked up and smiled. "Morning yourself. Wow, I can't believe you're up and walking after yesterday."

"I know, it's crazy," Charlie said.

"So tell me. How is this possible? You know I hate it when y'all vague text me."

"It was Ben," Charlie said. She leaned in close and told Lisa about Ben's visit, including what he'd said about Tom. When Charlie was done, Lisa leaned against the cushioned booth back. Charlie could see her cousin working over the details in her mind.

"So what do you think he meant about Tom?" Lisa finally said.

"I have no idea, but you can bet I'm gonna find out." Charlie folded her hands together and put her elbows on the table.

"I have no doubt," Lisa said, her eyes glittering. "So did it hurt?"

"No, not really. There was a little discomfort from the stone he used, but other than that it was the most bizarre and amazing thing I think I've ever experienced," Charlie said.

Lisa took a sip from her coffee. "So you and Tom have a picnic today?"

"Yep," Charlie said. "We're going over to the Palmetto Beach Park. Which reminds me, I need to put in an order for two box lunches. What about you?" Charlie asked. "What's your plan for today?"

"I've got an appointment later at Daphne's to get my hair trimmed. Then after that I don't know what I'm gonna do. I'm not usually very idle." Her long sigh indicated a level of boredom Charlie rarely saw in Lisa.

Charlie's phone began to ring and her purse vibrated. She unzipped it quickly and dug out her phone. She pressed the green icon and answered it.

"Hey, Jason," Charlie said, her gaze meeting Lisa's. "It's kinda early, isn't it?"

"Did I wake you?" he asked.

"No." She lowered her voice. "I have a dead chicken that continues to think she's alive and needs to be fed at first light. So I've been up awhile."

Jason chuckled. "I don't know if I should laugh or be scared."

"It is kind of funny," Charlie said. "What can I do for you?"

"How's your foot today?" he asked.

"Strangely enough, my foot is all better. It's not even tender anymore," Charlie said.

"How's that possible?" Jason said. "It was a gaping bloody mess yesterday."

"I'll tell you when I see you next. How about that?" she said.

"Great. Hopefully you can tell me this afternoon," Jason said. "You up for a little field trip?"

Dread coiled around Charlie's heart and gave it a squeeze and her heel twitched. "I don't know. Where's the field trip to?"

"I wanted to take you out to the place where we found the latest body. See what kind of impressions you get."

"Is Cameron gonna be there?" Charlie asked.

"Yes he is. Is that a problem?"

"No. Not as long as he minds his business," Charlie said.

"I will keep him in line. How about that?" Jason said. "Will you help me?"

"On one condition."

"What?" he said warily.

"I want Lisa to come. Is that okay?"

"Lisa? My Lisa?" he said, not even hiding the happy lilt in his voice.

"I did not realize that she belonged to you," Charlie teased. "Last time I checked Lisa didn't like to be thought of as a possession."

"You know what I mean," he said, instantly grumpy.

"Yes I do," Charlie said. "So can she come or not?"

"I don't see why not as long as she follows the rules," Jason said.

"Can you follow the rules?" Charlie asked.

Lisa tipped her head to one side and pursed her lips. "You know I can."

"Great. She's coming, too, then."

"What time can you be out here?"

"I'm busy until one-ish today. I'm having lunch with Tom. I don't know what Lisa's schedule is like." Lisa gave her a death glare. "Oh it looks like Lisa's schedule just opened up. So any time after one will be fine."

"Great, I'll send you directions."

"Wonderful. I'll see you around two?"

"Two is perfect," he said. "See you then."

Charlie pressed the red icon on her phone and disconnected the call.

Lisa folded her arms across her chest and shook her head.

"What are you playing at Charlie Payne?" Lisa asked.

"I'm not playing. I want you there for a reason. I'll explain everything over pancakes," she said as a waitress with blue hair approached carrying their plates.

* * *

CHAPTER 9

Ben walked out of his motel room and pulled the door tight behind him. He walked across the street to the Waffle Hut to grab some breakfast and figure out his next move. He'd arrived in the middle of the night and had barely slept, the hurt look on Jen's face haunting his dreams. There was nothing he could do about that now. He was here and he had a job to do. If he survived maybe he'd go back. Maybe. He wasn't even sure that she would have him now. And who could blame her? She needed somebody steady in her life. Somebody who could offer stability and health insurance. Somebody who wasn't him. It didn't matter how he felt about her, he had pledged his life to do this job and that's what he was going to do.

Ben sat down at the counter and turned the coffee

cup sitting in front of him upright. Within seconds a waitress in a faded yellow uniform with the name Florence embroidered above her left breast appeared and filled his cup.

"What can I get you, doll?" She pulled a pencil from the breast pocket of her dress along with an order pad. She perched the tip of the pencil against the grayish striped paper.

"What's good?" He asked.

"The waffles," she said flatly. "That's why they call it the Waffle Hut." There was no cheerful smile. No sparkling blue eyes. No good humor with a joke at the ready. The whole act of ordering breakfast left him empty. God, what was wrong with him? Six months ago he would've breezed into town, found his demon and done his job. Now all he could do was think about Jen and the day they first met. How adorable she had been. How calm and excited she had made him feel all at the same time.

He frowned, giving the menu in front of him a cursory glance. "I guess I'll have the waffles then."

"Okay, hon." She scribbled his order on her pad and stuck it into a spinning wheel at a pass-through to the kitchen before she moved on to the next occupied seat.

He glanced around at the sorry little restaurant. The clientele was mostly men, drinking coffee and eating waffles before heading to their jobs. The air stank of stale cigarettes and quiet desperation.

Ben pulled his phone from his pocket and began to search for any local shops that might possibly be run by a witch. Every community he'd ever been to had a witch and sometimes a whole coven. If he could find whoever supplied local witches with their herbs and crystals then he could figure out what the hell was going on here.

A quick Google search didn't yield much locally. Everything could be bought online these days. When further searches didn't point to a likely supplier, he bought a local paper from the machine by the door. It would be a sad day for him when little newspapers ceased to exist. He leafed through the pages until he found the police blotter. Among the reports of drunken and disorderly conduct by a couple of yokels and a neighbor dispute over a dead dog, one thing stood out.

A disturbance on Clarence Street had been reported by one Miss Myrtle Henshaw. The police had been called out to screams in the night and the loud clattering of trash cans being overturned. Miss Myrtle had reported seeing a dark figure fleeing from the house of one Megan Forrester. When the police knocked on Miss Forrester's door there was no answer and no sign of a struggle or forced entry.

Ben chuckled. It looked like a witch, and he was almost willing to bet that it'd smell like a witch once he got close enough. A witch hiding in plain sight. He added sugar to his coffee and waited for his waffles. Maybe if he was lucky, he'd be out of this town by dinnertime. Maybe.

* * *

Ben parked in front of the tidy craftsman style house. He noticed the neighbor across the street peeking out from behind her curtains as he approached the front door. He smiled and waved at her and she quickly ducked out of sight. He knocked and waited. Why not put on a good show? He quickly glanced over his shoulder toward the neighbor's house again. She seemed to have either taken up a different perch to spy on him or was minding her own business. He somehow doubted it was the latter. Ben placed his hand on the knob and gave it a turn. The antique brass doorknob didn't give. He tapped on the metal three times and whispered, "Unlock, unlock, unlock." His magic was always at the ready and it didn't fail him now. The lock clicked and Ben turned the knob and walked inside as if he belonged there.

He closed the door behind him.

"Megan?" He stopped and listened to the house. It didn't even creak. "Megan, my name is Ben Sutton. I'm with the Defenders of Light. I'm here to help you." No response.

Ben made his way methodically through the house

starting in the parlor to the right of the foyer. The house looked as if it had been completely restored. The dark oak floors, baseboards and wainscoting gleamed in the early morning light that poured through the front windows. From the looks of it, Megan didn't use the fireplace. She had placed a tiered candleholder where the logs should have gone. Built-in bookshelves flanked the fireplace and he gave the books and knickknacks a once over. If she was a hedge witch, working alone and not within a coven, she didn't put it on display. There were no books on magic or spells. There weren't even books on gardening or cooking. Just a lot of paperbacks. He pulled one off the dusty shelf and found a long-haired, bare chested man on the front cover. Ben chuckled to himself. A romance reader.

He noticed two things — a bare spot in the thick dust next to a miniature statue of the Greek goddess Persephone. Mixed with the dust was a glittery yellow residue. Ben traced his finger through the thick powdery layer and drew it up to his nose. The scent of rotten eggs made him gag before he had a chance to sneeze. Brimstone. Megan had definitely been conjuring. This was the kind of stuff that gave witches a bad name. He wiped his finger on the dark velvet armchair nearest the fireplace and scowled. Freaking hedge witches. Why couldn't they just follow the rules? Now he was going to have to hunt her down and take her in. No matter what her excuse was.

He crossed the foyer to the dining room and moved into the kitchen through the butler's pantry. A small oak kitchen table nestled beneath a bank of windows overlooking the backyard was set with one placemat and one glass half full of water. There were no dishes in the drainer and everything else seemed to be in order in the tidy little home. Still the energy of this house pulsed against his skin. Magic had definitely been practiced here recently. The energy of it hung in the air like a mist hanging over a summer lake.

Ben headed up the back stairs to the second floor. The eerie silence of the house made the hairs on his arms stand at attention. He opened and closed his hands a couple of times, ready to fight whatever came at him. A cursory inspection of the two bedrooms made him wonder when was the last time Megan had slept here. The headboard of the bed in the master bedroom looked dusty.

Ben went to the large window and opened the blinds. The room practically sparkled with the golden yellow dust. Dread coiled around his heart and squeezed.

"Where are you Megan?" he muttered. The only answer he received was silence.

CHAPTER 10

Charlie unpacked the large paper bag with the handle and the Kitchen Witch Café logo on the side.

"So I see you didn't cook," Tom teased as he spread the blue gingham tablecloth that Charlie had borrowed from her uncle's house.

She had brought him to Palmetto Point Beach Park and led him to the farthest picnic table underneath the last picnic shelter in the park. It had the best view of the ocean.

"You really don't want me to," Charlie said. "Trust me on this. I can make a mean scrambled eggs but that's about the extent of my cooking skills."

"It's fine," Tom said in a jovial voice. "I'd eat dirt as long as I got to be with you."

Charlie's stomach flip-flopped and she couldn't stop a smile from spreading across her face as she opened the plastic box holding their green salad. Tom took two paper plates and set them next to each other on the blue cloth. When the feast was all laid out they sat down next to each other and dug into the fried chicken, sliced tomatoes and cucumbers, green salad and potato salad. For dessert Jen had sent banana pudding.

"I like this place," he said, looking out at the seascape while he speared a cucumber on his plate. "You come here a lot?"

"Not really. I'd love to come more, though." She scraped half of the ranch dressing from a small plastic portion cup onto her salad and handed the rest of it to Tom. " It seems like the only time I get over here anymore is in the summer when I have Evan."

"Sure, that makes sense." He used up the rest of the dressing on his salad.

"I have a confession," Charlie said wiping her hands on the paper napkin Tom had laid by her plate.

"Really?" He tilted his head a little and gave her a sideways glance. "And what is that, Charlie Payne?"

"I brought you here for reason," she said.

He leaned in close and she could feel his breath against her cheek when he whispered, "Would the reason be foreplay?"

Charlie nudged him in the ribs with her elbow. Her

cheeks burned as if she'd stood in the sun too long. "Just cool your jets there, mister."

He laughed out loud and Charlie found herself enraptured with the sound. Oh good Lord — maybe Ben was right. Maybe Tom did have magic. It certainly felt like he was casting a spell on her.

"I'm just teasing," he said. "No pressure really. We have all the time in the world."

"Maybe you do," Charlie said.

He cleared his throat. "So what is this confession?"

"I'm actually kind of hoping that we're going to see a spirit today," Charlie said.

"Did you want me here for protection?" he quipped.

"Oh stop it."

"Who's the spirit? Do you know?" He picked up the little container of banana pudding and took a bite. A moan escaped his lips. "Oh my God, this is so good. I swear it's like Jen cast a spell on these bananas."

"Uh huh," Charlie said, focusing on her own plate. She had no idea whether Jen could cast a spell on her food, but she had her suspicions. "Who I'm looking for is the blue lady. Have you ever heard of her?"

"Of course. Everyone in a hundred mile range has heard of her. She's been dodging reapers for over 160 years. Why do you want to see her? Legend has it that any human who does is cursed."

"Right," Charlie said, her voice little shaky. "I've already seen her once this week."

"Did you?" Tom said, giving her cautious look. "Did she see you? It's the interaction, I believe, that invokes the curse."

"Yes, she saw me. We had a little chat."

"What did she say?" he asked warily.

"Not a whole lot really." Charlie pushed the salad on her plate around with her fork. "I got the feeling that in life she may have been psychic. I think she actually foresaw her lover's death."

"That's an interesting theory." Tom held his fork suspended over his food as he listened to Charlie's account.

"I also don't think that seeing her and speaking to her is a curse."

"Let me guess, you don't believe in curses," Tom teased. "What kind of a witch are you?"

"A witch that doesn't practice curses. I also don't believe for a second that a spirit can cast one. I felt kind of sorry for her. She's just looking for her love and he's never gonna come," Charlie said as a pang of sadness filled her chest.

"And you want me to help her." Tom gazed at her with awe in his eyes. He leaned close and kissed her on the cheek. "You're a good woman, Charlie Payne."

"I don't know about that," Charlie said. "I actually want to talk about her prediction for me before I hand her over to you and help her find the proverbial light."

"She's a tricky one," he said. "My brother William has been after her for years." He had resumed his lunch, with some gusto for a man who didn't require food for sustenance.

"Will it cause problems if you take her?" Charlie asked.

"No," Tom chuckled. "Some reapers are territorial but my family isn't. If I found her and was able to capture her, then William would strike her name from his book and move on to the next soul."

"Can I ask you a question about your family?" Charlie fiddled with the ridge around the handle of her plastic spoon.

"Of course. You know me, I'm an open book." Tom gave her a wink. There were things he wouldn't tell her, things she probably didn't really want to know and things he'd been bound to keep secret by oath.

"Right," Charlie said.

"How about, I tell you what I am allowed but no more. Deal?"

"Deal," Charlie swallowed hard. Now that she had the chance, the words wanted to stick in her throat. "I know that William is your brother. And Joy is your sister. Do you have a mother? Or a father? How does it ... how does it work exactly?"

"That is a very good question," he said. He took a scoop of potato salad and shoved it into his mouth. He turned his head to the side again and didn't take his eyes off of her. She wished for just one second she could see inside his head. He seemed to be regarding her with care, as if he didn't want to scare her with the answer. Finally he smiled.

"We were not born in the sense that you understand. So there is no mother and father. But we do answer to someone."

"Who?" Charlie asked.

"He has many names. Most cultures regard him as the angel of death or just simply death. He is as old as time," Tom said.

"You report to an angel?" Charlie asked.

"Not in the way that you think of an angel. In fact, we've wandered into very gray territory. This is how religions get started," he said. "Isn't it enough to know that we're all part of something larger than ourselves?"

Charlie sighed and speared the halved cherry tomato on her plate. Jen had grown them in her kitchen garden and they were sweet little bites of heaven when Charlie had an appetite. All this talk of death and angels, though, made her hunger disappear. "Yes, I suppose it is."

"Come on, let's finish our lunch and go for a walk on the beach." He took her hand and kissed her knuckles. "Who knows? Maybe we'll get lucky and run into your cursed spirit."

Charlie's lips curved into a smile. "Maybe we will."

CHAPTER 11

Charlie insisted on driving to the site to meet Jason and Cameron. She expected Lisa to put up more of a fight but once her cousin got a look at the map Charlie had printed she didn't complain. Lisa didn't like to drag her BMW through the country roads, especially not into the woods. Charlie just hoped the dirt road that Jason described wouldn't be too muddy.

"So how come Jason doesn't want you to go see the body?" Lisa asked.

Charlie drove along Highway 17 out toward Ravenel. "I asked him that when we started with the second victim instead of the latest. He said partly because she was in such bad shape. I think he was worried that it would gross me out too much."

"So what's the likelihood you'll even see her?" Lisa asked.

"Spirits don't always follow their bodies around. If it's as bad as he said, it may be too traumatic for her to think about staying with it. Denial is a strong emotion, especially for the dead," Charlie said. "I'm almost hoping that she's hanging around where her body was dumped."

"Almost, huh?"

Charlie shrugged. "Just 'cause I can see a ghost, doesn't always mean I want to see a ghost."

"Yeah, I get that. Although, it would definitely be helpful if she's there," Lisa said. She shifted her gaze to the map. "You're gonna turn left onto 162 up ahead."

Charlie got into the left-hand lane as she approached the turnoff. She stopped at the stop sign and waited for the oncoming traffic heading north on 17 to thin enough for her to make the turn. "I didn't think traffic out here would be this bad at this time of day."

"It's always busy on this highway these days," Lisa said.

She made the turn and headed down the two-lane road. The trees came almost up to the asphalt and in some places large oaks had hazard signs warning people of their presence, explaining that they had been there first. It was the road that had encroached. The trees on either side stretched overhead forming a shady canopy. Sunlight filtered through, splashing the dusky gray asphalt with dappled light that chased back the shadows. Charlie stuck close to the faded yellow centerline until Lisa directed her to turn right onto a dirt road.

Charlie took it slow, sand and gravel grinding beneath the wheels of her Honda. She held her breath as they approached a large puddle, testing its depth and the grip of her tires.

"There's another dirt road not too far from here." Lisa pointed up ahead, reading from the printed email Jason had sent with directions. "He says to look for the yellow mailbox."

"Uh huh, I see it up ahead," Charlie said. She turned right and inched forward on the compacted sandy road. Finally in the distance she saw Jason's black Dodge Charger. He got out of his car and waved them down as soon as they were within sight. Charlie pulled onto the narrow shoulder behind him.

Jason approached Charlie's car and she rolled down the window. He leaned down. "Hey," he said giving them both a smile. "I hope you're wearing walking shoes."

"How far is it?" she asked.

"About a quarter-mile through the woods," he said sounding apologetic.

"Great," Charlie muttered. She reached across to her glove compartment and opened it, pulling a dark green can with an orange top from inside.

"What's that for?" Jason said. "I haven't been swarmed by any mosquitoes out here."

"Mosquitoes. Ticks. No-see-ums. They may not love you, but they love me," Charlie said. She got out of her car and went to her trunk. Lisa followed her and Charlie turned her key in the lock. The trunk popped up and they both put their purses inside. Charlie shoved her keys in her pocket. "It's supposed to be a bad tick year. You'd be smart to let me spray you down, too."

"Yes, mom," Jason said in a sarcastic tone.

A fine mist began around Charlie's feet and spread up her legs as she saturated her jeans and tennis shoes with the deep woods bug spray, then squeezed her eyes shut and lightly sprayed her hair. Lisa did the same and then handed the can to Jason.

He rolled his eyes. "No thanks."

"Suit yourself," Lisa said and tossed the can into the trunk before closing it.

Lisa and Charlie followed Jason to a path in the woods. Pine straw crunched beneath her tennis shoes and the trees rustled and crackled with a strong breeze.

Charlie's skin began to thrum as they drew closer to the clearing. Jason and Lisa chatted and were friendlier with each other today than they had been yesterday. The drone of their voices buzzed in her ears like an indolent bee drunk on nectar. Her heart beat hard in her throat with each step. She could feel his energy pulsing. Was this what it was like for a deer wandering into a wolf's territory. Knowing the boundaries were there because they had been marked. Knowing at any moment the predator could strike. This place. This girl. It all belonged to him now. Would he defend it? She wouldn't know until she tried to cross his boundary. Until she became the deer.

"Charlie?" Lisa asked. "Are you okay?"

"I'm fine," Charlie said but the words were rote. Lisa gave her a pointed look. Jason may not have been one to pay attention, but Lisa was a different story altogether. Charlie sighed. "I can feel him. Okay? Is that what you want to hear?"

"Not really," Lisa said wryly. "But I'd rather you be truthful with me."

"What do you mean you can feel him?" Jason said. He scanned the surrounding woods.

"He's not here. That's not what I meant," Charlie chuckled. "I feel his energy. It's residual."

"What does that mean?" Jason asked, curiosity filling his voice.

"Sometimes people leave a signature. I'm sensitive to that energy. And his is strong," Charlie said.

"Oh," Jason said, leaving it at that.

"I don't feel it exactly the same way Charlie does, but I can feel darkness here," Lisa said. "Blood was spilled."

"Great," Jason said. "That just opens up a whole different set of questions."

"What do you mean?" Lisa asked.

"There wasn't much blood here when we found her. He didn't kill her here. He ..."

"Posed her." Charlie finished his sentence. "Right?"

"Yeah," Jason said. Deep worry lines formed on his forehead. Worry lines she knew too well. Charlie tried to give him a reassuring smile but her lips wouldn't cooperate and it turned into a grimace. He'd told her almost nothing about how the victims had been found. But the closer they came to the location, the clearer it became to her.

"I see him." She turned her gaze to the road behind them, and the whole scene unfolded before her. The sun had sunk below the tree line when he brought her to this place. The light dimmed and Charlie could hear crickets and cicadas. In her mind's eye, he drove a little further up the road. He didn't bother pulling over. His red brake lights glowed and he came to a stop in the center of the road and put the car in park. As he hopped out Charlie focused on his face. Maybe she could work with a sketch artist. At least that would be something. But he kept his head down and the murky light made it almost impossible to make out his features. She watched as he made his way to the back of the car. Charlie approached him carefully watching as he opened the trunk, taking note of the model of car he drove and the color. A powerful sense of remorse flowed from him. Inside the trunk was a young woman with red hair that had been braided and coiled on top of her head. Her eyes were closed but Charlie knew instinctively that the young woman wasn't sleeping. She was dead. He placed his hand against her cheek gently cupping it.

"I'm so sorry," he mumbled. Then he lifted her up and carried her away. Charlie followed him but he disappeared when he came to the clearing. She stopped in her tracks. Her vision cleared and the sun shined as brightly as it should for 2 o'clock in the afternoon. Charlie blinked away tears and took a breath. She was halfway up the path to the clearing. She glanced around and Jason and Lisa caught up with her.

"What did you see?" Jason asked.

"He drives a Grand Torino," Charlie said. "Or at least he did when he brought her here. It looked sort of dark yellow or maybe goldish brown. I can't be sure exactly because he brought her after sundown."

"That's great, Charlie," Jason said pulling a small notebook from the breast pocket of his polo shirt. "Did you notice anything else? You know, like a license plate?"

Charlie rolled her eyes. "Now, you know it doesn't work like that," Charlie chided. "I see what she shows me."

"And she showed you a Grand Torino?" Jason chuckled.

"I saw the car. I just happen to know it's a Grand Torino, that's all," Charlie said.

"Should I ask why?" Jason teased. "I didn't think you were into muscle cars."

"She's not," Lisa said matter-of-factly. "Marty Cobb."

"Exactly," Charlie grinned. "It looked a lot like his, except the color. I think his was red."

"Who's Marty Cobb?" Jason asked.

"He's a boy we went to high school with," Lisa said. "He was a senior when I was a junior and Charlie and Jen were sophomores.

"Any chance you know the year of that Torino?" Jason asked.

"No, sorry," Charlie said.

Lisa shrugged. "I could find out. I updated his will last year. I could call him."

"That would be great, babe. Thank you." Jason said scribbling into his notepad. "Was that it? Any other details?"

"He ... he was sad." Charlie frowned. "Remorseful. He told her he was sorry. It didn't make any sense to me."

"Any chance you got a look at his face?" Jason asked sounding hopeful.

"Not really. It was shadowy. There was one thing though." Charlie closed her eyes and commanded the memory of the vision to appear. In her mind, she stood beside the man at the trunk. He was nothing but a silhouette but something stood out. Her eyes opened and stared directly into Jason's intense face. "He had a pony tail."

"A ponytail. You sure?" Jason asked.

"Yes," Charlie said.

"That's good. That's really good, Charlie," Jason said. "As usual you amaze me with your details."

"I'm sorry it's not more," Charlie said.

"It's more than I had an hour ago. I'll take it." Jason gave her a reassuring smile and touched her arm. "I kinda wish Cameron was here to hear this."

"Why?" Lisa said.

"Cameron's not a believer," Charlie said. "It wouldn't matter if he was here, Jason. He'd think that somehow I had weaseled the information out of you."

"That's such bullshit," Lisa muttered. "I mean I understand being a doubter but if you have faith in her, Jason, then why can't he?"

"He hasn't seen what I have," Jason said. "And I was not a believer in the beginning, remember?"

"Oh yeah, I remember," Charlie said.

"Is he gonna put a damper on what you do see? I'll send him away if he will. I don't give a crap if he believes me or not," Jason said.

"It's fine," Charlie said.

"Will you stop doing that?" Lisa snapped. "It's not fine."

"Yes, it is," Charlie countered. "He's not important to me. It's more important that Jason believes in me."

"Awww, Charleeee," Jason grinned, his eyes full of mischief. "I heart you, too. Do we need to hug?" He opened his arms wide and walked toward her in a comical way.

"Jason Tate don't you dare," Charlie said laughing. "You know it will throw me off."

Jason stopped a foot away and swiped at the air in front of his nose. "Shoo, you stink like bug spray. Wouldn't want to get that all over my clothes, now would I?"

"Lisa, I can't believe you put up with this," Charlie said.

Lisa grinned. "Yeah, I know. It's a good thing he's good looking."

Jason gave her a hurt look. "Really? That's all I am to you? Eye candy."

"If the Skittle fits," Lisa teased.

"Okay you two, cut it out. You're gonna sap my mojo," Charlie scolded.

"Well we wouldn't want to do that," Lisa said. "Sorry, Charlie. We'll behave."

"Yeah, sorry, Charlie," Jason said. "So can I ask you a question?"

"I think you just did," Lisa said giving him a hard time.

"Har D har, har," Jason said exaggerating his face. "You are just a barrel of laughs today Lisa Marie Holloway."

Lisa giggled. Charlie couldn't remember the last time she'd heard Lisa giggle like that.

"You know you can ask me anything," Charlie said.

"It's not that I'm unhappy to see Lisa. But why were you so adamant that she come," Jason asked.

"Adamant? That's a little strong," Charlie wrinkled her nose.

"I'm going to help her," Lisa said.

"How?" Jason asked.

"I'm going to cast a spell that will prevent her from experiencing pain or any sort of physical manifestation of her visions," Lisa said.

"You can do that?" Jason asked.

"I'm going to try," Lisa said. "It was actually Charlie's idea."

"Yeah," Charlie said. "But Lisa has the magical capability to carry it out. I don't. Not on my own anyway."

"Wow," Jason said. "That's great, if it will protect Charlie."

"Let's just hope it works," Lisa said. "It's a spell I got from a witch doctor that Evangeline knows. I haven't had time to practice it, though."

"Is that dangerous?" Jason asked, concern deepening the lines in his forehead.

"Let's hope not," Lisa said. Jason's mouth gaped open.

"It'll be fine. Okay?" Lisa said patting him on the shoulder. "I promise. I wouldn't do anything that would hurt her."

"Okay," Jason gave them both a wary eye.

Charlie and Lisa traded glances. Both suppressing a grin. "Don't worry Jason. There is nobody in this world that I trust more than my cousins. Lisa's an exemplary witch. She won't let me down."

"Okay, if you say so," Jason said. "I guess we should hurry up. I left Cameron in the clearing by himself."

"Yeah, we better hurry," Charlie said, wryly. " We wouldn't want the bogeyman to get him."

CHAPTER 12

After a quick call to DOL headquarters, Ben found what he was looking for — a solid lead.

"In 500 feet turn right," the chipper voice of his GPS said.

"Yes ma'am," he said softly.

He noticed the sign before he even saw the half circle driveway. It read: Psychic Readings in large decorative letters. Next to it, hanging from the same wrought iron pole, was a placard with a laundry list of other services available. Tarot, séances, numerology, astrology and past life readings. Ben chuckled and turned into the driveway, parking behind a black Mercedes SUV. At least her clientele looked like they could pay.

He surveyed the small house that, from the looks of it, had been rezoned as commercial. The neat little brick ranch was wedged between a chiropractor in a nondescript white clapboard and an insurance agency in a beige saltbox.

A red neon Open sign flashed in the psychic's window. Ben got out, walked up the three steps to the front porch and let himself in. A bell tinkled above his head as he entered the former living room now transformed into a waiting room. The cool, patchouli-scented air circulated around him and he closed the door. A well-dressed older woman with a silver bob and an expensive manicure sat in one of the antique chairs flipping casually through a magazine. Had Lauren gotten this wrong? This looked like a standard psychic set up.

The older woman looked up at him, her eyes going over his body from head to toe. She smiled.

"I don't think I've seen you here before," she said in a deep sultry voice.

"No, I stopped by more out of curiosity." He had an impulse to cover his chest with his hands. He didn't like the hungry look in her eyes.

"Okay, Elinor," a voice came from behind a beaded curtain. A moment later a woman in her early thirties emerged. A bright colorful red scarf held her long raven curls away from her face. She wore a ruffled blue blouse over a red tank top tucked into a pair of dark yellow, skinny jeans with red flats finishing off her outfit. Ben had to think hard to figure out exactly who she reminded him of. Her pale white skin and rosy cheeks gave it away. He chuckled to himself. Snow White.

She flashed her large blue eyes at him and gave him a smile. "I'll be right with you."

Elinor rose from her chair placing the magazine back in its rack on the floor. He watched the transaction between them as Snow White handed the older woman a paper bag.

"Well, that's new. Is it a poison apple?" he asked, amusing himself.

Snow White threw him a confused look. The older woman took the paper bag and shifted her gaze to him.

"No, my dear. It's much better than that," she purred. "You're welcome to come with me to find out."

Ben smiled and held his ground. "That's a tempting offer. But unfortunately I've got business here."

Elinor picked up her purse from the floor and slung the leather strap over her shoulder. "Well if you change your mind, I own the bead shop downtown."

He halfway expected her to try to take a bite out of him but she just flipped her hair and left, the bell tinkling overhead.

"So how can I help you?" Snow White asked.

Ben pulled his credentials from his pocket. "I'm Ben Sutton with the DOL. I'm hoping you can answer a few questions for me."

She took the wallet from his hand and studied the

picture and credentials. She handed the badge back to him. "My business is on the up and up."

"We'll have to see about that," he said. "Is there someplace we can talk privately?"

"Sure," she said. "Come on back to my reading room."

He followed her through the veil of beads down a narrow hallway. At the end he could see sunny yellow wallpaper with flowers, a white tile floor and white cabinetry. "So do you just work here or do you also live here?"

"Are you also from the zoning commission?" she asked.

"No," he said. "Just curious. It looks like a nice set up."

"Well, technically this is my business," she said. They passed a bedroom with shelves lining the walls stocked with jars of ingredients. In the center was what looked like a kitchen island. A large mortar and pestle rested on the butcher block top next to a large leather-bound book.

"You have a spells and potions room," he said.

"Yes, I do. It's an additional service I offer select clients." She stopped and stared him in the eye. "There's nothing illegal about it."

"Maybe there is, maybe there isn't. I may just have to call in a squad to go through it."

"Are you kidding me?" she bristled. "Like I said, everything I do here is on the up and up."

"That's what they all say," he chided.

"You know, I really don't appreciate these sorts of surprise inspections. I should at least get a little notice."

"Well where would the fun in that be?" Ben quipped.

She stared at him in astonishment.

"Listen, I'm not really here to bust your chops over potions. I need help," Ben said.

She eyed him warily. "What kind of help?"

"I need to find a witch."

"Well, you found one," she answered tartly and started walking again. She directed him into a room on the right. The walls had been painted a dark purple and there were little silver stars and moons along the tops of the walls, bordering the ceiling. A rosewood table sat in the center of the room with two chairs facing each other pushed underneath. A deck of tarot cards rested on one side. Her side.

"Have a seat," she said sitting in the chair facing the door.

Ben pulled out the other chair and took a seat. He leaned forward with his elbows on the table. "You must do very well to afford the rent here."

"I have a lovely clientele. They take care of me and I take care of them," she said.

"Yeah, I bet. Wouldn't want to do anything to upset that clientele would we?"

She narrowed her eyes. "No, we wouldn't. Now what can I help you with?"

"I got a report stating there had been a witch in the area that has summoned a demon. This evidently happened a week or so ago. A child went missing – a baby. And an older couple that was killed."

"Right, I heard about that on the news," she said. "And you think that was a witch?"

"No. I think it was a demon. Whether he's working with her or possessing her, that remains to be seen."

"I don't understand how I can help you," she said.

"Why don't you tell me about the witches in this area? I don't have a registered coven here."

"Well I'm not surprised about that," she said. "Most of us here are in the broom closet. I get away with stuff because I'm a psychic. And that's a legal business. I might be scorned but nobody's threatening to burn my business down. Being a witch out in the open here, though, could be dangerous."

"How?"

"This is a small southern town with a church on every corner." She shrugged. "There are a few of us here, mostly hedge witches. We don't really gather together except on Mabon and Samhain. We're friends but nothing official. No coven leader."

"I'm gonna need the names of the hedge witches in the area."

She sat back. "Okay. I'm happy to help but ..."

"But?"

"I think you should get a reading."

"No thanks." He scowled. "No offense but I'm not one to put a whole lot of stock in the cards."

"It's just one card," she countered.

"Why?" he said.

"It'll tell me if you're going to hurt my friends or not. That's all."

Ben met her unwavering eyes. "Fine."

"Cut the cards." She pushed the deck toward him. He did as she asked. Then she shuffled them together again and fanned them out in a semicircle across the table. "Pick your card."

Ben reached for the first card in the center.

"Don't do it like that," she scolded and batted his hand away. "If you're gonna play, at least play right. You know how it works."

He blew out a heavy breath and closed his eyes. His right hand hovered above the table. An energy radiated faintly between him and the cards. His forefinger twitched and began to drag his hand from one end of the semicircle to the other and back before stopping. He opened his eyes and touched the forefinger to the edge of one of the cards between the middle and right end of the semi-circle.

He hated this sort of thing. Hated the pull of that card. Nobody was supposed to know the future. "That's why the world is round and why you can't see beyond the horizon," his mentor Will Tucker had told him once when he was just a boy, following Tucker around from job to job. "Knowing the future won't serve you anything but heartache, kid." Words Ben usually lived by. He looked into the young witch's eyes. She seemed to be studying his face.

"If you're scared ..." she began. A slight grin played on her lips.

"Ah screw you," he muttered and drew the card out and flipped it over. "Happy now?"

"Very." She pulled the card closer to her. "This is very interesting," she said studying the beautifully drawn card.

"Interesting how?" he asked, keeping his tone flat.

"This is the world card. It's that space between the ending of something and the beginning of something else. If you'd drawn it upright, it could have meant fulfillment or achievement. But you drew it upside down. You're struggling. A door in your life is still open and it's causing you strife. You need closure but you don't want it. If you pick another card, it will tell me more about your situation."

"No, thanks," Ben grimaced. "Just give me the names. And I'll be on my way."

"Fine." She gathered the cards back into a tidy deck and put his on top. "Let me get my address book."

Ben looked over his shoulder once she was out of sight, swiped the card he'd drawn and put it in his pocket.

CHAPTER 13

Ben scratched through another name on his list and tucked the piece of paper into his front pocket. Megan's name had not been on the psychic's list, but that didn't mean she wasn't a witch. He had good instincts about these things and the brimstone only proved something demonic had happened at that house. Hopefully, one of the witches on the list would know her.

He punched in the next address on the GPS app on his phone and began to listen to the pleasant computer voice that doled out the directions to the next witch he needed interview — Arista Carrington. The confident female speaker led him out of the little sleepy town of Acadia to rolling hills. After almost twenty minutes, she directed him to turn right onto a long, unpaved driveway.

When he emerged from beneath the tunnel of oaks, a large white plantation house with Doric columns and a wide brick front porch loomed before him. It looked almost like something out of a movie.

He parked at the base of the steps and got out. From the top of the porch, he looked back toward the driveway and could almost picture a carriage emerging from the corridor of oaks. When he rang the front bell it echoed through the grandiose house - ding dong ding. Ding dong ding. He waited a minute, listening for any sense of movement. He raised his hand to press the bell again but the door opened wide.

A regal, older woman with shoulder length silvery hair stood in the doorway. Her cold sapphire stare fixed him to the spot. She sniffed the air and narrowed her eyes. "To what do I owe this honor, Defender of Light?"

"How do you know I'm a Defender of Light?" he asked.

"I know a cop when I smell one," she said. "Whatever it is you think I've done, I know my rights. You have to prove it before you act."

"That kind of talk only makes me suspicious. You know that, right?" He could play this game too.

"Well, you people tend to act first and ask questions later. Nobody needs their magic bound up today. I have a potion brewing."

"I'm not here to bind anybody's magic today," he said. "I do have a few questions, though."

"All right." She folded her long thin arms across her chest.

"Are you Arista Carrington?"

"I am. And who are you?"

"My name is Ben Sutton. Do you mind if I come in for a few minutes?" He glanced behind her trying to see beyond the generous foyer.

Her thin lips flattened into a straight line, but she opened the door wider and gestured for him to enter. He stepped into the cool of the house. The scent of orange hung in the air, making his nose tingle.

The black and white marble tiles in the foyer gleamed. A remnant of days gone by, just like the staircase with the lustrous walnut banister. It curved up to a gallery overlooking the foyer.

"Come with me," she said, leading him into a living room decorated in all white. "Won't you have a seat?" She lowered herself into an overstuffed upholstered chair next to a coordinating overstuffed sofa. Ben sank into the sofa and scanned the room. The air smelled sweet and clean, with only a hint of orange. Not a speck of dust floated in the air.

"We received a report that a local witch may have summoned a demon. I've already talked to several witches in the area and none of them seem to know this witch."

"I'm not surprised. We all keep mostly to ourselves," she said.

"I figured that much out. I do have a lead on a Megan Forrester. From the looks of her house, she may be my culprit," he said.

Arista was all angles and lines, with just a hint of curve at the breast and hips. Nothing about her sharp pointed face suggested warmth or empathy. "So?"

"None of the other witches I've spoken to in this freaking town seems to know who she is. You people don't even seem to get together for high holidays." Irritation crept into his tone.

"There are no laws saying we have to," she replied.

"Maybe there should be," Ben said studying her body language. "There's less chance of someone going rogue when there's a coven. And more sense of community."

She shrugged one bony shoulder and rolled her eyes. "Community has never been my thing."

"Maybe I've got it wrong then," Ben said. He sat forward with his elbows on his knees and folded his hands together. "Maybe it isn't Megan at all. Maybe it's you."

Arista's sat up straight. Her jaw set with determination. "And tell me how you came to that brilliant deduction." She practically spat the words.

"Fairly easily. Maybe Megan doesn't really exist. Maybe she's made up. A scapegoat for all the other witches like you who want to do dirty deeds and not have to be accountable for them. What kind of potion are you making, Arista?"

"That's none of your business," she said.

"I would beg to differ with you. If it's anybody's business it's mine and the DOLs." He got to his feet and stared down at her. "Where is it?"

Southern women were notorious for their ability to conjure a look that could kill. And southern witches were no exception. The animosity in Arista's stare made the hairs on Ben's arms shrivel as if they'd been touched by heat. "Do I have to turn this house upside down?"

"You don't have the right to do that. Not without the correct paperwork."

"What makes you think I can't get the correct paperwork by the time I'm finished tossing this place?" he said. They stared at one another, neither willing to yield. Ben didn't have the patience for this sort of thing. And it was almost as if Arista sensed that about him.

Her chest rose and fell too quickly though. The pale skin at her hairline became dewy. If he could just hold out long enough. Surely she would break.

"What's it gonna be Arista? You show me what you're making and I don't tear this place down." A bead of sweat traveled down her hairline, disappearing near her ear.

"Okay let the tearing begin." He took one step away breaking her gaze. A familiar thrumming pulsated in his palms as he shifted his magic toward them. Two glowing yellow- orange orbs formed, hovering above his cupped hands.

"Okay," she said. "Just put your guns down. There won't be any need to burn anything down."

Ben closed his hands and the yellow orbs disappeared, the energy reabsorbed into his body. "I'll ask one more time then, what are you making?"

"If you must know I am making a potion to kill the demon."

"And why would you do that?"

Arista sighed and rolled her eyes in defeat. "Because Megan Forrester is my niece."

"So you've known this whole time," Ben said not bothering to hide the disgust in his voice.

"Yes I have known. The problem with Megan is that she's not actually a very powerful witch. I let her apprentice under me a few years back and well it was disastrous actually."

"Do you think she meant to summon the demon then?" Ben asked.

"I don't know." Arista dabbed at the sweat along her hairline, pushing it into her hair. "I would like to think that she did it by accident. She sometimes would screw up spells pretty badly."

"Yeah but a summoning spell ..." Ben said.

"I know. I'm probably making excuses that I shouldn't be. But she's the only family I have left."

Ben sighed and scrubbed his rough beard. "I'm sorry to hear that. You know this isn't going to end well for her. If that thing she summoned doesn't kill her, then if she's as bad a witch as you say she is, I will legally have no other choice than to bind her magic."

Arista's hand drifted to her throat and her face paled. "For how long?"

"Forever. Till she dies anyway," Ben said.

"And you want me to just give her over to you?" she said, sounding put out.

"This isn't about what I want. Or what you want. There's a demon on the loose in this town and it will continue to kill and wreak havoc until it's either dead or back in hell," he said. "I would appreciate a little help."

"And what if I don't help you?" She leveled her hard blue eyes on him.

His fingers twitched. It wouldn't take much to make her do what he wanted. You'll get more flies with honey, Jen's sweet voice floated through his head. He sighed. If he couldn't use force, then there was only one other thing to do.

"I walk away, leaving you with the knowledge that you could've saved your niece and helped stop that thing from killing another innocent. That blood won't be on my hands. It'll be on yours."

He held her gaze for a few seconds more, then turned to leave.

"Wait," she said. He turned. Her shoulders drooped a little. She sighed. "Fine. What do you want me to do?"

And it was guilt for the win.

"First, show me the potion. Then I need to talk to her. Can you get me in touch with her?" he asked.

"I can try."

CHAPTER 14

Charlie spotted her in the center of the fire ring. It was almost as if the ghost had been waiting for her.

"We found the body there," Jason began. He pointed to the space coming up in front of her. Charlie held up her hand to hush him. She walked through the scene, her eyes focused only on the spirit of the scantily clad, dirty young woman sitting in front of an ancient, blackened log. She had her knees hugged to her chest and her arms wrapped around the tops of her knees. Her reddish blonde hair was full of sticks and she bent her head, hiding her face. The braid she wore encircled her head and reminded Charlie of a Swedish milkmaid. Her body flickered in and out but there was no mistaking the sound of her crying. Deep and woeful, the sound carried on a heavy breeze that had picked up as Charlie approached her.

Charlie glanced at Jason and even Cameron to see if they had any reaction. Internally, she rolled her eyes at herself. Why would they? Lisa, on the other hand had stopped not far from the edge of the rocks forming the ring. Lisa's body stiffened and she reached inside her pocket and pulled out a small linen bag. Her thin fingers wrapped around it and held it close to her heart. Inside were things that Charlie knew were protective — a bit of dried lavender, a black tourmaline stone, bleached bones from a chicken, a tiny bag of salt and whatever else Lisa deemed necessary. The look on her cousin's face said everything that Charlie needed to know. Lisa heard it, too. Even if she didn't see the spirit, she could sense her.

Jason watched with his mouth open and Cameron sneered. One of these days she was going to have to have a talk with him about his bad attitude. Especially if it affected her work. She shook off his negative energy as best she could and approached the spirit with care. Startling an unknown spirit could be dangerous.

"Hello," Charlie said softly. The darkness of this place weighed heavy on her. It was as if someone had filled two sacks with sand and stones, tied them together, and dropped them on her shoulders. There was something besides the spirit here. A dark shadow Charlie could not quite get a reading on. It slithered around her, just out of view. If she concentrated she could see it hovering in her peripheral vision, but as soon as she turned her head, the shadow disappeared.

The woman continued crying against her arms. Charlie took a few steps forward. "I won't hurt you."

Still, the spirit wept. Charlie inched forward. "What is your name?"

The woman's shoulders hitched up and down as if with painful breaths. It was just a habit though. Spirits didn't really need to breathe, but every single one Charlie had ever encountered carried with it the memory of being human. So they did human things, like breathing and crying.

Charlie knelt in front of the spirit. "My name is Charlie."

"He changed my name," the woman whimpered.

Charlie's heartbeat thrummed in her ears. She put a hand on the ground to steady herself. The loamy soil of sand and dirt and clay pressed against her palm and filled the space between her fingers. "Who changed your name?"

"He did." The ghost's voice whispered across Charlie's skin. "I couldn't stop him. I couldn't ..."

"This isn't your fault. And he can't change your name. No one can do that. Unless you want them to," Charlie said.

"I thought it would be different," the ghost whispered.

"What?" Charlie asked.

"Death," the ghost whispered. "I thought there would be heaven. Or even hell. I never imagined I would still be here."

"There is more than just here," Charlie said. "I know it's hard to see right now because you feel like you're stuck. But there is another place. Maybe it is heaven, maybe it is hell. I won't know until it's my turn. But I know you don't have to stay here. I can help you. I need to know some things first."

"I'm not going anywhere," the spirit said. "He made sure of that. And now I have no choice."

The spirit raised her face and Charlie lurched backward. A scream caught in her throat. Where the woman's eyes should have been, there were dark bloody caverns.

"See? I have become exactly what he made me. A hideous creature." The spirit jumped to her feet and a black smoky shadow expanded from her back and she disappeared. The sound of beating wings filled Charlie's head.

"Good goddess, what has he done?" she muttered.

"Charlie, are you okay?" Lisa said, kneeling next to her. She shoved the little bag in her hands into Charlie's. "I should've made one of these for you and made you wear it."

Charlie rose from the sandy soil. She put the protection bag in her pocket and brushed her hands together to clean off any debris clinging to her palms.

Jason stood just out of reach.

"You didn't tell me that her eyes were missing," Charlie scolded.

"You could see that?" Jason asked, his voice filled with awe.

"Oh, yeah," Charlie said.

"You don't like to know too much. I've got a file in the car for you to go over if you want," he said weakly. "What did she say to you?"

"She said he changed her name. And for some reason, she says she can't move on because of him. Because of something he did to her," Charlie said, her stomach turning.

Cameron made a chuffing sound and Charlie stalked over to him.

"What the hell is your problem?" Charlie snapped.

"Nothing," Cameron said. "Your performance is very interesting. Almost believable."

"You know, I don't give a rats ass if you believe me or not," Charlie said. "But from here on out you need to keep your negativity to yourself."

"Or what?" Cameron challenged.

Charlie put her hands on her hips and locked her gaze on his. "You don't really want to mess with me, Cameron."

"Right," Cameron said raising his hands. "Because you're this oh so scary psychic."

Charlie narrowed her eyes. "Do you really want to find out what I am?" She stared at him, her gaze unwavering, refusing to even blink. After a moment Jason approached and clapped Cameron on the shoulder.

"Come on you two, don't fight," Jason said.

Lisa took her place next to Charlie, standing close enough for her arm to brush against Charlie's.

"If I'm going to help you, Jason, then I think it would probably be best if it was just you and me from here on out. Or even just me," Charlie said.

"Come on, Charlie, don't be like that," Jason said.

"Yeah, come on, Charlie don't be like that," Cameron echoed. "No one can see your theatrics if it's just you."

"Hey!" Lisa took a step forward. "You don't have to be insulting. Nobody's trying to make you believe anything."

"Come on Lisa, I know she's your cousin, but seriously? I mean you're smarter than that," Cameron said.

"You don't really know anything about me, Cameron," Lisa said.

"I know enough. And I'm sorry, I didn't mean to offend you." Cameron said, sounding contrite.

"I'm not the one you need to apologize to," Lisa said, crossing her arms.

Cameron pressed his lips together and crossed his arms. His defiance reminded Charlie of Scott and the way he would hem and haw when he was wrong about something. Charlie sighed.

"I don't need an apology," Charlie said softly. "What I need is to be able to work in peace. And you, Cameron, do not give me any peace. So if you want my help, Jason, then those are my terms. Just either me and you, or me on my own."

Charlie turned and walked across the fire ring toward the path. Overhead she distinctly heard the sound of beating wings. But when she glanced up there was not a bird in the sky.

* * *

"You know what I don't understand about Cameron?" Charlie said, digging out two pints of Haagen-Dazs ice cream from her freezer. "Butter pecan or chocolate peanut butter?"

"I'll take the chocolate peanut butter unless you want it," Lisa said.

Charlie pulled two spoons from the drawer next to her stove and put the pint of chocolate peanut butter down in front of her cousin. "It's all yours. It's not really my favorite. It's Evan's. I'll get some more before he comes back on Sunday."

Charlie sat down at the little bistro table across from her cousin and popped the top of the pint of butter pecan ice cream.

"You were saying?" Lisa said, taking a spoonful of ice cream.

"I don't understand why he has to be such a jerk about it. It's fine that he's not a believer. I don't really care." Charlie burrowed the tip of her spoon into the pint and lifted a bite of the rich buttery vanilla ice cream to her lips.

"It bothered you enough to chase him off. If you didn't really care, then you wouldn't have done that," Lisa said.

Charlie winced. Leave it to Lisa to sting her with the truth. She scowled and took another bite. "Fine. So I care a little bit," she sighed. "It wouldn't be so bad if his energy wasn't so draining. I swear I don't know how he and Jason are friends."

"Jason was the same way when we first met him, remember?" Lisa said, prodding the hardened ribbon of peanut butter in the center of the frozen treat. "And he came around."

"Yes, but not without some convincing." Charlie laid her spoon on the placemat next to the cover of the ice cream.

"True." Lisa met Charlie's eyes. "Maybe that's what it's going to take."

Charlie grimaced. "Yeah, I know. But that means I have to poke around in his head and maybe even call on the spirits haunting him."

"Are there always spirits?"

"Not always." Charlie chuckled and put the top back on the ice cream. "Hell, maybe I'll get lucky. Maybe he's not haunted at all. Maybe he's just a jackass."

"Well, you won't know unless you try to read him."

"Fine," Charlie said, trying to shrug off her irritation. "Is Jason bringing him to Friday night dinner?"

"Yeah, that is if he even comes. They've been working late every night since Sunday," Lisa said sulking.

"You've only noticed because you're not working late, too."

Lisa rolled her eyes. "And your point is?"

"He's crazy about you, Lisa. That's all. And I think you complaining that he works too much is the pot calling the kettle black." Charlie chuckled.

"Dammit, Charlie Payne," Lisa said as she scowled. "I hate it when you make sense."

"Not nearly as much as Cameron does," Charlie said and Lisa laughed out loud.

CHAPTER 15

Charlie tidied up her cottage, unable to get the image of the spirit she had seen that afternoon out of her head. It wasn't the first time she'd seen a spirit trapped by her own self-image at the moment of her death. What she couldn't figure out, though, was whether the spirit was actually wearing wings.

Jason had told her after they left the scene that the killer often left behind a pair of beautifully crafted wings made of metal and leather. She had smelled metal in her vision. Had felt the heat of the room where he kept her captive. Why would the spirit adopt something the killer had contrived for her? It didn't make any sense. There was only one person she knew who knew as much about spirits as she did. She ran the dust mop over her hardwood floors quickly and when she was done she picked up her phone and sank into her overstuffed couch.

She jotted off a text. How's your schedule?

Always open for you, he replied. Charlie grinned from ear to ear.

I had a very strange experience today.

Want to talk about it?

Would love to. Do you want to come over?"

Would love to. :-) Should I drive? Or would other means be all right with you?

Charlie glanced at the clock and thought about it for a moment. If he drove, her cousins would know that he had come over after eleven pm. At a minimum, there would be questions to answer. And at worse, there would be unending teasing.

Other means would be perfect. I'll see you soon.

Her stomach flip-flopped and she hopped to her feet to take a quick turn around the house, scanning for dust she'd missed and to empty the trash.

A knock came at the front door just as she gathered the plastic string of the trash bag and tied it in a knot.

Charlie rinsed her hands in the sink and caught sight of herself in the glass pane cabinet next to the sink. She finger combed her hair and pinched the apples of her cheeks. It would have to do. She called up a smile right before opening the door. Tom stood on her porch unaffected by the heavy darkness of the night.

"I'm so glad you texted me," he said. He swept into the room and Charlie could almost hear his invisible reaper robes ruffling even though he wore his sleek jeans and a polo shirt. She frowned and closed the door.

"What is it?" he asked.

"Nothing," she said forcing her lips to curve into a smile. "How are you tonight?"

"I am wonderful now that I get to see you." He stepped close. He brushed a strand of hair off her face and tucked it behind her ear. "Is this okay?"

Charlie nodded and closed the gap between them. She put her hands on his hips and brushed her lips across his. "More than okay."

He wrapped his arms around her and kissed her deeper. Charlie's belly exploded with butterflies and heat. He pulled away a little breathless. "We should stop."

She gazed into his dark amber eyes. "I don't want to stop. Do you?"

"God no," he said. "But you texted me because you wanted to talk about something. I came to listen. Not to seduce you. I promise."

Charlie laughed. A curious expression wrinkled Tom's brow.

"It's not really seduction if both parties are willing. And you're sweet. It's one of my favorite things about you," she said. She hugged him close, nestling against his neck breathing him in. He wore a musky cologne but beneath it was another smell. A very human smell. Charlie pulled away and looked him in the eye.

"You smell sweaty," she said grinning. "Is that part of your glamour?"

A wide smile stretched across his face. "Do you like it? Or is it too much? Daphne taught me how to do it. She is an absolute gem when it comes to glamours."

Charlie laughed. "Yes, she is. And no, it's not too much. I had no idea that a glamour could actually affect smell."

"Daphne says a good glamour should affect all five senses," Tom said.

"Well she would know. She's queen witch around here when it comes to that." Charlie snuggled in close again and kissed his neck. He shuddered and wrapped his arms around her pulling her tighter against him. "And yes I do like it," she purred. "It's kinda manly."

"So tell me about the strange encounter you had," he asked.

Charlie sighed and pulled away, leading him over to the couch. She described her experience as they settled on either end, and even closed her eyes to help her remember every detail.

When she was done she opened her eyes and met his gaze. "I don't understand. I've never seen a spirit with wings before. What does it mean?"

"You told me that in the vision you had he kept talking about making you an angel," Tom said.

"Yes. He did. But he couldn't really make an angel. Could he?"

Tom slicked his hair back and said, "No, of course not. He's not divine." Tom picked up her hand and placed it between both of his. "There are some legends, though."

"What kind of legends?"

"There are many different supernatural creatures who feed off of the energy of the human soul. Some have very specific rituals for preparing the souls for consumption. Perhaps he's being controlled by one. He could be like you. Sensitive. And it could be that this creature has preyed on him and is making him do its bidding."

"You mean like a spirit?"

"Not a spirit like you mean spirit. Not a human spirit. But it could be an evil spirit. Some cultures call them demons."

"Demons," she said thoughtfully. "I thought they were just a myth. Something Christianity invented to act as a scapegoat for bad behavior."

"Demons exist in every culture on the planet, Charlie. I am a supernatural creature. Some might think me a demon. Or an angel. As we discussed earlier."

Charlie sat forward and put her head in her hands. She sighed. "Sometimes I feel like my head is going to explode with all this information."

"I'm sorry it isn't what you want to hear." Tom rubbed a circle in the center of her back.

"How can I be sure? That he's not just some sick murderer. I mean Jason showed me the autopsy reports this afternoon. This guy rapes these girls postmortem," Charlie said.

"Maybe it's part of the ritual. To bind them to his master. It wouldn't be unheard of to defile the body. Perhaps as part of the girl's death. Symbolic defilement of the soul," Tom said.

"What you are describing is just a whole other level of evil," she said.

"Typically, that is the motivation of the demon. Well, that and food. And nothing tastes better than a human soul. Why do you think I carry a scythe?" he asked.

"I thought it was to reap the soul," she said.

"Sometimes I use it for difficult souls. But it's also a weapon against other supernatural creatures who would try to steal the soul away from me at the moment of reaping," Tom said.

"Who was supposed to reap her?" Charlie asked.

"I don't know. She wasn't in my book. She may not have been in anyone's book. It may not have been her time. It is been my experience that most murders are not written in the reaper's book," Tom said.

Charlie sat back and looked him in the eye. "Just

when I think I understand the supernatural world, I learn that really I don't have a clue."

"You have far more knowledge than most humans, Charlie." He took her hand in his again and kissed her knuckles. "Is there anything I can do to help?"

"You could kiss me again," she said. "Make me forget all this even if it's just for a little while."

"I can do that." He smiled and leaned in close. He pressed his warm lips against hers and Charlie let herself get lost in it. It had been a long time since Charlie had wanted someone the way she wanted Tom. After several minutes of kissing she gathered her courage.

"Tom," she whispered into his ear. He dotted her neck with gentle nibbles.

"Mmmm?" He didn't stop.

"Do you want to move this to the bedroom?"

Tom pushed himself up and looked her in the eyes. "You sure? It's a big step."

"I'm sure." A smile stretched across her face. She wiggled out from beneath him and rose to her feet then held out her hand for him. "Come on."

* * *

CHARLIE FOUND HERSELF WALKING THROUGH THE WOODS again, headed toward the circle where she had seen the angel girl. Maybe it wasn't a fair representation. Angel girl. She was not really a girl, nor was she an angel. But someone had convinced her she was, and when her spirit manifested, she had wings.

Charlie looked to the sky trying to determine the time of day. Trying to remember how she got there. Trying to find the source of the goosebumps that had risen on her arms. Thick mist hovered above the ground giving the dense pine tree forest the sense that it was floating in the clouds. A chill skittered across her shoulders and she stopped on the path and glanced around. Someone was watching her. She could feel it. Feel someone's eyes on her back. Why was she alone? Where was Lisa? Where was Jason? Or even Cameron. She would have settled for his skeptical presence no matter how annoying.

"I know you're here," Charlie called. "I can see you." It was a lie meant to manipulate her watcher. She scanned the woods carefully for any movement. Something dark appeared in her peripheral vision and she turned toward it. A flutter of wings ruffled and settled behind the girl. Her name had been Bethany in life. Charlie let out a slow breath and turned to face her. She seemed more solid than she had the last in their last encounter.

But of course she would. This is just a dream, Charlie's mind interjected.

"I know you," Charlie said. "What I don't know is why you're here."

The spirit tipped her head. The dark black holes in

her face were gone. That had to be a good sign, didn't it? That even though this was a dream, the girl saw herself as she was in life. Well mostly. The wings attached to her fluttered just a little along the edges. "He's watching you. Watching you all. Be careful. He's hunting again."

"For another girl?" Charlie asked.

"Be vigilant. He's hunting again," the angel girl said.

"I'm working on a way to free you," Charlie said.

The angel girl shifted her gaze to Charlie, her expression mournful, her lips curved into a weary smile. "It's too late for me. Be vigilant."

"We will stop him. And I swear on all that's holy to me, I will find a way to free you," Charlie said.

"Be vigilant," The spirit whispered. Something rustled in the woods and Charlie looked toward the noise, searching for the source. She couldn't see anything obvious, but her senses didn't believe her eyes. The hair on her neck stood up. The sound of wings flapping drew her attention again and when she looked back the angel girl was gone.

Charlie scanned the sky but there was no sign of her. "Dammit," she muttered. "Couldn't you at least show me where he kept you?" She waited a beat.

A breeze rustled through the canopy of trees and something dark played at the corners of Charlie's eyes. She turned her head slightly to see if she could get whatever was teasing her, trying to frighten her, to come into focus. Her heart hammered its way into the back of her mouth. She could barely make out his features, and they were unlike anything human that she had ever seen. His eyes were as black and shiny as polished obsidian and his skin the palest of gray. Deep purple veins marbled the skin and if he had not blinked she might have thought him a statue. He moved closer, and placed a clawed hand upon her shoulder. Charlie couldn't move. He leaned in, his stinking hot breath puffed out hitting her cheek. She tried to move her head so she could look him in the eye but her neck would not cooperate.

"Charlie Payne," his voice slithered through her head. "As I live and breathe."

Charlie swallowed hard and tried to speak but the words clogged her throat.

"Who are you?" her mind cried.

"You know who I am. I think you know what I am." He said his words dying off into a low growl.

"How do you know my name?" She thought.

"You are legend. You and your whole family. Seekers of light and truth. Blah blah blah. How boring you all are," he said.

"You know my name, tell me yours," she said. "That's only fair."

"What makes you think I care about fair?" he growled. "We are legion. That is all you need to know."

Every hair on her body stood at attention. But this

was exactly what he wanted. He wanted her afraid. He wanted her cowering in a corner. Just like the spirit of every girl he had ever defiled. "That's pretty chicken-shit if you ask me."

He growled again, this time deeper. She had struck a nerve. Good. She could use that. "You know what I think? I think you're too scared to tell me your name. Too scared to show me your face. All that makes you is a coward."

His growl gave way to a roar. It filled her head hot and angry and reminded her of a lion and alligator. Something hard struck her across her cheek. Her vision exploded with a burst of pain and white light, and she fell to the ground.

"You will say my name one day, Charlie. They all say my name right before I eat them. I cannot wait."

Charlie held her cheek and blinked until her vision cleared. She heard the rustle of the nearby underbrush and turned her head trying to catch a glimpse of him, but he was gone.

CHAPTER 16

Charlie awoke with a start, sat up straight in bed and grabbed her phone off of her nightstand.

"Bad dream, love?" Tom asked.

Her breath caught in her throat and she turned her gaze toward his voice. Tom was next to her, propped up by pillows with one of her books resting across his lap. In her bed.

The memory of his arms around her, stroking her hair after their love-making flooded her mind. She'd drifted off to sleep and had been sure he'd be gone when she awoke. Why would he stay? He didn't need sleep. "You're still here."

"Of course I am. Where else would I be?" Tom asked.

"I thought you'd be gone."

"Do you want me to go?" he asked.

"No. No, that's not why I said that. I ..." she struggled to find the right words.

"Are you all right?" He placed her hand over hers.

"Yes." She smiled, trying not to be distracted by his nakedness. "I'm fine." She fought the urge to run her hands across his well-muscled chest, push the book off his lap, and wrap herself around him, skin to skin. But the demon's voice echoed through her head. They all say my name, right before I eat them. The girl's voice echoed through her head. He's hunting again. She faced forward, focusing on the phone in her hands. Who was she going to call? It wasn't as if Jason could help her with this. Maybe Evangeline or Jen, or even Lisa might know more about what she was dealing with. "Shit," she muttered. "I don't know who call."

"What happened?"

"I saw the spirit again. The girl that was killed. But..." She put the phone back on the nightstand and stared down at her hands. "There was someone else there too."

Tom edged closer and put an arm around her shoulders. "Who?"

"He wouldn't tell me his name and he wouldn't let me look at him either. Not directly anyway," she said.

"What were you able to see?" Tom asked, his voice full of steady seriousness. A pang filled her chest. She loved that there was not one ounce of disbelief in his voice.

"Pale gray skin. Veins. Dark purple veins. And black eyes. Not a lick of white in them," she said. "I could only see him from my peripheral vision though."

"A demon." Tom said the word absently.

Charlie peered into his face. A deep line formed between his eyes.

"What else did he say?"

"He knew my name. Said he knew my whole family. He wouldn't tell me his name though."

"No, I'm sure he wouldn't," Tom said.

"Why?" Charlie asked.

"If you know his name then it gives you power over him. You could control him, or banish him, or even kill him. If you don't know his name the best you could ever hope for is to send him back to the netherworld," Tom said.

"So there is a hell?" Charlie asked.

"Only for creatures like him. As I told you, he's a supernatural spirit. They live separately from humans, and that includes their souls. But they're attracted to both your lightness and your darkness. He can feed off the energy of both," Tom said.

"He said I would say his name, right before he ate me," Charlie's voice shook. "Is that why he killed those girls? To eat their souls?"

"I don't know," Tom said. "Maybe."

"I have to text Jason." Charlie grabbed for her phone again.

"Why?" Tom asked. "What does he know of demons?" Did she detect hurt in his voice?

"He needs to know what he's dealing with isn't human," Charlie said.

"Will he accept that?" Tom asked.

"I sure hope so," she said. She jotted off a text. She stared at the screen, waiting for any response.

"Your chicken stuck her head in here briefly, by the way," he said.

Charlie chuckled. "She's not really my chicken."

"Oh, she's your chicken all right. I think I must scare her. Because she appeared and perched on the footboard for barely five seconds before she disappeared again."

"Maybe so. Are you sure there's not a reaper for animals?" Charlie asked.

"If there is, I've never met one." He laughed as if he hadn't taken the question seriously.

Charlie glanced down at the screen again, then looked at the clock on her nightstand. The red digital numbers read two forty-five a.m.

"He must be sleeping pretty heavy." Charlie sighed.

"It's very early, or very late depending on your point of view," Tom said. "Would you like me to go wake him?"

Charlie imagined that scene unfolding — Tom appearing in Jason's bedroom in full reaper form before transforming into his human glamour; Tom tapping Jason on the arm to wake him; Jason pulling a gun from beneath his pillow. Charlie shook her head.

"I don't think that would be a good idea. I really don't want you to get shot today."

"Fair point," Tom said. "Maybe I'll just wake Lisa instead. She's with him most nights now, right?"

"Hey." Charlie sat up straight. "Good idea."

She jotted off another text.

"Really? You want me to go wake her?" He closed his book and placed it on the nightstand.

"No, you stay put." Charlie placed her hand on his thigh. She stared at the screen. Within a minute, three dots appeared on the screen. Lisa was typing. Charlie grinned.

What's up? You okay? Lisa's text read.

I had a dream. I need to talk to Jason and he's not answering.

I'll wake him up.

Thank you. :)

Less than a minute later Charlie's phone buzzed in her hand with a text from Jason.

What's up?

The killer isn't human.

What? You don't think it's a ghost do you?

Not exactly. More like a human that's been possessed.

Three dots appeared and disappeared then reappeared a few minutes later.

"I think I broke him," Charlie said.

"What do you mean?" Tom said.

Finally another text appeared.

All right. I don't know what to do with that. Lisa tells me that human possession is a real thing.

Lisa would be right.

So, what? He's possessed by a demon?

"Do demons have magic?" Charlie asked. "Could they cast a glamour, like you?"

"Yes and no. The have their own sort of magic. All supernatural beings do, but as far as I know they cannot cast a glamour. They aren't truly corporeal on this plane. He would have to possess someone," Tom said.

Charlie pursed her lips and gave him a quick nod. "Right."

Yes. He's being possessed by a demon.

Well that's just great. Fan-freaking-tastic.

It doesn't mean he can't be stopped. But I do know he's not done. He threatened to come after me.

Shit! What can I do?

Nothing you can do. I've got it handled on my end. I do know what he's after though. Why he's killing.

Why?

He wants their souls.

You have got to be fucking kidding me.

You kiss your mama with that mouth?!

An eyeroll emoji appeared and Charlie snickered.

Sorry mom.

LOL. It's okay. I feel exactly the same way. Go back to sleep. We'll deal with this in the morning.

Ok

Charlie put the phone down on the nightstand and turned her attention to Tom.

"Now, what should we do?" She gave him a sly smile.

"I'm sure we can think of something," he said reaching for her.

Charlie crawled onto his lap, straddling him. She brushed her lips across his. He wrapped his arms around her, pulling her against his chest. She deepened the kiss. "I'm sure your right Mr. Sharon."

CHAPTER 17

Charlie walked in to the small satellite office for the sheriff's department and greeted the deputy at the front desk.

"Hey, Darren," Charlie said, handing him a cup from the tray of four coffees in her hand.

"Hey, Charlie." He grabbed the coffee without hesitation, opened the lid, and took a long sniff. "Thank you. You always bring us the best coffee." He reached into the middle drawer and pulled out two packs of sugar, ripped them open, and poured them into the rich black liquid. "What can I do for you this morning?"

"Is Lieutenant Tate here?" she asked.

A strange smile spread across the deputy's thick lips. His gaze shifted over her shoulder. "Uh, I believe he is."

"Great," she said. "Any chance I could get a visitor's

pass? There's something I need to tell him about a case he's working on."

The deputy eyed the box in her hand. "Are those muffins?"

"Yes they are." She smiled and set down the tray of coffees, then opened the box for the deputy to see the confections her cousin had made. "Would you like one?"

"I would. Thank you," he said plucking a blueberry lemon muffin from the box and peeling the paper away. "You know I would love to help you out. But Lieutenant Tate said that if you came by to give him a call before I let you back." He broke off a piece of the muffin and popped it into his mouth. A little moan started in the back of his throat and he closed his eyes. "My God, this is so good."

Charlie resisted the urge to scold him for talking with his mouth full. She really needed to remember to ask Evangeline to show her how to use a suggestibility spell. Charlie forced a smile. "I'll let my cousin know that you like them. Would you mind giving Lieutenant Tate a call for me to let him know I'm here?"

The deputy took another bite of the muffin and nodded his head. "Sure thing." The words came out a little garbled.

Charlie gritted her teeth but kept a smile painted on her face. She closed the box of muffins and picked up the tray of coffees again placing them on top.

A large round clock kept time and Charlie glanced at

it every thirty seconds or so. As she waited, she paced. By the time Jason poked his head out into the lobby ten minutes later, Charlie's face was hot and her impatience hovered close to the surface.

"Hey, Charlie," Jason said, giving her a wary smile. His eyes were drawn to the box. "Whatcha got there?"

Honey, Charlie, not vinegar. She took a deep breath.

"I brought y'all some muffins and coffee from the café. Although I'm not sure the coffee is still warm at this point, since I had to wait so long."

"Yeah," Jason rubbed the back of his neck. "Sorry about that. We were in the middle of something when the deputy let me know you were here."

"I thought we were gonna meet this morning and discuss what I told you last night," she said, giving the deputy at the desk a sideways glance.

"Yeah," Jason nodded.

There was something about his demeanor that set Charlie on edge. She narrowed her eyes. "What's going on Jason?"

"Nothing," he said.

The little bell that often went off in Charlie's head when someone lied to her rang wildly in her ears. Charlie stepped closer and lowered her voice. "You know better than that. Please answer my question."

Jason gently put his hand on Charlie's elbow, guiding her to the side of the lobby. Charlie could feel the deputy's eyes on them, watching their every move. Their closeness smacked of impropriety. It didn't matter how big the county was, in this little corner of it, gossip could infiltrate the community at the speed of sound. Deputy Darren Murray was married to one of the biggest gossips, besides Daphne, in the greater Palmetto Point area. The last thing she needed was for Lisa to hear some ridiculous rumor about her and Jason having a spat in public. Charlie pulled her elbow out of Jason's hand, careful not to spill the coffees. She took a step back.

"What are you doing?" Jason whispered.

"I'm saving my reputation and Lisa's," Charlie said softly. "Why are you lying to me Jason?"

Jason put his hands on his hips and sighed. His lips pressed into a straight line and he glanced at the deputy behind the desk. "Murray can you give her a visitor's pass please?"

"Sure thing, Lieutenant," Darren said. He pulled a white laminated badge from the side drawer and tapped the sign-in log with the pen. "Charlie if I could just get your John Hancock."

"Sure thing," she said. After she signed her name she clipped the white badge to the collar of her pale pink blouse.

She followed Jason back through the maze of offices to a conference room. Sitting at the long wooden table were Beck and Cameron.

"Good morning, I come bearing gifts," she said, placing the box of muffins on the table and setting the tray of three coffees next to it.

"Lord have mercy," Beck said, hopping up from his seat. "It almost makes me believe you could read my mind, Miss Charlie. Now I hope you remembered my favorite." Beck lifted the lid of the box.

"I think what he meant to say," Jason rolled his eyes and punched Beck lightly on his upper arm. "Is thank you, Miss Charlie."

"Yes," Beck nodded. "Thank you, Miss Charlie." He plucked a peach, streusel-topped muffin from the box, peeled half the paper back and took a bite. "Mmm-mmm-mmmh."

Cameron rose from his seat and took one of the coffees from the tray. "Thanks, Charlie." He eyed her with care. "At least I know this will be better than the swill they've got here."

"Well I'm happy to oblige," Charlie said. The words were automatic, polite. Always polite. Something she had learned from her parents before they died, more from her father than her mother. Her mother had been born in upstate New York and, while Sandra Keegan Payne believed her children should be raised to be polite, it was her father who understood and drilled it into her from the time she was a very small child. Being polite was akin to being invisible. Which she would later learn was an important skill to have, especially for someone like with her gifts.

"I thought you didn't really want to have anything to do with me or this investigation while I'm here," Cameron said. He certainly knew how to pick at the scab between them.

"I don't," Charlie said softly. "But I have new information and it's important."

"Right," Cameron said. He took a sip of his coffee. "Jason filled us in on it this morning."

"You did?" Charlie asked. She turned to look at him and was surprised to find him shuffling papers as if his life depended on it. He didn't meet her gaze.

"I did," he said. He still didn't look up.

Charlie's stomach wound into a knot and dropped deep into her belly. "Jason?"

"I've been thinking about it." He swallowed hard. "And I'll take your information into account."

"Into account?" Charlie said incredulous. "How are you gonna stop him?"

"With a bullet if I have to," Jason said, finally meeting her gaze. Charlie's cheeks heated and she folded her arms across her chest.

"You don't believe me?" Charlie said. She didn't even try to hide the hurt in her voice. Hadn't they gotten past this?

"Charlie," Jason straightened in his chair. She could

see him thinking carefully about what to say next. "You know I believe you on a lot of things. Otherwise, I wouldn't pull you into the cases that I have."

"You just don't believe me about this," she said.

"No, I don't. I'm sorry," Jason said. "If you told me it was a ghost I'd probably be right there with you, but demons?"

Charlie shook her head and bit her lip to keep it from quivering. From the corner of her eye she could see Cameron wearing a smug expression. She would not cry no matter how angry this whole thing made her. Cameron did not deserve the satisfaction. She cleared her throat.

"All right. Fine," she said. "Let's just hope that bullet you put in him actually stops him. Although I should probably warn you that if he's being possessed by a demon, I can guarantee you that it won't." She shifted her gaze from Jason to Beck and finally to Cameron. "Good luck. You're gonna need it."

Charlie turned and headed out into the hallway, noting the empty offices as she passed them. The deputies were already out and about keeping watch over the county.

"Charlie wait," Jason said from behind her.

Charlie kept her eyes forward and her feet moving. Her long legs afforded her a speed that Jason could only match if he jogged a little. She passed through the door leading to the lobby and Jason touched her elbow.

"Please wait," he said.

Charlie stopped and rounded on him. She jerked her arm away. "I don't want to hear it, Jason."

"Let me walk you to your car. Please? I'd like to explain," he said.

"There's nothing to explain. You think I don't understand your doubt? And what I'm proposing?" She lowered her voice and looked him directly in the eyes. "You think I don't know how crazy this sounds?"

Jason glanced over at the deputy behind the reception desk. He frowned. "Come on. We can discuss it on the way to your car."

Charlie let out a disgusted sigh. "Fine."

Jason followed her to the parking lot and they stopped and faced one another once they reached her blue Honda.

"I know you're mad," Jason began.

"I'm not mad," Charlie said. "I'm disappointed."

"Ouch. Man, you go straight for the throat, don't you?" A grin tugged at one corner of his lips.

"Yep," she said, not amused.

"Demons?" Jason said. "It's just ..."

"I know," Charlie said. "I know. It makes him more dangerous than anything or anyone you have ever met before, except maybe Tom."

Jason rolled his eyes and made a scoffing sound in the back of his throat.

"Jason I'm not kidding. From what I know, when a demon possesses a human being, it can be unstoppable. It can and will stay in that host body until another one becomes available," she said.

"Charlie, why does it always have to be supernatural with you? Why can't it be some guy who is just a straight up murderer?" Jason asked.

"Maybe it is. I pray to the goddess above that it is. But based on my dream I know it's not." She shrugged. "And when you hang out with a coven of witches, you're gonna end up surrounded by the supernatural." She smiled. "Wear your vest. Wear your pendant. I'll have Lisa make up a protection bag for you. Carry it with you everywhere."

"I don't need all that," he whispered.

"Yes, you do. Now promise me."

The grin faded from his lips. "All right. Fine. I promise."

"Good," she said.

Jason pressed his lips together. He seemed to be studying every line of her face. "What are you going to do?"

"He knows my name. I'm gonna do the only thing I know how to do, " she said.

"What's that?" Jason asked.

"I'm gonna find him and I'm gonna stop him before he takes another girl," Charlie said. "And I'm gonna banish him back to wherever he came from before he has a chance to move to another host."

"What makes you think you can find him before we do?" Jason said, his voice full of skepticism.

"I know where to look now," she said softly. She patted him on the shoulder before climbing into her car. Charlie put the car in gear and pulled away. In her rearview mirror, she could see him standing in the parking lot, watching as she drove away. "Blessed goddess, watch over him. Watch over them all."

CHAPTER 18

Charlie knocked on the forest green door of Lisa's condo and waited. She probably should've texted first. But when she left the sheriff's station it was like some other person had put her car in gear and driven her over against her will. Some unseen hand guiding her. A minute later the door opened wide and Lisa's beautiful countenance met her.

"Charlie? What are you doing here?" Lisa glanced at her wrist, touched her gold watch. "I didn't think we were getting together till later."

"We weren't. But I just left the sheriff's department." Charlie scowled. "Jason didn't believe me."

"I know," Lisa said softly. "I'm so sorry."

"I don't understand. I thought he was on board last night," Charlie said.

"He was, till Cameron overheard us," Lisa said.

"What?" Charlie asked.

"Come on in." Lisa opened the door wide and stepped back so Charlie could pass. "I'll tell you everything."

Charlie got settled on one of the chairs at the breakfast bar dividing Lisa's kitchen from her living room.

"You want some coffee? Or maybe some iced tea?" Lisa asked.

"No, thank you," Charlie said. "I just want to know what happened."

Lisa nodded and took a seat in the other chair at the breakfast bar. "After you texted Jason this morning, we couldn't go back to sleep. Evidently Cameron is a very light sleeper and came into the kitchen while we were discussing the ins and outs of demons."

"So Cameron somehow convinced Jason I was crazy," Charlie said.

"Not crazy – just backwards. I think his actual words were a ridiculous excuse grounded in superstition," Lisa said.

"What did you say?" Charlie asked.

"I told him he was wrong, and he told me he was disappointed in me. I saw no point in arguing with him after that. You can't change somebody's mind that doesn't want to be changed."

"He changed Jason's mind," Charlie said defiantly.

"I don't know that he really did," Lisa said. "Jason was

having a hard time with it. You know he's more of a see-it-and-believe-it kind of guy. Not the other way around."

"Dammit," Charlie muttered. "I don't know what to do. This thing is already hunting according to the spirit of his last victim."

"You talked to her?"

"She was in my dream," Charlie said. "She kept telling me to be vigilant. I just wish there was some way that we could track him down."

"It's too bad Ben's gone," Lisa said. "He would know how to work outside the system. He might even have a way to track the demon."

"Oh my goddess that is it," Charlie said.

"What is?" Lisa said.

"We need to call Ben," Charlie said.

"You sure that's a good idea? He hasn't contacted Jen since he left," Lisa said. "He may not want anything to do with this."

"Ben cares deeply for Jen. I know it. In my gut – which I trust way more than anyone's words. I also know he wants to do the right thing. And the right thing would be to help us. And he came to see me the night he left."

"To say goodbye," Lisa said.

"Exactly. You don't do that kind of thing if you don't care. I think he'll help, he may not be able to leave his job but he can at least answer my questions."

"And then what?" Lisa said.

Charlie shrugged. "You wanna go demon hunting?"

"Girl you are crazy," Lisa said.

"Come on. You don't have to work and I only have one eight-hour shift tomorrow, and I'm sure I can get someone to cover it."

"What about the storm that's coming?" Lisa asked.

"If it hits, and it won't until Monday night, that gives us plenty of time. Now are you in or are you out?"

Lisa folded her arms across her chest. A frown tugged her lips into an upside-down crescent. "You better not get us killed, Charlie Payne."

"Don't worry, I won't," Charlie said, giving her cousin a sly grin.

* * *

CHARLIE SAT AT ONE END OF LISA'S WHITE DENIM COUCH and Lisa sat at the other. She stared at the phone in her hand. The contact on the screen had a photo of Ben and Jen with their cheeks pressed together. It had been a happy day when she took that picture one late Friday afternoon on her Uncle Jack's back porch. She took a breath and selected the option for Send Message. She thought it was funny that she and Jason texted all the time but she almost never texted Ben. For some reason, he preferred to call her and talk.

She had asked him about it once, and he said that texting was too impersonal. He liked to hear a person's voice. It was easier to know what they were feeling from their intonation. It had secretly made her smile and reminded her that inside and out, Ben was a witch. Still, she was too afraid to just press the icon on the phone and call him. Being rejected in a text seemed much easier. She took a deep breath and tapped out a short message. Then put the phone down on the clear acrylic coffee table in front of the couch.

"Now what?" Lisa asked.

"Now we wait," Charlie said.

Charlie glanced around at her cousin's carefully decorated living room. It could have been in a magazine for modern minimalism. All the fabrics were functional and easy to clean, but there was a formality to the furniture. Clean lines, no clutter. The only thing that struck her as cozy about the place was the fat yellow tabby curled up in the apple green chair flanking the couch. Even the cat's sculpted, cardboard scratching post was beautiful and fit with the decor.

The phone rang and vibrated at the same time traveling across the table a little ways before Charlie could pick it up. Her heart sped up at the sound. She glanced at the screen and read Ben's response. *Call me* was all it said. Charlie tapped his name and another menu dropped down and she pressed the Call icon and then the Speaker icon. A few seconds later the phone began to ring. He let it ring twice before picking it up.

"Hey, Charlie," Ben said, sounding mildly surprised. "You know how much I hate texting."

"I do," she said. "But I was scared that you were gonna say no."

"You know I would never say no to you. What can I do for you?" She could hear the smile in his voice.

"It's kind of a long story," Charlie said.

"Okay. Why don't you give me the abridged version," he said.

"I'm helping Jason on a case. Someone or something has killed three young women over several months. I dreamed about one of them last night. She was very different from most of the spirits that I encounter in dreams," she said.

"Different how?" he asked. She pictured him concentrating on her words with a deep line between his brows.

"She had wings. Black, shadowy wings."

"Okay," he said, "Tell me more about her."

"It's not really her I'm worried about so much, as it is the other creature I encountered," Charlie said.

"In your dream?" Ben asked.

"Yes," Charlie said. A thick pebble of dread formed in her throat making it difficult to say the words. It was one thing to disassociate herself from the idea of a demon but something altogether different to relive the account of that creature she met. She closed her eyes.

"Charlie? You okay?" he asked. Despite all his swagger and confidence, at heart she knew he was just a healer. The same way her aunt was a healer. And that knowledge was enough for her to push through.

"I'm fine. It was a demon."

"In your dream?" Ben said with quiet alarm in his tone. "You're sure?"

"Pretty sure. He had black eyes, the claws, the marbled skin. And he would never let me look at him directly."

"No, he wouldn't. Any chance he told you his name?" Ben asked.

"No," Charlie said. "I asked but all he would say was legion."

"Of course he did," Ben said dryly.

"Did I screw it up? Should I have pushed him harder?"

"No, you didn't screw anything up. I promise. He wouldn't have told you no matter what you said or did, of that I'm sure."

"Tom told me that if I knew his name I could control him and even banish him. Is there any other way?" she asked.

"Tom's right. Knowing a demon's name is unfortunately, the only way to banish him," Ben said.

"But if we get that, he can be banished, right?" Charlie asked.

"Yes, it can. Your reaper friend might be able to help you with that, once you know its name. Is it possessing someone?" Ben asked.

"I think he's possessing the man who killed these girls." Charlie sighed and paused for a moment as if checking her mental notes. "Is there any chance you're just about done with your job?"

"I wish I could say yes. I'm in a holding pattern at the moment. I've got a meeting Friday afternoon with the witch that allegedly summoned the demon and snatched a baby in this town," Ben said.

"Oh, Ben," Charlie said her hand drifting to her throat. "You be careful, okay."

"I will be. You, too. You should take a look at Jen's secret shelf," Ben said. "There are a couple of books there that might help you find the guy being possessed. And there's a binding spell that will actually trap the demon inside his body."

"Why would we want to trap him?" Charlie asked.

"If you trap it inside the body and the guy dies, so does the demon."

"I thought they could reanimate a dead body," Charlie said.

"They can usually, but there's a hitch," Ben said.

"A hitch?" Charlie asked, feeling a little sick to her

stomach. A hitch was never a good thing in her experience.

"You have to cut its head off and carve the heart out of its chest."

"Are you kidding me?" She leaned forward and held her head in one hand.

"I wish I were," Ben said.

"Why on the goddess's green earth can't it be easy? Can't I just stab him through the heart with a wooden stake or something? Like a vampire."

"Yeah, that whole stake thing doesn't really work on vampires. It's a myth," Ben said.

"Great," Charlie said. "That's just great."

"Listen, I gotta go. Call me if you need me. I'll do whatever I can from here to help," Ben said.

"Thank you," Charlie said. "You take care of yourself and be careful."

"You too," Ben said.

Charlie tapped the Phone icon and ended the call.

"Did you hear that?" Charlie sighed. She shifted her gaze to her cousin's face and was met with a look of disgust.

"I am not cutting that thing's head off. We're just gonna have to figure out a way to banish it," Lisa said.

"Looks like you and I aren't gonna be enough," Charlie said.

"No. We're gonna need the whole coven for this. And maybe Tom," Lisa said.

"So, did you know that Jen has a secret shelf?" Charlie asked.

Lisa narrowed her eyes. "No I didn't. I wonder what all she has on that secret shelf?"

"Dark spell books, apparently," Charlie said.

Lisa frowned. "That little witch. She's been holding out on us."

"Come on." Charlie rose from the couch. "Let's go get some lunch at the café. No time like the present to find out what books she has that will help us catch this thing."

* * *

CHARLIE KEPT WATCH OVER THE DOOR TO THE CAFÉ. Her nerves buzzed with anticipation, waiting for the bell to ring, announcing someone's entrance. The bell stayed silent. She sighed and stabbed a piece of cornmeal-encrusted okra with her fork and popped it into her mouth. The crispy coating did nothing to soothe her nerves.

"A watched cauldron never boils," Lisa said under her breath. She loaded the tines of her fork with a cube of ham, some cheddar cheese and a piece of lettuce then dipped it into the small cup of dressing on the side of her plate.

Charlie scowled. "I just don't know what's taking them so long."

"I'm sure things are crazy at the store, like Dottie said. You know how people can be before a storm," Lisa said.

"I know, but they're only expecting a cat one hurricane. That's not even that bad," Charlie said.

"They're all bad, Charlie." Lisa rolled her eyes. "And nobody wants to run out of bread, milk and water. I don't even drink milk except on cereal, and I always stock up when there's a storm coming."

"That does not make any sense Lisa Holloway. Especially if the power goes out. It's not like you can drink it," Charlie said, unconvinced.

"You can always take a carton of milk and a cooler and eat cereal for a couple of days till they get the power back on," Lisa said.

"I'd rather eat cold SpaghettiOs," Charlie said. She didn't bother with her fork and grabbed the fried chicken leg. The crunchy batter broke into pieces, littering her chin and plate.

The bell tinkled and Charlie jumped at the sound. Lisa threw a glance over her shoulder toward the door and they watched as Jen, her father Jack, and her daughter Ruby walked in to the café. Lisa turned back and gave Charlie a smug grin.

"See, I told you. You just had to stop watching the door," Lisa said.

Charlie rolled her eyes. "Whatever. I don't think that would have made them walk through that door any sooner."

Ruby raced across the restaurant and hopped up on an empty stool near the cash register.

Jack Holloway spotted Charlie and Lisa sitting in a booth along the back wall. He grinned and waved, then tapped Jen on the elbow and pointed in their direction. Charlie and Lisa both waved at the same time.

Jen flashed a quizzical smile at them but didn't approach the table. She gave them a quick wave and headed behind the counter. Dottie stopped Jen at the register and Charlie watched as Jen wrapped her apron around her waist and listened intently to whatever Dottie had to say. Jen nodded and reached for a coloring page and a box of crayons from the cubby beneath the register, then grabbed a carton of milk from the small refrigerator beneath the back counter. She placed the coloring page in front of Ruby along with the milk and crayons.

Jack Holloway walked toward them with a grin on his face. "Afternoon ladies. Scoot over sweetie," he said and pushed his way into the seat next to his daughter. Lisa slid her plate to the right to let her father sit down. "If it isn't two of my favorite people."

"How many favorite people do you have, Daddy?" Lisa said.

"Six or seven tops," he said with a sly grin on his face.

"Hey, Uncle Jack," Charlie said. "How was the store?"

"Insane." He scrubbed his hand across his salt and pepper beard. "I tried to tell Jen we could just drink toilet water, but she wasn't having it."

Charlie giggled. "Now, I cannot imagine why she objected to drinking toilet water."

"I know," Jack said, his good humor shining in his voice. His blue eyes glittered with mischief.

"Are you gonna take the boat out of the water?" Lisa asked.

"I've got a little time. I'll probably drive the boat around to the landing in the morning," he said.

"If you need help, I'm free this week," Lisa said. Charlie kicked her cousin beneath the table and gave her a what-the-hell look. "Ow."

Jack's gaze flitted between Charlie and his daughter. "I appreciate that, sweetie."

"Just let me know." Lisa scowled at Charlie before taking another bite of her salad.

A few minutes later Jen approached the table. She placed a fresh glass of tea in front of her father. "Hey, girls. I wasn't expecting to see you today."

"It's Wednesday. When don't you see me on a Wednesday?" Charlie quipped.

"I wasn't talking about you, Charlie," Jen said, her gaze homing in on her sister.

"What? I usually bring my lunch to work," Lisa said.

"Daddy, do you want something?" Jen shook off her sister's remark and took her order pad from the front pocket of her apron.

Jack rested his forearms on the table and folded his hands together. He looked over Charlie's half empty plate. "Fried chicken looks good. If you don't mind."

"Sides?" Jen asked.

"Green beans and corn please," he said.

"You want a slice of pie?"

"I do," Charlie said.

Jen grinned. "Let me guess. Lemon meringue."

"Unless you have key lime," Charlie said.

Jen shook her head. "You are so predictable. Key lime it is. Daddy?"

"I'll have a slice of key lime pie too, thank you very much," he said.

"Coming right up." Jen turned and headed back to the kitchen.

"When y'all are done eating can you help me unload the plywood I brought out of storage for the windows for the café and for Daphne's?" Jack asked.

"Sure thing," Charlie said. She scooped up a bite of macaroni and cheese and savored it. "Did you get a new truck?"

"I sure did," Jack said. "It'll be much easier to take the boat out of the water and put it back in." He beamed. "Plus, it's pretty."

A few minutes later Jen appeared with a tray carrying her father's food and two slices of pie. "Can I get y'all anything else?"

Charlie and Lisa exchanged a glance.

"When we finish lunch we need to talk to you," Lisa said.

"About what?" Jen asked, wariness edging into her voice.

Charlie's gaze shifted sideways toward her uncle, and she thought carefully about how to answer. "Just something that Ben told me."

The smile on Jen's lips disappeared. "You talked to Ben?"

"I did," Charlie said.

Jen hugged the tray against her chest. "Is he okay?"

"He's fine," Charlie said. "But he did mention something very interesting. Thought you might find it interesting too."

"What?"

Charlie glanced at her uncle again. He was salting and peppering the scoop of buttered sweet white corn on his plate, seeming not to pay any attention to the conversation. Jen's gaze followed her cousin's line of sight. Charlie shrugged. "Nothing important. We can talk about it later."

"Oh. Okay," Jen said. Someone called, "Waitress," from a nearby table. "Well that's my cue. I'll talk to y'all later." Jen headed toward the customer needing her attention.

"You know you can say anything in front of me," Jack said, looking up from his plate. He picked up his fork and slid it into the corn kernels.

"We know, Daddy," Lisa said.

"You know what I think?" Jack said. "I think there are too many damn secrets you girls keep." He brought his fork to his lips and emptied it into his mouth.

Charlie's stomach suddenly soured. She hated lying to her uncle, even if it was for his own good. Charlie met Jack's gaze and pushed her plate away.

* * *

Charlie grunted and adjusted her end of the 8' x 4' long piece of plywood. Lisa backed through the entrance door holding the other end. Jen directed them into the storeroom.

"It's not gonna fit," Lisa said.

"Yes it is," Jen said, sounding exasperated with her sister. "You just have to trust me. This is not my first rodeo."

"I don't know how you're gonna get it out, once we get it in," Lisa complained. "Why don't you just board up the windows now instead of storing it, wouldn't that be easier?"

"No. Boarding them up now would scare off the customers," Jen said. "Plus if I store it now for this storm, I'll have it in case there are others later in the season. So quit fretting over it," Jen reassured her. "I promise you it will fit, and I promise you I'll be able to get it in and out."

Lisa made a sound in the back of her throat but didn't continue to argue. They carefully rounded the corner into the storeroom, wedging Lisa between the shelf holding sacks of rice and flour and other ingredients.

"Now what?" Lisa said, irritation edging into her voice.

"Put your end down," Charlie said. "I'm gonna back up a little bit so you can get out. Then I'll just slide it into the storeroom."

Lisa glanced around as if she were trying to make sense of her cousin's proposition. Lisa lowered her end of the long plank onto the floor, and Charlie dragged it backward at an odd angle, freeing her cousin. Lisa stepped between two ceiling-high shelves on the opposite side. Charlie squatted and lowered her end of the plywood, then carefully slid it forward. The long plank of engineered wood began to tip to one side and Lisa stepped in to keep it upright. Charlie pushed and Lisa guided the plank in front of an empty wall. When they got it into place, Charlie and Lisa stepped back to admire their handiwork.

"See? I told you it would fit," Jen said, joining them. "Now, we've only got three more pieces to unload."

Lisa folded her arms across her chest and scowled at her sister. "No."

"What?" Jen's gaze shifted from Lisa to Charlie. "Did she just say no?"

"I believe that's what she said," Charlie said.

"Lisa Marie," Jen began.

"Jennifer Elizabeth," Lisa countered. "I'm not helping anymore until you tell us about the secret spell books you have."

Jen's cheeks flushed pink, and she automatically shushed her sister. "Be quiet. Somebody could hear you."

"I'm sure they've heard worse," Lisa muttered. "I'm serious. I'm not moving another inch until you tell us."

Jen gritted her teeth and closed the storeroom door. "Is that what Ben told you?"

"He said you have a secret shelf," Charlie said. "We just assumed that it meant spell books."

"Ben is a blabbermouth," Jen grumbled.

"So you do have a secret shelf?" Charlie asked. "Does it have more than spell books?"

"Maybe," Jen said, not meeting her eyes.

"Were you ever gonna tell us?" Lisa asked, sounding a little hurt.

"No," Jen admitted. "I never thought we would have to use them."

"What kind of magic do they contain that you wouldn't want to use it?" Lisa asked.

"There's some dark stuff in them," Jen said. "Not anything we would ever use in our rituals or practice."

"Why do you have them then?" Charlie asked.

"Well I didn't set out to buy them. I found them at an estate sale and recognized the danger immediately, and I didn't want them to fall into the wrong hands." She gave Charlie and Lisa a defiant glare. "So I bought them."

Charlie overlooked her cousin's defensiveness. "Well Ben seemed to think there might be something in one of them that would help us. Me in particular."

"Help you how?" Jen asked.

Charlie told Jen about her dream and about the reception she received from Jason and Cameron that morning. Jen listened, never taking her eyes off of Charlie's face. When Charlie finished, she shrugged. "I'm gonna need all of y'all's help if we are gonna find this guy."

"All right," Jen said. "I'll be done here after three. Then we can start going through the books and see what will help."

Charlie threw her arms around Jen shoulders and hugged her cousin close. "Thank you so much." An electric buzz started in her chest, chasing away the cold cloud of doubt. They were going to find him. They were going to find him and they were going to banish him. Charlie could feel it in her bones.

***

Charlie and Lisa followed Jen up the steps to the attic of Jack Holloway's house. Jen shut the door tightly behind them. Charlie's eyes widened in alarm. Jen patted Charlie's arm with reassurance. "It's okay I'm not gonna lock us in. I just don't want Ruby to follow us up."

It'd been years since Charlie had been in this attic. The last time, they must've been twelve or thirteen. Lisa had just learned a new spell and had asked Jen and Charlie if she could practice it with them. The spell had backfired when Lisa lit the wrong candle in the wrong order resulting in a sudden flash of the flame. Charlie had almost lost her eyebrows that day.

She approached the top floor warily. The smell of musty boxes tickled her nose. The attic stretched across one half of the house and Charlie could only stand up straight in the center of the space. Even then, she had to duck to go beneath the naked lightbulb on the center beam where the eaves joined together. Shelves holding plastic containers with labels on them were tucked up under the eaves. There were boxes of decorations for most of their high holidays, Samhain, Yule and Beltane. Other boxes held books and old photographs.

Charlie spotted a picture of their grandmother, Bunny, sticking out of an old shoe box. She picked it up and smiled, despite the pang of longing that filled her chest. Bunny's beautiful, angular face, wrinkled from years of laughter, grinned at the camera. The old woman sat on the front porch swing of her little house with a white enameled wash pot filled with green beans, yellow crookneck squash and small red potatoes that she'd grown in her garden.

Bunny grinned from ear to ear, her arms slung around the shoulders of her granddaughters, Lisa and Charlie. Both girls wore a silly smile. Bunny had made a game of picking the beans and raced the girl's to see who could pick the most vegetables. In the end, Bunny picked the most, but she always put a handful of her beans into the girls' pile so that they would win.

Lisa glanced over Charlie's shoulder and touched a hand to her back. "Bunny sure could make anything grow."

"She sure could. And she always made it fun," Charlie said. A pang of nostalgia filled her chest.

"She did." Lisa smiled. "That was a good day."

"Yes, it was," Charlie brushed her thumb over Bunny's smiling face and put the photo back into the box.

At the end of the long shelf, Jen shifted boxes around until she found the one she wanted. She pulled it off the shelf and placed it on the floor. The top flaps had been locked into each other so the box was closed without having to tape it. A quarter-inch layer of salt was spread across the top. Jen pulled on the flap closest to her and all of them lifted up and fell open. Salt scattered onto the floor.

Charlie and Lisa knelt on either side of Jen and peered into the box.

"Jen," Lisa said, panic in her voice.

"I know," Jen said.

"Is that a book of the dead?" Charlie asked.

"Yes," Jen reached into the box and removed all three books. "And someone's book of shadows and a grimoire."

Charlie picked up the book of shadows and opened it. "Evangeline's been after me to start my own book of shadows."

"Evangeline's right," Jen said.

"Why were you scared these would fall into the wrong hands?" Charlie asked.

"Well normally I wouldn't be. There's nothing wrong with the book of the dead as long as you respect the dead. Just like there's nothing wrong with the book of shadows or a grimoire. Both are good ways to document your own personal journey as well as magical research and spells that you may want to pass down," Jen said.

"I don't think we should be playing around with the dead," Lisa said.

"I guess I don't understand," Charlie said. "I talk to the dead all the time."

"I know," Jen said. "But you don't try to command them. There are spells in this book that can not only conjure the dead from beyond the veil but can also make them do your bidding."

"Oh," Charlie said. Her hand floated to her throat and her stomach flip-flopped. All she had ever wanted was to help the dead reach their destination. She sure didn't want to pull them back from that place and try to control them. Just the idea of it made her feel sick.

"Why do you think Ben thought of these books?" Charlie asked. "I mean he's not suggesting that I . . . we, conjure the dead is he?"

"I don't know?" Jen said. "Maybe."

"How could that help us find the demon?" Charlie asked.

"Well, you think he's possessing someone, right?" Lisa asked. Charlie nodded. "Then the best way to find the demon is to find the man he's inhabiting. What better way to do that than to talk to the women that he's killed?"

"I don't know," Charlie said. "It just seems sort of disrespectful."

"I know." Jen patted Charlie on the elbow. "But sometimes desperate times call for desperate measures and as much as I hate to admit this, there are spells that could help you achieve your goals."

"But how high is the price?" Charlie asked.

"Listen, I've looked through them all and the owner did dabble in dark magic. That's the real reason I took them. I didn't want them to end up being used by anyone. But ..."

"But you're proposing we use them now," Lisa said.

"Maybe. Maybe some good can come from them," Jen said.

"Is there anything in there about locating a person?" Charlie asked.

"I could do a location spell without any of this darkness." Lisa waved her hand over the box. "But I've got to know specifically who I'm looking for."

"Your spirit. The one from your dreams," Jen said. "You said she's been a little cagey. Not wanting to stay around. What if we called her and asked her to talk to us?"

"You mean forced," Lisa said.

"I don't know," Charlie said. "I don't like the idea of that. At all."

"It's not like we're gonna kidnap her or force her to do anything horrible on our behalf," Jen said.

"I know. It just feels wrong," Charlie said.

"I hate to admit this, but," Lisa began, "Jen may be right. She's seen his face and where he kept her. All we want from her is some information. When we're done, you can have Tom escort her to where she's supposed to go."

"I guess if Tom could get her away from him and help cross her over, maaaaybe it might be okay," Charlie said.

"We'll need some of her personal effects," Jen said.

"Hair would be best. Preferably with the root still attached."

"I can give Jason a call and see if they catalogued anything like that into evidence," Charlie said.

"What about her apartment?" Lisa said. "You think Jason could get us in?"

"Probably," Charlie said. "Why? What are you thinking?"

"I'm thinking there's gotta be a hairbrush somewhere in her apartment. And that we should see if she has any other personal effects that we could use," Lisa said.

"All right then," Charlie said. "I'll give him a call."

* * *

CHARLIE, LISA AND JEN WAITED IN LISA'S CAR IN THE parking lot of Bethany McCabe's apartment complex. Charlie glanced at the watch on her wrist.

"Don't worry, he said he would come," Lisa said.

"I know," Charlie said.

"What are you worried about, Charlie?" Jen asked.

"I'm not worried." Charlie's cheeks heated at the lie. She turned her head, looking out the window, hoping her cousins wouldn't notice.

"Charlotte Grace," Jen said in a tone usually reserved for Ruby and sometimes her father. "You want to try that again?"

Charlie shifted in her seat and crossed her arms. "No. Not really."

"If she doesn't want to talk about it ..." Lisa said.

Charlie let out a little irritated growl from the back of her throat. "Fine. I'm worried."

"About what?" Jen asked.

"I'm worried that Jason won't show up. Not because he's breaking his word. But because Cameron has somehow convinced him otherwise. Cameron's a bad influence if you ask me."

"You're jealous," Lisa teased.

"No, I'm not," Charlie said.

"You are." A grin spread across Lisa's face. "You couldn't care less that he and I are dating, but have someone else move in on your crime-solving territory and you turn positively green."

"Hush your mouth Lisa Holloway. I'm not jealous." Charlie tightened her arms across her chest. She hated it when Lisa was right.

"Don't worry, Jason still loves you," Lisa said. "I wouldn't take it personally that he doesn't believe in demons. It's not really about you. Or even Cameron. If he ever ran into one, he'd believe."

"Well let's just hope it doesn't come to that," Jen said. "Demons are dangerous creatures, and they should not be messed with, especially not by humans."

Jason's black Dodge Charger pulled into the parking lot.

"He's here," Charlie said, pulling on the door handle and opening the door. She jumped out of the car to greet him, her gaze flitting to the passenger seat. It was empty. She let out a sigh of relief, raised her hand and waved.

Jason parked one space over from Lisa's car. As he got out of the car he waved but his expression was tight, wary.

"Hey," Jason said. "So I'm here. What is it that you need to get from the apartment?"

"We need to get some of Bethany's hair, if possible," Charlie said, keeping her tone neutral.

"Do I want to know why?" Jason asked.

"Probably not," Lisa said.

"I'm gonna try to get Bethany's spirit to talk to me. She doesn't seem to really want to sit down and have a chat, so were gonna force the issue," Charlie explained.

"And you need her hair to do that?" Jason asked.

"Yeah, I do," Charlie said.

Jason's gaze bounced from Charlie to Lisa to Jen and back to Charlie. His shoulders slumped a little with defeat and he pointed to the nearby stairwell. "Come on. I'll let you in."

Charlie and her cousins followed him up the steps to the second floor landing. Bethany's apartment was on the left. It had been sealed by the sheriff's department, and the yellow tape warning people that it was a crime scene and not to cross, was still in place. Jason tore the tape and pulled a Leatherman tool from the sheath hanging from his belt. He opened the knife and sliced through the seal on the door, before inserting the key into the deadbolt.

"You're in luck. The landlord's been after us to release this back to him so he could get it cleared out," Jason said. "But I haven't been willing to do that just yet. In case we needed something else."

Charlie and her cousins entered the well-appointed living room. "Should we wear gloves?" Charlie asked.

"No," Jason said. "CSU's already been over it. If you find something that you think might be helpful to me, though, let me know before you touch it."

"You got it," Charlie said. "Where's her bedroom and bathroom?"

Jason pointed to the hallway beyond the small kitchen. "That way."

"This really shouldn't take but a minute or so," Charlie said. "I'll check her bedroom."

"I've got her bathroom," Jen said.

The two of them walked down the hall with Jen taking the first right into the bathroom and Charlie heading in to the bedroom at the end of the hall.

A fourposter bed dominated the room along with a heavy matching dresser and mirror hanging on the far wall.

The nightstands were clear of any clutter but a thin layer of dust had already fallen, dulling the shiny varnish of the mahogany. The bed was covered with a floral comforter and more pillows than was necessary. Charlie checked the drawer of the nightstands closest to her and found a small notebook and a Catholic prayer book. She thumbed through the notebook. It appeared that Bethany had been writing down her dreams. Charlie skimmed the text. It looked like Bethany's dreams were more akin to nightmares. Charlie sat down on the edge of the bed and read through several pages.

MAY 9 — I DREAMED ABOUT THAT CREATURE AGAIN. CHASING me through the woods. Always chasing me. Why won't he leave me alone? I know it's just a stupid dream but sometimes I wake up and it's so real. I can't shake this feeling.

THERE WERE THREE MORE PAGES OF SIMILAR DREAMS. THE last entry made Charlie's blood go cold.

MAY 14 — I FINALLY GOT A GOOD LOOK AT IT IN MY DREAM last night. It was the most hideous thing I've ever seen, with skin so pale it looked purple. I could see his dark veins and those eyes. Black. Just pure black. I swear it's like evil is *chasing me. I don't know how to stop it. Praying doesn't help. Maybe I'll talk to my priest.*

"JASON!" CHARLIE CALLED AS SHE GOT UP FROM THE BED.

Jason, Lisa and Jen all hurried into the room.

"What's going on?" Jason asked.

"She was dreaming about him," Charlie said.

"Dreaming about who?" Jason asked.

"Dreaming about the demon. He was stalking her in her dreams," Charlie said.

"Where does it say that?"

Charlie pointed out the entries to him she felt were most pertinent. Jason looked up at her. "Charlie, it's just a dream."

"I'm not so sure about that," Charlie said.

"Can I see that?" Jen asked. Charlie handed her the book and Jen read through the last three pages.

"Look at this," Jen said. "She's been documenting her dreams for a while now, but it doesn't really change to him until May. Something happened. She must've come across him somewhere and he took a liking to her. Jason, did you recover a calendar?"

"Yeah, I think there was a calendar on her desk," Jason said.

"Maybe we should look at that to see if there were any places that all three victims went to," Charlie said. "Something that wouldn't stand out. And something way before they were taken."

"Yeah, I guess we pretty much just focused on the days they went missing. It's worth another check." Jason pulled a small notebook from the breast pocket of his polo shirt and wrote down the information. From his back pocket he took a folded up evidence bag. "I'm gonna confiscate that." He held it open for Jen to drop it in.

"Did you find a hairbrush?" Charlie asked.

"No. No sign of a comb or brush," Jen said. "Did y'all take those into evidence?"

"I don't think so. But I can check," Jason said.

"Well there goes that idea," Charlie said, feeling a little relieved that she didn't really have to summon Bethany McCabe's spirit.

"Jason, did Bethany have long hair or short hair?" Lisa asked.

"All the pictures I've seen of her she had a ponytail, so I guess long hair. Why?" Jason said.

"You're not off the hook just yet Charlie," Lisa said. She walked out of the bedroom, her footsteps muffled on the carpet. Charlie heard a door open and the sound of something heavy being shuffled around.

"Do you need help?" Charlie called.

"Yeah, Jason can you bring me your knife?" Lisa asked. The three of them left the bedroom and found Lisa at the breakfast bar in the kitchen. Propped against the bar was a vacuum cleaner that Lisa had turned upside down. She fiddled with a pale gray plastic piece holding the round carpet brush in place. Jason handed her his Leatherman tool and the gray piece of plastic flipped open to one side and Lisa carefully lifted the brush out of its holder.

"How much you want to bet all this hair is hers?" Lisa asked.

Charlie smiled weakly. "Great."

They all looked on as Lisa used Jason's knife to scrape some of the hair free from the vacuum cleaner brush. "Jen, do you have anything in that monstrous bag of yours that could hold this?"

Jen dug through her messenger bag until she found a tin of mints. She opened it to reveal she had repurposed it. Several black ponytail bands filled the space. She took them out and stuffed the nylon covered elastic bands into an inner pocket, then handed the empty tin over to her sister. Lisa put the small ball of hair into it and closed the top. Jen took the tin and put it into another pocket inside her messenger bag.

A loud cracking pierced the quiet of the apartment, making all four of them jump.

"What the hell was that?" Jason headed back toward the bedroom with his hand on the hilt of his weapon. "Holy shit!"

Charlie raced back to the bedroom. Her cousins not trailing far behind. She stopped just inside the doorway next to Jason. The oversized mirror that had hung on the wall above the dresser was now face up, balanced precariously on the edge of it. Charlie took a step forward and the mirror fell, landing with the frame against the bed. The sound of the glass shattering set Charlie's teeth on edge. Slowly, she approached the mirror, stepping over the few shards that had fallen out of the frame. They should've cleared the house with sage before they started work. Mirrors could be portals for spirits. Charlie internally chastised herself for not thinking of it sooner.

A low growl reverberated against her skin making her heart jump into her throat. Charlie stopped a few feet away from the mirror. Transfixed by what she saw in the cracked glass. Scratched deep into the mirror was the word mine. As she watched, the mirror clouded over and Charlie could see in the hazy glass the form of a creature, pale with marbled skin, growing smaller and smaller until it disappeared.

CHAPTER 19

They gathered in Charlie's living room. Charlie lit the sage, letting it flame up for a moment before she held it over a small silver bowl and blew it out. The trail of white smoke curled up toward the ceiling of her house. She handed the lighter to Lisa and Lisa lit the sage smudge in her hand. As soon as it produced smoke, she gave the lighter to Jen to light her bundle of sage.

"Mother goddess," Jen said, "bless this house and keep it free of all evil that might try to do us harm."

"So mote it be," Lisa and Charlie said in unison.

"So mote it be," Jen echoed.

They each headed in different directions with a smudge of sage and a white feather. Charlie wasn't taking any chances. They filled every corner of the house with the cleansing smoke. When they were done smudging, she poured a line of salt in front of every mirror in the house.

"There," Jen said, tamping her sage smudge out in the silver bowl and laying it against the inside wall. "Nice and clean."

"And just in time," Charlie said. She heard two car doors slam. "Sounds like Evangeline and Daphne are here."

Jen went to the door and opened it. The two women greeted Jen warmly and climbed the few steps up to Charlie's front stoop.

"Y'all come on in," Jen said.

"Hey, Charlie," Daphne said she took a deep sniff. "I smell sage."

"Yeah, we just cleansed the house," Charlie said. "Thank you all so much for coming. I really appreciate it."

"Jen said it was important," Evangeline said. She put the white canvas bag that she often carried down on the floor next to the front door. "Now what's going on? What's so terrible that Jen couldn't tell me over the phone?"

Charlie took a deep breath. What if they wouldn't help her? She had her own objections to this whole thing. She couldn't imagine Evangeline not having objections, too.

"Charlie, honey, what's going on?" Evangeline asked.

"I need to summon a spirit. And I didn't want to do it

by myself. I thought if you were here, that somehow it would make it better."

Evangeline's sharp blue eyes widened. "When you say summon, what exactly do you mean?"

"I mean call forth and hold captive. At least long enough to question her. Then a I'll call on Tom and have him take her to the other side," Charlie explained.

"Oh, Charlie," Evangeline said. "You're talking about dealing with dark things."

"I know. And I wouldn't ask if it wasn't important." Charlie waited, studying her aunt's face contemplating her request. Charlie knew it wouldn't be an easy decision. The balance between light and dark, between positive and negative energies was delicate and had to be respected. The very act of summoning could backfire on them, allowing darkness to prevail, and throwing everything out of kilter. Charlie took a deep breath. She couldn't think about that now, there were bigger things at stake. Matters of life and death. If there was fallout, she would deal with it.

"What is it that you expect the spirit to help you with?" Evangeline finally said. The crack of light and hope spread across the dread in Charlie's chest.

"I believe the spirit of the young woman is being held captive by a demon."

"You're sure?" Evangeline asked, sounding horrified.

"Yes ma'am. He's laid claim to her, convinced her that she must serve him," Charlie said.

"She said those words?" Evangeline asked.

"Not exactly. But I can tell you that when somebody dies and their spirit remains here, they almost always appear to me the way they saw themselves. Sometimes a little younger but nothing outrageous. The first time I saw this woman, she was crying and had black wings attached to her back. I don't know how, but this demon has convinced her to see herself that way in death. She told me it was too late for her. And I can't believe that. I just can't."

Her aunt's beautiful face deflated with defeat. "It is a powerful thing to call up the dead. Something not to be taken lightly. This cannot be a solution for you every single time that someone is in dire straits."

"No ma'am," Charlie said. "It won't be."

"So what do you want to do? You want to summon her here? You know I'm not a big fan of defecating where you eat," Evangeline said.

Charlie bit back a smile. "Yes ma'am."

"We should really do this in nature, preferably in a protection circle. Not here," Evangeline said.

"Yes ma'am," Charlie said with her cousins echoing.

"Where do you suggest we do this mama?" Daphne asked.

"Marcene Lewis has a field where the regional council

sometimes performs rituals. I could give her a call and see if we can use it," Evangeline said.

"Actually, I was thinking we could go back to the place where her body was found," Charlie said. "I'd need to call Jason and make sure it was all right, but there's a stone circle already in place and the ground is charged with her blood."

Evangeline latched onto Charlie's hand and gave it a hard squeeze. Her wizened gaze bore into Charlie, making it impossible to look away. "You sure you want to do this?"

Charlie let out a shaky breath and nodded. "Yes ma'am. I am."

"All right then. We will stand with you as your family and as your coven," Evangeline said.

"Thank you," Charlie wrapped her fingers around Evangeline's. "You have no idea how much I appreciate your help."

"You're welcome," Evangeline said. "I'm still not convinced this won't rain darkness down on all of us."

"Don't worry Evangeline," Jen said. "I'll make sure that we each have the strongest protection possible."

"All we can do is hope that it will be enough," Evangeline said.

"It will be," Jen said. "It has to be."

* * *

THE NEXT MORNING, THE FIVE OF THEM WALKED ACROSS the gravel road to the clearing. Rocks crunched beneath Charlie's feet.

The air pressed heavier and heavier against Charlie's shoulders the closer she got to the fire circle. Jen touched a hand to the center of Charlie's back and Charlie almost jumped out of her skin.

"Sorry about that," Charlie said.

"No apology necessary." Jen kept her hand flat against her cousin's back. The warmth soothed Charlie's ragged nerves and she hoped she was doing the right thing.

Once they were inside the fire ring, Charlie stepped back and let her aunt assess the situation. Jen reached inside her messenger bag and pulled out several small linen sacks strung on long pieces of jute. She slipped one over her head and then began to pass out the protection bags. They each put one over their head and let it rest against their chest. Evangeline took five large stones from the fire ring and placed them inside the circle around the charred remains of some long-ago fire. Each stone represented the point of a star. A pentacle.

Evangeline opened the canvas bag slung over her shoulder and removed five slender boxes. By the size of the boxes a stranger might have thought there was jewelry inside. But the boxes held something far more sacred, the wands belonging to each member of the coven.

Evangeline had done a quick blessing before they left Charlie's house. Each witch removed her wand from the box and handed it back to Evangeline. Evangeline dug through her canvas bag for more supplies. Including five black candles for protection, five books of matches and five white tealights in glass holders, that she had already anointed with blessing oil, to form the circle. She distributed these to the cousins. She also opened a plastic container that held a slice of bread and a sliced apple. Offerings for the spirit.

"Take your white tealight and place it on top of the stone in front of you," Evangeline instructed. "Charlie, since you'll be performing the ritual, you should stand at the top point."

"Okay," Charlie said and moved toward the stone representing the top most point of the star. She glanced down at the rock, looking for a place for the candle holder. The jagged surface didn't offer much for holding the candle so she turned the rock over. The other side was flatter. It took a little finagling, and digging but she got the rock to balance and placed the small glass candle holder in the center. She glanced around at the others. They were all stooped next to the rock in front of them, waiting.

"Light both your candles," Evangeline said.

Charlie tore a match from the book with the logo of a local pizzeria on the front and dragged the tip across the striker on the back. The head of the match burst into flame and Charlie touched it to the wick of the white candle and then the black candle. She blew out the flame, folded the used matchstick back into the matchbook and put it into her front pocket.

Charlie stood up with her black candle in one hand and her wand in the other. She looked to her aunt and then to her cousins to ensure they were all in place before she began the invocation.

Charlie took a deep breath. She held a small faceless doll with some of Bethany's hair stitched to its head and placed it in front of the tealight. "Spirits of the North and South, hear our call. Spirits of the East and West, hear our call. We bring this offering as a remembrance of your time in the mortal realm."

Charlie looked to her aunt, and Evangeline bent down placing the bread and slices of apple inside the circle. When Evangeline stood up Charlie continued. "We invoke your guidance. We beseech you to assist in our time of need. We invoke your presence to assist in our time of need. We invoke you by name, Bethany Ann McCabe. Stolen daughter of the world, come forth from the shadows and cross the veil. Wronged child of the spirits come forth and show yourself."

They all stared at the charred wood in the center of

the circle. When nothing happened Charlie searched the faces of her aunt and cousins. It wasn't working. Maybe she just didn't have the power needed to do this. Evangeline must've seen the panic on her face. She gave her niece a reassuring smile and nodded. Keep going, her aunt mouthed. Charlie's hands shook a little and she called up a weak smile.

"We invoke you by name, Bethany McCabe. Stolen daughter of the world come forth from the shadows across the veil. Wronged child of the spirits, come forth and show yourself," Charlie said.

The long dead embers in the center of the fire ring stirred. A thin stream of smoke curled upward. The coals beneath the blackened log glowed red for the first time in months.

"We invoke you by name, Bethany McCabe. Wronged child of the spirits come forth and show yourself." Charlie said.

The smoke grew thicker and darker until the form of a woman's body appeared. The apparition flickered at first then became more opaque than any spirit Charlie had ever seen before. The woman's long silver hair hung around her shoulders and her sharp angular features were echoed in the faces around her. Jen let out a gasp and Lisa muttered something that Charlie couldn't hear.

"Mama?" Evangeline said.

"Were you expecting the Queen?" the spirit of Bunny

Payne said, then cackled. Charlie could not stop the smile from spreading across her face.

"Bunny!" Charlie said.

"The spirit turned and faced Charlie. Her face full of light. Even in death, good humor glittered from her eyes. "Charlie girl. Looks like you finally decided to be the witch I knew you could be."

Charlie shrugged. "It took me a while, but I finally did."

"That makes me happy," Bunny said. "Now why have you called me back from the other side?"

"Well that's funny, because we didn't call you," Charlie said. "I was trying to call the spirit of a young woman who was murdered. She's been reluctant to talk to me, but I think I can help her."

"So she hasn't passed?" Bunny asked.

"No, she's dead," Charlie said.

"No, silly," Bunny said. "She hasn't passed over through the veil."

"Oh, no ma'am, she hasn't," Charlie said. "I believe she's being held captive."

"Held captive by who?" Bunny said. A quizzical look on her face.

"It's kind of a long story," Charlie said. "But I believe that it's a demon."

"Oh dear," Bunny said. "And you called me to help? I never figured you'd approve of necromancy, Evangeline."

Evangeline straightened up a sick look on her face. "It's a rather desperate situation, Mama."

"Bunny, it's not Evangeline's fault, it's mine," Charlie said.

"I understand," Bunny said. "But Evangeline is the leader of this ragtag coven of witches, is she not?"

"Yes ma'am," Charlie said.

"I take full responsibility," Evangeline said.

"Well I can't judge too harshly. It's not as if I didn't ever call on my ancestors for help," Bunny said. "You're gonna need a stronger invocation to pull her away from him. What we really need is a book of the dead."

"I have that," Jen said. "That's where we got the invocation that called you."

Bunny clapped her hands together. "Wonderful. Can you bring it here and show me, Jenny girl?"

Jen glanced at Evangeline. She bit her lower lip and hesitated.

"It's all right," Bunny said. "I'm not gonna disappear. That's the dangerous thing about calling a spirit from the other side. They may decide to stick around."

Charlie felt the sting from her grandmother's words. She looked at the candle burning in her hand. Her cheeks felt hot.

Jen reached into her messenger bag and retrieved the book of the dead. She tucked her wand into the front pocket on the flap and began to put the candlestick down on top of the rock next to the tea light.

"Jennifer Elisabeth," Bunny scolded. "Don't you dare put down that black candle."

Jen looked stricken and snatched the candle back into her hand. The flame flickered and almost blew out.

"Sorry," Jen managed in a meek voice.

"No, I'm sorry honey," Bunny said. "I didn't mean to scare you. It's just you should never enter a circle with a spirit without some protection, even when it's someone you love. Especially if it's someone you love. What if I'd been some demon pretending to be me?"

"Are you some demon pretending to be Bunny Payne?" Lisa asked in her best lawyer voice.

Bunny cackled. "Of course not Lisa Marie. But it's good practice. And as we all know ..." Bunny waggled her finger and they all echoed her words as she said them, "practice is the back bone of a strong craft."

Charlie's chest filled with lightness chasing away the dread. "Could you find her?"

Jen stood next to the spirit, rifling through the old book in her hands. Bunny cast a gaze at Charlie her dark blue eyes sharpening.

"What was that girl?" Bunny asked.

"You're on the side of the veil now. And you're a spirit. You can see things I can't see and I can see a lot," Charlie said. "Do you think you could find the spirit that we're looking for?"

"Well I suppose I could try," Bunny said cautiously. "Could be tricky, I don't want to be captured by any demon, that's for sure."

"Could he do that?" Daphne asked, a hint of panic in her voice.

"I couldn't say for sure, Cricket," Bunny said, using the pet name she had for Daphne when she was a little girl.

"He'd have to let go," Charlie said. "He's possessing a human right now. My guess is he thinks he has her and has no worries about her escaping. Which is why she was able to come to me in my dream last night and warn me. Please Bunny? If you can help us it would mean the world to me."

Bunny's ghostly hand drifted to her chest and she pressed it over her left breast. "Well I've never been able to say no to you, Charlie girl. I will try to find her."

"Thank you," Charlie said. "Thank you so much Bunny."

"You're most welcome child," Bunny said.

"How long do you think," Charlie began but stopped when her grandmother's spirit flickered and then disappeared. Charlie let out a sigh. Spirits. They could be so unpredictable, even when they were your grandmother.

"I was not expecting that," Evangeline said.

"Bunny?" Jen asked.

"I thought if anything, we would call up something dark," Evangeline said. "I'm still not sure that we haven't."

"Aren't you glad to see her, Mama?" Daphne asked. "I am. I missed her."

"Oh no, it's not that. I'm glad to see her, if it is actually her," Evangeline said.

"It's her," Charlie said. "It feels like her. Plus it's just like Bunny to warn us about stepping inside a circle with a strange spirit, even though she's the spirit."

"Yes," Evangeline said. "I suppose that's true."

A loud popping sound like a bubble breaking rippled across the circle and Bunny reappeared with another spirit in tow.

"Get back, Jenny girl," Bunny said, holding up her hand and putting her vaporous body between the other spirit and her granddaughter.

Jen jumped out of the circle, taking her place behind the stone representing the third point of the star.

The spirit of Bethany McCabe rounded on Charlie. "Why are you doing this? Why have you brought me here? I told you what you needed to know. He is hunting. Be vigilant."

"I know," Charlie said. "But I need more than that. I need to know where he is. Where did he keep you?" Charlie's lips quivered with the next question. "Where did he kill you, Bethany?"

Bethany let out a primal cry full of rage and sorrow. Bunny flickered in and out before disappearing.

Charlie became vaguely aware that her aunt had begun a quiet chant and that her cousins joined in. Against the soft drone of her cousins chant —

mother goddess hear my plea,
protect us from the shadow's harm,
bind the circle,
let no spirit flee,
until our mission here is done.

Bethany swept her hand forward and the gravel surrounding the remains of the fire swirled up as if it were dust caught in a storm. She thrust her arms out toward Charlie and the dust moved with her motion. Charlie took a step back, raising her candle in front of her chest.

Mother goddess hear my plea, Charlie began to chant along with her coven.

The gravel smacked the edge of the circle as if it had hit an invisible wall, spreading up and down into a mushroom-like cloud before raining debris back to earth.

The spirit screamed again – a wail so loud it made Charlie cover one ear in a vain attempt to muffle it. Bethany charged at Charlie and was thrown back toward the center when she hit the edge of the circle. She landed on the fire pit with enough energy to send the charred wood flying.

The spirit charged at her twice more, each time she was thrust backwards. Finally, the spirit laid down in the center of the circle staring up at the sky. Her chest rose and fell with heavy breaths, but Charlie knew this was just a habit, something left over from being human.

"Please let me help you," Charlie said. "Please."

"I've already told you. You can't help me." She sounded calmer, sad, broken.

"Yes, I can," Charlie said. She knelt, hoping Bethany would look toward her. "If you take me to him we can banish him. We will break the tether holding you to him."

Bethany's hands brushed across gravel and pieces of charred wood. The spirit sat up and set her gaze on Charlie. "You promise?"

"I promise," Charlie said.

Bethany shifted her gaze staring off into nothingness. "That's good. Perhaps we'll be in time then."

"In time for what?" Charlie asked.

"He's found another, and he's bringing her home now."

Charlie's heart sped into a fast steady drum against her ribs. "Bethany, you need to take us to him now."

"I can only show you the way. And only you can come," Bethany said. "I don't have the energy to lead you all."

"Okay," Charlie said. "How do you want to do this?"

Bethany stared at Charlie. "You need to come inside the circle."

Charlie threw a quick glance at her aunt. Evangeline continued to chant softly, but a new alarm darkened her eyes and she shook her head no.

Charlie took a deep breath. "You promise you're not going to run away if I take down the circle?"

"I promise," the spirit said.

"Evangeline," Charlie said softly. "You can stop."

"Charlie," Evangeline said.

"It's okay, really. I have to do this."

Bunny reappeared as soon as the circle protection was lowered. "Charlie girl, I don't know about this."

"You can come with her old woman," Bethany said. "You have your own energy."

"Who are you calling old, young lady?" Bunny said, sounding offended.

"Bunny, now is not the time," Charlie said. Charlie stepped inside the circle. "All right, what do you want me to do?"

"You need to sleep. That will be the easiest way for me to show you," Bethany said. "Lie down and close your eyes."

Charlie glanced around at the hard gravel-covered ground. "I don't know if I can sleep here."

"Lie down and close your eyes," Bethany said.

Charlie scowled, blew out her black candle and

stretched out on the ground next to Bethany. Tiny rocks dug into her back, head and butt. She shifted, trying to find a comfortable position. Then finally sat up. "This is not gonna work here."

"He's not looking for me here, and your circle offers me protection, just as it does you."

Evangeline, Jen, Lisa and Daphne all stepped closer inside the circle of rocks. "Charlie, I have a yoga mat in my car. Would that help?" Daphne asked.

"It's worth a try," Charlie said. Daphne hurried off to her SUV parked behind Jen's truck.

"You know you don't have to actually fall asleep," Evangeline said. "You could go into a trance. The spirit should be able to guide you, just as easily as in a dream."

"Evangeline, I don't think I've ever been in a trance before," Charlie said.

"Sure you have," Jen said. "You probably just didn't call it that. But any time you have a vision or you do a reading you go into a meditative state. This is just a deeper version of that same thing."

Charlie had not thought about it that way before, but Jen was right. She did meditate lightly whenever she did her readings. "I don't have to lie down for that."

Daphne reappeared carrying a purple yoga mat. She handed it to Charlie. Charlie kicked some of the gravel out of the way until she formed a rectangle large enough for her to sit in a half-lotus position. Charlie unrolled the yoga mat and folded it in half.

"I need something to help me focus," Charlie said. "Do you have a black tourmaline or a sodalite crystal with you by any chance, Jen?"

"Let me see," Jen said. She grabbed her messenger bag and dug through until she found a velvet drawstring bag that she always kept with her. She untied the string and pulled open the top, poking a finger inside. She looked over each crystal before removing three. A black tourmaline. A blue and gray sodalite crystal, and a clear quartz crystal. "Here."

Charlie didn't argue. She placed the black tourmaline in her left hand and the sodalite and quartz in her right before lowering herself into a half-lotus position. She glanced up at her aunt and cousins. "Maybe y'all can form a circle around me. If that's okay."

"That's perfectly okay, sweetheart," Evangeline said. "And a good idea. Come on girls."

Evangeline, Jen, Lisa, and Daphne joined hands stretching as far as their arms would allow into a circle around Charlie and the spirit.

Charlie closed her eyes, and squeezed the crystals, pressing them into her palms. She breathed in and out then held her breath for a half second after her lungs filled, and before she slowly released her breath to the count of ten. The air around her stilled and she didn't even hear birds and squirrels in the trees. She cleared her mind and focused on the feeling of the crystals in her hands. The smooth cool surface. The energy pulsing from within each stone. She counted backward as she released her last breath.

Ten, nine, eight ...

"Charlie girl. Can you hear me?" Bunny's voice. Melodic and full of good humor.

"I'm here," Charlie said.

Seven, six, five ...

"Charlie girl, where are you?" Bunny called.

"Here I am," Charlie said.

Four, three, two ...

"Charlie," another voice whispered harshly. Bethany's voice. "Open your eyes."

One.

Charlie opened her eyes and she was no longer in the circle surrounded by the safety of her aunt and cousins. She stood next to Bethany beneath the cover of a live oak tree. A frayed rope hung from one of the high branches and an old rubber tire leaned against the base of the tree, dry rotting. Sticks and branches stuck out where a bird or maybe a rodent had made a nest. Charlie shivered.

"There," Bethany said, pointing to the two-story farm house in the distance. It may have once been white but had grayed with age and was covered in a layer of thick dust. There was a porch beneath a shed roof held up by four square columns. Two wooden steps led up to the porch and two rocking chairs leaned against the wall next to the front door. An old porch swing creaked in the slight breeze rustling across the property.

"Can he see me?" Charlie asked.

"I don't know," Bethany said. "Maybe. Or maybe not. Maybe your coven keeps you from being seen. But he can see me."

Charlie shifted her gaze to the spirit standing next to her and for the first time she saw the collar around Bethany's neck. It looked to be made of iron. Her black wings stretched up and out from her shoulder blades.

"Did he make angels out of all of you?" Charlie asked.

Bethany locked eyes with Charlie. "He didn't make us into angels. He made us into demons. Or at least the beginnings of demons."

"How?"

Bethany's lower lip quivered and she looked back to the house. "He's back. And he has a fresh catch."

Charlie heard an engine coming up the long dirt and gravel driveway. The wheels kicked up dust as it passed the tree, heading around to the back of the building.

"Come on," Charlie said. She took a deep breath and left the safety of the shadows beneath the tree. She blinked and when she opened her eyes, she and Bethany were standing at the back of the house, watching a young man get out of the truck. He headed to the truck bed.

Charlie glanced down at the license plate, and caught only part of the sequence of letters and numbers before he opened the tailgate, blocking the plate.

"I saw part of his license plate," Charlie said aloud hoping that her cousins could hear her. She read the three letters aloud, repeating them once, so if nothing else, she might remember them when she came out of her trance. Jason could at least run a partial through one of his databases.

Once the tailgate was down, a body-like shape wrapped in a green canvas tarp appeared.

"Oh good goddess," Charlie breathed. "Has he taken another girl?"

"Yes," Bethany said. The man lifted the petite form over his shoulder and Charlie heard a cry.

"Please," the woman's voice said. "Please let me go."

Charlie's heart lurched into her throat. She had to do something. Had to stop him. But how? This vision was nothing more than a shadow of possibilities and Charlie felt like Scrooge being led around by the ghost of Christmas future.

"I need to wake up," Charlie said.

"Then wake up, Charlie girl," Bunny said. Charlie turned toward her voice and her grandmother snapped her fingers.

Charlie's eyes flew open and she jumped to her feet. "He has another girl. I have to call Jason."

Lisa fumbled her phone from her pocket and quickly dialed Jason's number. "Hey – Charlie needs to talk to you." She didn't give him a chance to argue or question, instead she thrust the phone toward Charlie.

Charlie slipped the black tourmaline into her front pocket and took the phone. "Hey – I think I know how to find him. All I have is a partial plate and a make and model of a truck. Will that be enough?"

"Let's hope so," Jason said.

"I think . . . I think he's taken another girl, Jason," Charlie said.

"Then we don't have any time to waste. What's the plate number?" Jason asked.

* * *

"What do you mean you don't want me there?" Charlie asked. She stared at the phone in her hand, listening to Jason's voice over the speaker. "I don't understand."

"Cameron, Beck and I are gonna go check it out. If we find probable cause, we'll arrest him. Then you can come in and do your thing. But I don't want you there until it's safe."

"Jason, it's not safe for you," she said. "You don't seem to understand what you're dealing with."

"Charlie, I think between the three of us we can take

him down if we have to," he said. "And we will have backup there as well."

"Jason, please, just tell me the address. Let us meet you there."

Charlie could hear his hesitation over the phone. Could picture his face, deliberating. Weighing the options. Would it be more dangerous for her to be there? Maybe. Or maybe not.

"If," Jason sighed. "And it's a big if . . . if I let you come you absolutely have to stay out of our way. The last thing I want is for you to get shot or worse."

"Nobody wants to get shot," Charlie said. "That is not part of the plan."

"All right then, promise me," he said.

"What?" Charlie said.

"You heard me," he said, not amused. "Promise me that you will stay out of our way."

Charlie pursed her lips and rolled her eyes at the phone. "Fine, Jason. I promise. On one condition. If you and your merry band of brothers get in trouble because, well, you know, it's a demon, you will back off and allow us to do our work."

Silence. Charlie frowned. "I can hear you breathing. I know you're still there."

"All right, fine. Deal," Jason said. "Just so you know, the only reason I'm making that deal is because I don't believe he's possessed by a demon, at least not how you mean."

"We'll see," she said. "Address please."

Jason rattled off the address and Charlie dug in the center console for a pen and piece of paper. An old grocery receipt and one of Evan's nubby pencil's was the best she found. She quickly jotted down the name and address and hung up the phone. She turned to Lisa in the passenger seat. "How's it going?"

Lisa sat with the book of shadows from Jen's box across her lap. Concentration lined her face and she didn't look up.

"I think I found a spell that will work," Lisa said. "I wish there was a way for us to test it first."

"I guess there's nothing like trial by fire," Charlie said.

Lisa nodded and flipped the page. "We're going to need a few ingredients."

"Well, hopefully Jen will have them. Lord knows, she has everything else in that bag of hers," Charlie said.

"Let's hope so," Lisa said. She reached in her purse and took a blank piece of paper from her leather planner and stuck it inside the book as a bookmark. "Where are we going?"

"A little south of Ravenel," Charlie said. "Can you text Daphne and Jen this address please?" Charlie handed Lisa the receipt and pulled out onto Highway 17.

***

"Up on the right," Lisa said, pointing to the orange reflector on the side of the road. "That's your turn."

Charlie's heart beat hard in her throat as she braked and flipped on her turn signal. "I sure hope Jason's here already."

"What do you want to do if he's not?" Lisa asked.

"I don't know," Charlie said. She glanced in her rearview mirror to make sure Daphne and Jen were still behind her. Evangeline had to return to the restaurant. But that was okay. The four of them still made a strong team. Charlie had no doubts that she and her cousins could take down this demon.

Charlie's stomach flip-flopped when they drew closer to the house and she saw the oak tree. It looked exactly like it had in her trance. The frayed rope swung in the breeze and the old rotting tire leaned against the trunk. Charlie's fingers thrummed with anticipation. He was here. She could feel him. Feel the darkness. Feel all the pain and suffering he had caused, emanating from the house. There was no sign of Jason yet. Charlie put the car in park and stared at the front door. She saw a curtain move in an upstairs window.

"He knows we're here," she said.

"What do you want to do about it?" Lisa said.

Charlie looked in her rearview mirror. Daphne had

parked her black SUV behind her. "I want to confront him."

"Charlie," Lisa said. "I know that you feel responsible. Especially since we think he's taken somebody else, but we don't even know if Jen has all the ingredients we need to banish him. Maybe we should wait for Jason."

Charlie looked up at the house. She saw one pale hand on the curtains and a silhouette of his head and upper body. She could feel his eyes on them, watching, wondering.

"We don't have time," Charlie said.

"Charlie, you promised Jason," Lisa said. "I heard you. You break that promise and he may never trust you again."

A scream shattered the still quiet air. The sound of it cut through Charlie's heart. "That's just a chance I'm gonna have to take."

Charlie opened the door and got out of her car. Lisa scrambled after her and Jen and Daphne joined them.

"Did you hear that?" Charlie asked.

"Yes," Jen said. She reached inside her messenger bag and retrieved her wand.

"Hang on," Lisa said. "You sure you want to do that? This place will be crawling with cops soon."

"I know, but they're not here yet," Jen said. "I'm not going in there unarmed."

"Jen's right. Get your wands," Charlie said. She

opened the back door of her car and dug through her purse for her wand. She removed it from its protective box and held the carved piece of elm tightly in her hand by the leather-wrapped grip. Evangeline had helped her make it. The feel of it against her palm sent an electric current up her arm into her chest. When they met between the two cars, the witches held their wands. Ready to do battle, if need be.

"So what is the plan here exactly?" Daphne asked.

"That's a good question," Lisa said. "What is your plan, Charlie? We can't just charge in without some sort of reason."

"We're not the police, Lisa," Charlie argued. "We are not going to arrest him. And we don't need probable cause."

"No, what we need is a little charm," Jen said.

"What do you mean?" Charlie asked.

Jen reached into her messenger bag and pulled out what looked to be an inventory sheet. She stood up and handed the page to Daphne. "Work your magic. Make it look like a list from the Women Voter's League."

"Okay," Daphne said, her voice full of uncertainty. "I can do that but I'm not sure what the point is."

"We're just four concerned citizens making sure that our rural residents are registered to vote," Jen said.

"Okay," Daphne said, looking down at the page. She

brushed her blue-tipped bangs from her forehead. "There's not an election for months."

"I know that. But it's the only thing I could come up with off the top of my head. I don't have any food with me to use as a charm," Jen said.

"Can you do it Daphne?" Charlie asked.

"Of course I can," Daphne said. "I can make anybody see just about anything I want them to."

"Wonderful," Lisa said wryly. "Then let's make him see a list of potential voters that need to be registered."

"You got it," Daphne said. "We don't know his name though, right?"

"Lisa do you still have that receipt I gave you? With the address?" Charlie said. Lisa nodded. She'd tucked it into the front of the book of shadows, which she still had in her hands. She handed Charlie her note.

"Gabriel Curtis," Charlie said, reading his name.

"You got it," Daphne said. She touched her wand tip to the paper and whispered an incantation. Charlie watched as the letters rearranged themselves to form the document that Jen wanted. When she was done, Daphne handed the paper back to Jen. "One glamorized document, as requested."

"Thanks," Jen said. "Come on Charlie, you're with me."

"Wait, what are we doing?" Lisa asked.

"Why don't you and Daphne go around back," Charlie said. "But stick together."

"Come on Lisa, we've got this," Daphne said. Lisa rolled her eyes.

"Don't do anything until we've actually made it inside the house," Jen said.

"I just want to make sure that my objections to all of this are on the record," Lisa said. "We should wait for Jason."

"So noted," Jen said.

"Jason will forgive me," Charlie said.

"Not if you're dead," Lisa said.

"Gosh, you're morbid," Jen said.

"Don't worry. If I'm dead I'm not really gonna be worried about his forgiveness," Charlie said. "Come on Jen."

Jen and Charlie walked to the porch. Charlie focused on the front door, trying to ignore the wave of nausea going through her. The darkness inside the house had a heartbeat. A steady rhythm that pounded inside Charlie's head the closer she moved to the place. Charlie touched her hand to her belly trying to get control of her feelings. She could not let them overwhelm her. Too much was on the line. Jen glanced sideways.

"Charlie, are you all right?" Jen said in a low voice as they climbed the steps.

"I'm fine," Charlie said. "I'll be fine."

"We don't have to do this," Jen said. "We can wait for Jason." The door opened startling them both.

"Hello. Can I help you?" the man asked. He wasn't very tall, but he had an athletic build that reminded Charlie of Scott. Of course he would be fit. How else could he overpower and lift a 125-pound woman like a sack of potatoes? Charlie's stomach turned. His wavy brown hair was chin length and he had it tucked behind his ears. Something about his pale blue eyes was haunting. Vacant. That was the word that played on the tip of Charlie's tongue. He had a vacant look about him. No one was home. Which made sense in a way, if he was being inhabited by a demon.

"Hi," Jen said stepping forward. She thrust her hand out. "My name is Jen Holloway and this is Charlie Payne and we're with the Women Voters' League."

"Hello," he said.

Jen glanced down at the paper in her hands. "You're Gabriel Curtis, right?"

His feet shifted, and he blinked, long and slow. "Yes."

"Well, Gabriel, we go from house to house, especially in rural parts of the county, making sure that people who are eligible to vote, can. Are you registered to vote?"

"Excuse me?" He asked as if he had not been listening. He kept staring past Charlie toward Lisa and Daphne.

"I said are you registered to vote?" Jen said. "I know people think the elections are months away and there's plenty of time. But time is one of those things that just always seems to slip away from us."

"I'm not very political." He waved her off. His soft voice bordered on creepy. It gave Charlie the shivers despite the June heat. He pointed toward Lisa and Daphne. "Who are they?"

Jen glanced over her shoulder. "Oh, they're with us. Women Voters' League."

"Hmmm," he said. "Pretty."

A scream filtered down from the top floor of the house, spreading like a dark mist. Charlie and Jen stood frozen, staring at him. He seemed unfazed by the blood-curdling sound.

"T.V.'s on upstairs. Didn't realize the sound was up so loud," he said casually. His lips tugged up at the corners but there was nothing natural about the smile and it never touched his eyes.

"It didn't sound like the T.V." Charlie said, holding his gaze. The wand in her left hand vibrated and she kept its tip pointed at the ground, trying to make it as inconspicuous as possible. A loud banging noise from the second floor rattled the house.

The man raised his eyes skyward and began to shut the door. "I have to go."

Charlie stuck her foot in the door. "Not yet."

Energy pulsated through Charlie as she raised her arm. A blast of red light exploded from the tip of her wand. The door flew open, splintering the wood and knocking Charlie on her butt. The man jumped back and held his hands up. Jen stepped in and held her wand up while Charlie recovered from the recoil.

"What the hell is this?" He said.

"Where is she?" Charlie asked dusting her backside off.

"What are those?" He said. "They're not guns. What are they?"

"Just hush," Charlie said. She stepped on the porch and waved Lisa and Daphne inside. Within a couple of minutes they joined Charlie and Jen in the depressing little living room. An old brown couch with a ripped arm, set in front of a T.V. Beer cans littered the top of a dusty old coffee table, and the smell of rotting meat permeated the air.

The witches encircled him. His gaze swept over them, sizing them up, as if he were trying to determine whether they were a real threat or not. The sound of weeping and a ragged call for help echoed through the house.

"Jen, why don't you go upstairs and free her," Charlie said. Jen nodded and headed to the staircase. Charlie watched her cousin ascend the steps from the corner of her eye.

"Wait a minute," he protested and took a step forward. "You can't just come in here. It's trespassing. I should call the cops."

"Why don't you do that?" Charlie pulled her phone from her front pocket. "Here, you can use my phone."

He narrowed his eyes. A smile played on his lips, this time it was more natural. More true to his nature. More evil.

"I know what you are," Charlie said.

"And what am I?" he asked. His face lit up. He was playing with her.

Charlie's jaw tightened. She didn't like to be trolled. "You know exactly what you are. A demon."

"Looks like you got your wish." Lisa glanced over her shoulder and watched as Jason's black Charger sped up the gravel driveway followed by two sheriff's cruisers with their lights on. "The cops are here."

His gaze shifted to the open door. His eyes widened and he looked around at the witches as if he was trying to determine whether to fight them or run. He grabbed a heavy book from a nearby shelf and pitched it at Charlie then turned and ran down the hall alongside the staircase.

Charlie held her hand up to deflect the book. It fell to the floor. "Dammit. He's getting away." Charlie started toward the hall and Lisa grabbed her arm yanking her back. "Let me go, Lisa."

"No," Lisa said. "He is a serial killer. Let Jason handle it."

Charlie jerked her arm out of her cousin's hand. "You're wasting time. You saw that look. He's possessed by a demon. I thought you were going to help me."

"I ..."

"Just forget it," Charlie said, taking off after him. "I'll take care of it myself."

Lisa called after her, "How? You don't even know the spell?"

"No, but you do," Charlie yelled, reaching the door. "Now, are you coming or not?"

Lisa threw up her hands and took off after Charlie "You win. Come on, Daphne. Hurry"

The three of them reached the back of the house, letting the screen door slam behind them. A pasture of golden, waist-high grass stretched out to a grove of trees, beyond the dead grass in the backyard. Charlie saw Gabriel stop when he reached the top of the white rail fence and look back at them. He gave them a two-fingered salute before jumping down and wading into the grass. He began to run and Charlie picked up her pace to a jog.

Lisa was the real athlete of the group and she broke out ahead of Charlie, scaling the fence with ease and keeping a tight grip on her wand. Charlie pushed herself to catch up. Her one advantage was her long legs. Daphne stopped at the fence, bent over with her hands on her knees, gasping for air. Charlie paused for a second.

"You all right?" Charlie asked.

"Go," Daphne said between heavy breaths, waving her on. "Get the bastard."

Charlie nodded and boosted herself over the fence,

managing to hold onto the wand. She raced through the path of broken grass. A bloodcurdling scream echoed over the tall grass and Charlie pushed herself harder, fighting the burn in her thighs. Just when she thought her lungs might explode, she caught up to them.

Lisa had somehow tripped him. Charlie realized the scream had been his. He lay on the ground with his arms stretched above his head and bound at the wrist by two thin, blue streams of light. His legs were bound and despite flailing his body and fighting against his restraints, he couldn't break his arms and legs free. It was as if Lisa had staked him to the ground.

"You caught him," Charlie said.

"Like you said, we couldn't let him get away," Lisa said.

Charlie rubbed the stitch biting into her side and chuckled. "They're not gonna be far behind us. How hard is the exorcism going to be?"

"Pretty dang hard without all the stuff we need," Lisa said.

"So, it can't be done?"

"I didn't say that. A witch isn't worth her salt if she can't improvise, right? " Lisa said.

Charlie smiled. "Right."

"You stand on one side of him and I'll stand on the other," Lisa said.

"Okay." Charlie took her place.

"You still have the protection bag Jen gave us?" Lisa

asked. Charlie nodded. "Good, take it and pour the contents into your hand."

Charlie did as she was told then watched Lisa empty her bag into her palm. A mix of salt and nine herbs made the base of the protection spell enclosed in the bag. But there were also several crystals and the bone of a chicken.

"Hold out your hand," Lisa said. Lisa picked through the salt mixture and plucked the black tourmaline and white quartz crystals from her palm before she poured the salt and herbs from her bag into Charlie's hand. Lisa knelt next to him and placed the white quartz on his forehead and the black tourmaline in the center of his chest.

"Okay, sprinkle the salt and herbs over him," Lisa said as Charlie covered Gabriel from head to toe. He grimaced and turned his face to the right, spitting salt away from his lips. Lisa pointed her wand at the crystal on his heart. "Point your wand at the crystal on his head," Lisa said then she began the incantation.

Demon head, demon heart,
    I command you.
    I cast you out of this body.
    Leave this realm. Go home.
    To the netherworld where you belong.
    Demon head, demon heart,
    Leave this realm. Go home.

To the netherworld where you belong.

CHARLIE LISTENED AT FIRST AND JOINED IN ON THE SECOND chorus. Her wand tip began to glow pinkish red and a stream of energy extended to his head. Gabriel flailed against his bindings, but showed no signs of pain, just irritation at being bound. She watched carefully, waiting for some small sign that the demon was leaving his body, but Gabriel only yanked his arms and feet. There was no screaming. No thrashing. No growling or cursing at them. None of the things Charlie expected.

"It's not working," Charlie said.

"You have to give it time," Lisa said. She began to chant again.

Charlie could hear the deputies in the distance drawing closer. Jason's voice called, "They're over here."

"What are you doing?" Jason said as he entered the space with his gun drawn. His gaze bounced from Charlie and Lisa to Gabriel bound on the ground. He glanced back over his shoulder at the deputies gaining on them.

"Stop that right now," he hissed. "Put your wands away," he said and knelt beside Gabriel. "Let him go."

Lisa lowered her wand and the energy holding Gabriel in place dissipated. Jason grabbed Gabriel's wrist. He jerked him up to a seated position and reached for the cuffs on his belt. Gabriel struck Jason with his free hand hard in the side, and shook his other hand free. Then he struck Jason in the face catching him off guard and knocking him backward. Lisa screamed. Gabriel clambered to his feet and headed into the grass. Jason managed to recover and chased after him. "Stop!"

A shot rang out. The loud thunderclap-like sound was too close and made Charlie's ears ring. Everything seemed to slow down as she watched Gabriel fall forward.

"Get them out of here," Jason commanded one of the deputy's. The next thing she knew, Charlie was being ushered away from the scene. Her heartbeat drummed in her ears. She kept trying to look over her shoulder, to see what had happened. Was Gabriel dead? She caught little glimpses of Jason and another deputy dragging Gabriel to his feet. His shoulder was bloody from being shot, but he seemed conscious, at least for now.

Jen and Daphne waited by the back door. A look of relief flooded Jen's face and she rushed forward throwing her arms around Charlie and Lisa at the same time.

"Oh thank goddess you're okay," she said. "We were so worried. We heard a shot."

"Jason got him," Lisa said. "Did you find the girl?"

"Yeah, I did," Jen said. "She's in pretty bad shape. He worked her over."

"It didn't work," Charlie said. She let out a defeated sigh. "He didn't react at all."

"Probably because we didn't have all the things we needed," Lisa said.

"What did you need that wasn't in your protection bag?" Jen asked. "It may be basic but it should have done the job."

"Evidently we needed a star anise," Lisa said.

"No," Jen disagreed. "That's optional."

"Optional or not, the spell didn't work," Lisa said.

They all turned and watched Jason and one of his deputies walk across the yard with their prisoner in tow. A blood-covered Gabriel cut his eyes toward the witches. Jason kept his gaze forward. His expression stoic.

"Jason looks mad," Lisa said.

"He'll get over it," Charlie said.

"I'm not so sure," Lisa said.

"The deputy we talked to said they're gonna want us to give a statement," Jen said. "I don't really want to lie."

"So don't," Charlie said. "Tell them the truth. Tell them that I had a vision and we were following it. I don't mind being the crazy one. We waited for the police but we heard a scream and we felt like we had to act. Don't lie. They're just gonna take the statement and file it away."

"You seem awfully sure," Daphne said.

"Charlie's right. This guy will cut a deal. He'd be an idiot not to. He had a girl chained up in his house. There's no way to explain that away," Lisa said. "We should all tell the truth. Except for maybe the part where

I used a binding spell to hold him in place and where we tried to exorcise him."

"How are you going to explain how you stopped him?" Charlie asked.

Lisa shrugged. "The truth, I tripped him. I don't have to tell him exactly how. It's not pertinent. And that is the one thing you should know when dealing with the law. Never give them too much information."

* * *

"Do you know how dangerous and stupid this little stunt of yours was?" Jason asked not doing a good job of controlling the tremor or volume of his voice. His cheeks and chest heated. He couldn't believe he had to have this conversation with her. "One thing. I asked you to do one thing. But no, you couldn't wait ten minutes for us to get there."

"We heard her scream," Charlie said. She sat in a chair in the interrogation room at the sheriff's station. She'd folded her arms across her chest and she wouldn't look at him.

"I don't care. You can't just go off halfcocked. What if he had killed you?"

Or Lisa, his mind added. The image of the two women standing over Curtis with their wands pointed at him played over in his head. The blue streams of energy binding him to the ground. The red energy connecting with Curtis's body as they chanted. It sent a shiver down his spine just thinking about it. He knew they were powerful. He'd seen it with his own eyes. But ... it was always for good. Never in a million years did he think he'd see them do something so ... vengeful. It scared him more than he wanted to admit.

"I would not have let that happen," Charlie protested.

"You don't know that," Jason said. "He could've had a gun for all you know." He leaned in close and lowered his voice. "And I don't care what kind of magic you work, I know you can't stop bullets."

Charlie finally looked up at him, fury burning in her blue eyes. "We had it under control."

"I saw you pointing at him, Charlie, with that wand of yours. You were torturing him."

"No I wasn't. We were trying to cast out that demon."

"Charlie, there is no demon," he said, his voice rising again. "There never was. He's just a bad man."

"Of course he's a bad man. A demon can't really make you do anything you don't already want to do. He wanted to kill those girls. The demon just made it easier."

"Just stop it," Jason said. "Do you hear yourself? You are obsessed."

"I'm obsessed." She rolled her eyes. "You're just ... You're just scared. You know, he wouldn't have gotten away if you didn't ask us to take the bindings off. You wouldn't have that black eye now and he'd be sitting in jail instead of in some hospital recovering from a gunshot. We had it under control until you interfered."

"You had it under control?" He stood back up and threw his hands into the air. "You had it under control! You essentially broke into his house. You assaulted him. You put yourself and your cousins at risk of death. You know, I ought to arrest you for obstruction of justice."

Charlie's jaw tightened and she narrowed her eyes. She thrust her wrists out defiantly. "Go ahead if it'll make you feel better. I did what I had to do. You didn't hear her screaming. If you feel I've jeopardized you or your case in some way then you go right ahead and arrest me. I stand by my actions."

Jason put his hands on his hips. Frustration burned a hole in his chest. He licked his bottom lip and didn't look at her as he spoke. "I can't believe I'm about to say this, but I don't think we should work together anymore. I appreciate all the work that you've done and the help you've given me, but I think you're too emotional."

The energy in the room shifted and the air stilled. His skin broke into goosebumps and the hair on his arms stood at attention. She stood up and glared at him.

"I'm too emotional," she said too calmly. Her gaze locked onto his. "You have got to be kidding me. You know what you can do with your 'too emotional' bullshit

Lieutenant?" Her fingers gestured air quotes. "You can take it and shove it where..."

One heavy knock on the door stopped her mid-sentence. Beck stuck his head into the room. "Y'all just about done in here? I need to take a statement."

"Yeah, we're done," Jason said to his partner. Beck opened the door wider and led Jen into the room.

"I'll get a deputy to walk you to your car," Jason said.

If Charlie's stare could've killed, Jason knew he'd be dead. "No thanks. I know the way."

Charlie breezed past him and he shivered. He'd been given the cold shoulder before, especially from the women in his life, but this felt different. If he hadn't known better, he would've sworn the temperature in the room had actually dropped.

CHAPTER 20

Friday afternoon, Ben waited in the upstairs bedroom of Arista's house. He stood close to the window overlooking the grand lane waiting for some sign that Megan might appear. Arista said her niece had sounded normal on the phone. As if nothing was wrong. But Ben knew that was a lie.

If Megan had summoned a demon, it would need a body to inhabit in order to do any sort of real destruction, and demons craved destruction like sugar addicts craved donuts and ice cream. They needed it, and they let nothing stand in their way of getting it. The problem with demon possession was that they could inhabit a person and then remain dormant for years. After all, demons had nothing but time and patience. They could hang around unnoticed endlessly until the time was right.

Only then would they awaken, take control, and begin to feed—that addiction for destruction becoming the thing they lived for. Ben had never seen a demon willingly relinquish its power to annihilate. Driving a demon out usually took the host's sanity with it. Ben didn't have the heart to tell Arista that part. That her niece would never be the same.

He left his post by the window, went to the bed and opened his messenger bag. He had a few supplies with him that would force the demon to show itself, if indeed it was there. And if it wasn't, Ben's tools of his trade wouldn't harm Megan.

From his bag, he pulled out a small stainless steel flask filled with water he'd arranged to have blessed by a Christian priest and a silver-plated hunting knife a High Priestess in his home coven had blessed, then dipped in salt water and allowed to dry. He wouldn't even have to cut Megan and draw blood to see if this worked. Just a touch to her skin with the knife tip should be enough of a threat. He snapped the leather sheath holding the knife to his belt at the small of his back, testing to make sure he could easily release the retention snaps holding the knife in place. When he felt comfortable with the accessibility of the weapon, he tugged his shirttail over it to make it less conspicuous.

He drew one more thing from his bag. A small Latin prayer book. He was not a Christian by any stretch of the imagination. He kept the pagan high holidays such as Yule, Ostara, Beltane, Litha, Mabon and Samhain.

He could also use spells to drive away an evil spirit or demon. But driving a demon away always seemed like he was just making it someone else's problem. He wanted to deal with the creature and nothing seemed more effective to him than the exorcism ritual that the Catholic Church had come up with a few hundred years back. He thumbed through the small leather bound book and found the page detailing the exorcism. He actually knew the ritual by heart even though he rarely did any demon hunting these days. He just liked to stay on top of his game. To be ready for whatever the world threw at him. And his boss, Lauren, she could always be counted on to keep him on his toes, that's for sure.

He tucked the book into the back pocket of his pants and shoved the flask of holy water into his front pocket. He would need a vessel of some sort to capture the demon. Some demons could be captured and put into glass bottles as long as the glass was opaque and a cork dipped in salt was used to trap it. But it wasn't foolproof. The only thing he had ever come across that was unfailing for holding whatever kind of spirit he encountered, human or non-human, was his amulet. He had captured spirits with it countless times, the most recent being a real SOB named Tony Smoak. Charlie's reaper friend had helped him dispose of Smoak and now the amulet hung around his neck, waiting for its next captive. He ran his finger along the thick silver chain, pulled the oval amulet into his hand and held the stone against his palm for a moment. The energy of it thrummed against his skin, sending a cool sensation up his arm, spreading through his chest and torso, down into his legs. He let it go, and it landed with a gentle thud on top of his gray T-shirt. Even through the thick layer of cotton the energy of the stone still vibrated.

Ben closed the messenger bag and shoved it underneath the bed, out of sight, then went back to the window. A few minutes later a red Jeep Cherokee drove up the lane and parked in front of the house. Arista had made Ben move his truck around to the back of the house and park in the garage that had once been a stable. If they were going to catch this demon there could be no sign that Arista was cooperating with the Defenders of Light. He actually admired Arista for helping him. This was dangerous work and she knew it. Guilt or no guilt.

Ben crept down the staircase to the foyer, stopping in the shadows to listen to the two witches argue.

"What's this all about Arista?" Megan asked.

"This isn't easy for me. You know I think of you as my daughter."

He could not see Arista but he imagined his tall, elegant friend pacing back and forth in front of the couch, stopping every once in a while to tuck her long, silver hair behind one ear or to raise her hand in an animated fashion.

"What are you getting at?" Megan asked.

"I need to know what you've been doing," Arista said flatly.

"I don't understand what you mean," Megan said.

"I think you know exactly what I mean," Arista said. "Miles and Rowena Carpenter."

"What about them?"

Even from where he stood, Ben could hear the bristle in Megan's voice.

"They were murdered and their baby – that sweet, ten-month-old boy – was abducted." Sadness tinged Arista's voice.

"So?" Megan lowered her voice and irritation edged into her tone.

"Okay, I'll just come right out and ask. Did you kill them? Did you take that baby?"

"What?" Megan's voice rose higher. "No, of course not. What on earth would give you that idea?"

Silence fell between them and Ben finished descending the steps.

"I gave her that idea." Ben stepped into the living room. Arista stood on one side of the coffee table, her arms folded tightly across her chest. Megan sat in one of the overstuffed chairs. Her dark auburn hair looked wild and curly, a halo of frizz surrounding her head.

"Who the hell are you?" Megan got to her feet. Her dark green eyes looked him up and down.

Ben pulled his credentials from his pocket and opened the wallet so she could see his I.D. "I'm Ben Sutton. I work for the Defenders of Light. Are you familiar with them?"

"Vaguely." Megan's feet shifted uncomfortably. She wouldn't look at him. Instead her eyes darted around the room as if she were looking for an escape.

"Arista called you here because I wanted to speak to you," Ben said. "Why don't you have a seat?"

"I don't want to," Megan said meekly.

"Sit," Ben instructed. Megan rolled her eyes, but she didn't argue.

Arista took a seat on the end of the couch near Megan. She leaned forward with her arms propped up on her knees, studying her niece's face.

"Where were you three nights ago?" Ben asked.

"I was ..." Megan swallowed hard. "I was at home."

"Anyone with you who can verify that?" Ben asked.

"No. I live alone," Megan said. "You're not the police, so why are you asking me these questions?"

"Actually, I am the police when it comes to witches and their use of magic," Ben said. "Especially when that magic leads to murder."

"Murder?" Megan muttered. "I did not murder anyone!"

"No? How about summoning a demon then? Which is also against the law, at least for witches." Ben held a steady gaze on Megan and she didn't seem to be able to look away from him. She didn't answer, but she did squirm, hugging her arms across her chest. "Did you summon a demon, Megan?"

"No. How could I? I'm not a very good witch. Just ask my aunt," Megan's eyes cut toward Arista.

Arista opened her mouth as if to protest but stopped. Her jowls drooped a little as she frowned. "Oh Megan, that's not true."

Ben narrowed his eyes. Carefully, he slipped the flask from his front pocket. "You know, somehow I just don't believe that. You know what I think? I think you did summon a demon. I think you did it to be taken more seriously as a witch. What's his name, Megan? Who did you summon?"

Megan shifted again and swallowed hard. She settled her gaze on her aunt. "Are you just going to let him accuse me of stuff?"

"I think you need to answer his questions, Megan," Arista said. "It would be better for everyone if you did."

"You mean it would be better for you. I know my rights," Megan said. "The burden of proof falls on him."

"Yes it does," he said. He moved between her and the door.

Megan's mouth drew up into a determined grimace.

"Megan, honey," Arista said on the edge of panic. "Let me help you. Okay?"

"The way you helped me now? By calling the cops on me? I thought we were family, Arista."

"We are family, sweetie," Arista said.

Ben stepped closer, twisting the metal cap from the flask, ready to take aim. "Megan, have you experienced any lost time?"

"What?" Fright darkened Megan's green eyes. "What do you mean?"

"Do you wake up, not knowing how you got some place? You can't remember whole chunks of time. Hours. Maybe even days," Ben said.

"I ... I don't know. Maybe. The last couple of weeks have been sort of hazy." She hugged herself tighter and rocked a little from side to side.

"Like living in a dream," Ben said.

"More like a nightmare," Megan whispered.

"Tell me about the nightmares, Megan." Ben knelt in front of her, holding the flask tightly in one hand.

Megan shook her head. Her eyes became glassy with unshed tears. "I ... I can't."

"Why not?"

"I ... I don't know." Her voice dropped. "It's like I open my mouth to say something but the words won't come. Like they're stuck." The tears pushed their way onto her cheeks.

"Or like someone won't let you speak?" Ben asked.

"Yeah," she whispered. "I've tried to scream. I open my mouth, but there's no sound."

"And you can see yourself, doing these horrible things, unable to stop yourself," Ben said. "Like kill that couple and take their baby."

"It's not me. It can't be me." Megan breathed the words. She closed her eyes and swiped at the trail of tears on her cheeks.

"Who is it, Megan? Tell me his name," Ben said softly.

"I can't," Megan insisted.

"Do you hear his voice? Inside your head. Telling you to do things, things you don't want to do?" he asked.

"I'm not crazy, " Megan said, her voice full of defiance.

"No one is saying you are," Ben said. He leveled his gaze on hers. "What's the name of the demon, Megan?"

Megan's jaw flexed. Ben could see the internal struggle on her face. Finally she spat out the words, "I ... can't."

Ben narrowed his eyes. "You wanted to say something else, didn't you?"

"Yuh-yuh," Megan stuttered and grunted, her face reddening. She grabbed hold of her neck as if she were choking.

Alarm filled Ben's chest and he touched her arm. "Megan? What's going on?"

"Cuh-can't bruh-bruh-bruh-eeeathe—"

Arista moved in closer. "Megan? Honey? Help her!" Her eyes pleaded with Ben.

"It's okay Megan, you don't have to answer me," Ben said. Suddenly, Megan's breath rushed from her body. She heaved forward into her aunt's arms, coughing and clutching at her throat.

"Dammit," Ben muttered. "I'm really sorry about this, Megan."

"What?" Megan glanced up at him. He hoisted himself to his feet and with the flick of his wrist, a spray of the holy water splashed Megan in the face.

Megan flung herself backward into the chair, swiping madly at her face. "It burns! What did you do?"

"Revelare nomen tuum!"

Ben chanted three times while he doused her with the holy water.

Megan scrambled up onto the chair and crouched. Her slim face morphed into a savage mask. A loud hiss escaped her mouth as she batted the place on her face where the holy water had struck her. She blinked and her corneas turned deep red as if they'd suddenly filled with blood. Her pretty green irises disappeared, obscured by a round black pupil.

"There you are," Ben said. He'd seen a few demons in his time and was prepared for the black eyes. The red, on the other hand, was something he'd never seen before.

A sound emanated from deep inside of Megan's chest,

a mish-mash of growls that sounded like no wild animal he'd ever heard. The primal noise made the hair on the back of his neck and his arms stand up. He shook off the fear and tightened his grip on the flask.

"Very scary," he mocked. His other hand found the hilt of his knife. His fingers deftly unsnapped the leather strap holding the knife in place.

The demon inhabiting Megan's body glanced at his moving hand. Her lips spread into a wide sneer. "Do you think you can hurt me, Defender of Light?"

"Hurt you? Why would I want to hurt you? Hurting you hurts Megan," Ben said.

"So you care for this sack of meat I'm wearing? How peculiar," the demon taunted.

"Yeah, I care about other humans. I'm weird like that," Ben said. "It's time for you to go."

"No, Defender of Light," the demon hissed. "It's time for you to go."

Megan launched herself toward Ben with the full weight of her body. Even though she couldn't have stood taller than 5'2" and weighed a hundred-and-ten pounds soaking wet, she managed to knock Ben backward, making him lose his balance. The two of them spilled onto the floor. Ben's flask slid across the carpet. The holy water glugged from the opening, drenching the fine, cream and tan Persian rug. The demon hopped to its feet before Ben. It reared one leg back and kicked Ben in the head before he could get out of its way. Red and white stars bloomed before his eyes and his ears began to ring. Ben shook his head and tried to get up. Megan lunged at him with unexpected strength, knocking him onto his side. She stalked over to the marble fireplace and grabbed the shiny brass poker. Ben slipped his hand behind his back and unsheathed the knife.

"Megan, please," Arista begged. "Don't do this."

Megan stopped in her tracks and stared at her aunt. Disgust twisted her lips. She swiped at the air with the poker and Arista flung backward. Her aunt hit near the ceiling and fell to the floor in a crumpled heap.

"This wasn't how I wanted things to end," Ben said. He got to his feet and held the knife out in front of him.

"You think you can kill me?" The demon asked. "You're not fast enough. I will snap your neck before you can even get close to me." The demon raised its arm in the air, hand half-open, with fingers bent as if they were wrapped around Ben's neck.

Ben's hand flew to his throat. He tried to take a deep breath but something blocked air in or out. Ben dropped the knife onto the carpet. Heat flooded his cheeks and his eyes watered while he scratched at the skin on his neck. Every bone in his neck and spine stretched as he lifted into the air. He pointed the toes of his heavy boots, trying to hold onto the floor without any success. How could this tiny young woman, who, by all accounts, barely had any magic of her own, choke him and lift him up as if he weighed nothing?

She can do anything I want her to, a deep unearthly voice growled through Ben's mind. Including kill you.

The world grayed at the edges and Ben felt himself shaking back and forth like a lifeless doll. Then he was sailing toward the wall next to the fireplace. The last thought to go through his head before everything went dark echoed through his mind: He never told Jen the truth and now he would never get the chance.

CHAPTER 21

Charlie slipped her hand into Tom's and descended the three steps of her front stoop. He lifted her hand to his lips and kissed it.

"Are you sure you want to go tonight?" Tom asked. "He'll be there."

"I know." Charlie gave him a smile and let her gaze drift across the expanse of bright green grass separating her uncle's house from the small cottage she rented from him. The sun had not quite set in the sky and the white clapboard house glowed like a beacon in the dying golden rays. She took a deep breath. "Are you ready? I mean it's not like they don't know already. Well Jen knows anyway. It's a big step."

"If Jen knows, they all know, right?" Tom smirked.

"None of my cousins are brilliant secret keepers," Charlie said.

"I don't know about that," Tom chuckled. "Lisa knows how to keep a secret or two, being a lawyer and all."

Charlie gazed up at him, a smile playing on her lips. "Well, that's true."

"It's good that we're telling them officially." Tom squeezed her hand and gave her a soft smile. "I like things to be out in the open."

"Except the fact that you're a, you know," Charlie teased. "Everyone knows except uncle Jack of course, and the kids. And I'd like to keep it that way."

"Of course," Tom said. He smiled and her heart fluttered. She knew the face he wore was a glamour, a façade to cover his real face, but she didn't care. He was beautiful. There was no other word to describe him. He had even changed his hair a little for her. She had mentioned that she liked men with longer hair and the next day his hair had grown an inch and was thicker and curlier than the day before. She had to scold him and tell him that hair didn't grow that fast on human beings and that he would need to gradually grow it out.

She'd blinked and his hair was suddenly an inch shorter. She had wrapped her arms around him and run her fingers through his dark mane and he had kissed her deeply for the first time. She shuddered at the memory and reached up and quickly kissed him on the cheek.

"Thank you for understanding," she said.

"You know it's always been a puzzle to me?" he began. "How is it possible that Jack Holloway is surrounded by witches, and even supernatural creatures such as myself, and he has no clue about them? You all act as if you're normal."

"I can't say for sure what my uncle knows or doesn't know. I've never asked him. Never quite had the guts. But he's not a fool. And I know Jen and Lisa would object vehemently to doing anything that might mess with his memory." Charlie shifted her gaze back to the house. "My guess is he probably does know on some level that the women in his life are all ... different. I doubt very seriously, though, he's put the word witch to it. And if he has, I don't think he would ever say. It's much easier to delude yourself if you don't actually speak the words out loud, you know?"

"Yes," Tom said, a thoughtful expression on his face. "I can see that."

Charlie stopped at the bottom step of the wide back porch to her uncle's house. The windows and backdoor were closed up tight to keep the late June heat out, but music still managed to escape. Evangeline must have picked it because it was old classic rock. The harmonies of Kansas singing about southern skies drifted from the kitchen. It wrapped itself around Charlie and warmed her heart.

"Come on, let's go get this over with," she said and stepped onto the bottom stair.

Tom slipped his hand out of hers and wrapped it around her waist, hugging her to him. "It's going to be fine. They like me."

"Yes they do. They like you very much actually." Standing on the bottom step, she stood a few inches taller than him. She grinned and wrapped her arms around his shoulders and kissed him properly this time. When she pulled away, she brushed her hand over his cheek. "Of course, that doesn't mean they won't be concerned. Especially Lisa. You still kinda scare her."

"Scare her?" Tom sounded a little offended. "Why on earth would I scare her?"

"She still thinks you're too close to Death. With a capital D."

"For the thousandth time, I am not death. I do not choose who lives or dies. I merely collect the soul and deliver it to its destination," he said, an indignant grimace twisted his lips.

"I know that." Charlie laughed and pressed her lips against his. "I'm just saying that's how Lisa sees you. That's all."

The screen door creaked open and Charlie looked up to find her cousin Lisa standing at the top of the steps with her hands on her slim hips. Her strawberry blonde hair was plaited into a long fishtail braid that flopped over one shoulder. She wore denim cut offs and a vintage navy Clash T-shirt.

"Are y'all gonna stand out here all night?" Lisa asked.

Charlie met her cousin's teasing gaze. "We're thinking about it. Depends on what kind of reception we're going to get."

"You're never gonna know unless you come inside." Lisa motioned for them to climb the steps. "Hi, Tom."

"Hello, Lisa." Tom offered her a warm smile. Charlie could sense her cousin's apprehension but she appreciated Lisa's little olive branch. Most of the time she just ignored Tom.

Charlie tucked her arm in the crook of Tom's elbow and pulled him up the steps. "I guess it's now or never."

The pair walked into the kitchen and found a familiar scene. Evangeline was at the stove and from the smell of it she was frying shrimp while Jen tended a small fryer on the counter. Charlie moved in close and watched her cousin drop a handful of perfectly breaded summer squash into the fryer. The golden oil bubbled up once the vegetables submerged.

"Yum!" Charlie said. "You need any help?"

Jen glanced sideways toward Tom and a wide grin crossed her lips. "Nope. Hi, Tom."

Tom stood awkwardly at the end of the table in the middle of the large kitchen. "Hi, Jen."

"Tom you look parched. Would you like a beer? Or some iced tea?" Jen said.

Tom's eyes darted between Charlie and Jen, his expression wary. "Tea sounds wonderful."

"Why don't you go join my dad? Jason and his friend are also in the living room. Do you remember the way?" Jen asked.

Charlie bristled against the mention of Jason. Tom locked his gaze on Charlie as if he were looking for guidance. She smiled and nodded, then gestured toward the door leading to the dining room. "It's fine. I'll bring you your tea. You want lemon?"

"No, thank you." Tom winked, and disappeared through the doorway.

"So you're making it official?" Lisa leaned against the counter opposite her sister. "You're really dating death."

"Hush your mouth," Charlie and Evangeline hissed simultaneously.

"Tom is not death," Charlie lowered her voice. "How many times do I have to tell you that?"

"Doesn't matter how many times you say it. I'm not particularly convinced," Lisa quipped.

" I don't particularly care whether you're convinced or not," Charlie said, giving back as good as she got.

"All right you two, that's enough," Evangeline said. "I have these lovely shrimp and flounder fillets and nobody needs a sour stomach because of your bickering. I think it's wonderful if Charlie's happy. Ultimately, that's all that matters."

"Thank you, Evangeline. I appreciate that," Charlie said. She took a glass from the cabinet, and filled it with ice. A pitcher of freshly made tea sat on the table in the middle of the large kitchen and Charlie filled the glass.

"Lisa, can you mix up that potato salad on the counter next you?" Evangeline asked.

"Me?" Lisa said sounding appalled and terrified at the same time. "I can't cook. Why do you think I come here?"

"Oh good goddess above," Jen muttered. "Get out of the kitchen if you're not gonna be any help. Why don't you go entertain Jason and Tom?"

Lisa folded her arms across her chest and pushed off from the counter. "Fine."

"Here, why don't you take this to Tom, and I'll set the table," Charlie said.

Lisa took the glass and gave Charlie a knowing glare. "I know what you're doing. You can't avoid him forever."

"I do not know what you're talking about, Lisa Marie," Charlie said nonchalantly and followed Lisa into the dining room.

Daphne was nowhere to be seen but the extra leaves had already been put in place, making the table long enough to seat twelve. Nine plates had been set out but there was no silverware or napkins. Charlie went to the sideboard and took a stack of white linen napkins and placed one by each plate. A moment later Daphne came in through the door that led to the foyer. She struggled with an extra chair.

"Here let me help you with that." Charlie rushed to her cousin's aid. The two of them lifted the heavy chair placing it near the end of the table then rearranged the other chairs because they were lighter and easier to maneuver.

"Uncle Jack should really get some folding chairs for company instead of keeping these old things around," Daphne said. She ran her hand through her short bob.

"Or maybe we should just let Jen do the lifting," Charlie teased. "She's the one that can pick up those sacks of flour and sugar."

"Good idea," Daphne said. "I saw Tom come in."

"Oh?" Charlie moved to the sideboard and began to fiddle with the forks. She counted them out to make sure there were enough for each plate.

"And in case no one tells you this tonight, I think it's wonderful. And screw what Lisa thinks."

Charlie smiled and gave her cousin a grateful look. "I appreciate that. It's not easy to date someone if your family disapproves."

"Oh, I know," Daphne said. "Why do you think I never bring anybody home?"

"What?" Charlie asked.

"What?" Daphne took a handful of dinner knives from the sideboard and began to place one by each plate.

"Daphne, don't play dumb with me. What does that mean? Are you dating someone?"

"Just forget I said anything," Daphne said.

"Daphne..."

"Hey, Charlie," a man's voice said from behind her.

Charlie turned and found Jason Tate standing in the doorway. Her body stiffened. "Hey."

"Hey, Charlie," Cameron said moving in behind Jason. He wore a stiff blue button down and dark gray slacks.

"Hey, Cameron." Charlie regarded him with caution. "It's kind of hot for that get up, isn't it? Or is there just some FBI rule that you have to be uncomfortable all the time?"

"It's pretty much a rule." Cameron gave her a half-grin. He patted his hand against his stomach. "Naw, really I just wanted to look nice. Jason said Friday dinners are kind of a big deal."

"That's very sweet." Charlie kept her tone neutral. "But Jason exaggerates."

"I did not tell him to wear a freaking button-down," Jason rebuffed, grinning. A glimmer of hope shined in his hazel eyes but Charlie ignored it and looked him up and down. He wore a navy polo shirt and a pair of khaki shorts and a pair of tennis shoes that had seen better days. She wasn't ready to make up. She wasn't sure she would ever be ready. "I have no doubt about that. If you'll excuse me, I've got to get another place setting."

"Sure," Jason nodded, the hope in his eyes fading. He disappeared back into the living room. Daphne followed him out but Cameron hovered near the end of the table.

"Listen, Charlie," Cameron began, "I was hoping we'd have a chance to chat."

"Oh?" Charlie said coolly.

"Yeah, I think we got off on the wrong foot throughout this whole investigation and . . ."

"Did Jason make you say that?" Charlie asked unable to hide the surprise in her voice.

"No. No, of course not." Cameron sounded offended. "I'm still not sure about whatever ability you have. I like to deal in hard facts, not whatever it is you do."

Charlie cut him off. "Okay. This was lovely while it lasted." Why did everything Cameron say feel like a pebble in her shoe? Not quite painful, but more than just mildly annoying. Tonight was a good night. A night for celebration as far as she was concerned. They'd gotten a killer off the streets and it happened because of her 'whatever it is you do.'

"Listen, you don't have to believe in me. I'm just glad that Gabriel Curtis is on his way to jail."

He nodded. "Me, too." He seemed to struggle for his next words. "No matter what Jason says, we can't deny that you were instrumental in finding Curtis. That's all I'm trying to say."

"All right." Charlie folded her arms across her chest.

"Truce?" Cameron held out his hand.

Charlie sighed. Up till now, she'd done everything she could to avoid touching him, to avoid seeing inside his life and his head. Reluctantly, she took his hand in hers. An electric jolt traveled from the place where their hands met up her arm into her chest. The pressure around her heart tightened and for a moment she could barely breathe. A vision flashed inside her mind. Sights and sounds overwhelmed her senses. Two boys wearing different colored polo shirts and khaki shorts ran across a field. Charlie recognized Cameron's dark brown eyes and wavy dark hair. The other boy was a near mirror image of Cameron. *Twins.*

"Come on, Kyle." Cameron prodded the other boy. His voice echoed through her head. "Hurry or it'll get you." He sped up, heading toward the fence in the distance.

"Cameron," the other boy said. He paused a minute and held his side, gulping in air. " Cameron, wait!"

"Keep up, Kyle!" Cameron called back to the other boy. "Mama will be mad if we're late."

Brothers. Twin brothers.

Charlie blinked and met Cameron's wary gaze. "You have a brother named Kyle."

Cameron jerked his hand out of Charlie's and took a

step back, the connection broken. Charlie swiped at her cheek.

"Did Jason tell you that?" Cameron said, his voice almost a growl.

"What?" Charlie asked. She opened and closed her hand several times. Her fingers still twitched with the electric connection. It clung to her skin and she thought for a second if she touched him again, her whole hand might catch fire. "No. Of course not."

"You're lying," Cameron said.

"I beg your pardon?" Charlie bristled at his accusatory tone. Anger crept up into her throat, and her chest and neck heated.

"Just stop," Cameron said holding up his hand.

"No, you stop. Are you seriously going to come into my uncle's house and call me a liar to my face?"

"Everything all right in here?" Jason said, turning back into the dining room. "Charlie?"

"Why don't you ask him?" Charlie folded her arms across her chest. "He's the one who's calling me a liar."

"What did you tell her?" Cameron said.

"Tell her about what?" Jason said perplexed.

"Kyle," Cameron said.

"I never said anything to her," Jason held his hands up in surrender. "I swear to God."

"You sure?" Cameron said. His eyes flitted from Jason to Charlie and back to Jason.

"Absolutely," Jason said. "Why would I tell her something like that?"

Cameron gave Charlie a hard stare but directed his words at Jason. "To make your point."

"Come on man. You know me better than that," Jason said, sounding hurt.

"Then you told Lisa, and she..." Cameron started.

"You hush up. Right now. Do you hear me?" Charlie pointed her finger at him and used her mom voice. She could take insults all day but she wasn't going to let him disparage Lisa. Especially when Lisa was innocent. "Nobody told me anything." Charlie glanced at the door and lowered her voice. " I saw you with him, when you touched me. Why do you think I've been avoiding shaking your hand? When I touch people, I see things about them. Personal things."

Cameron clenched his jaw and shook his head. His brown eyes narrowed and he showed no signs that he believed her. "I don't know what your game is. And I don't know how you convinced Jason to play it but nobody can read minds." The air around them grew heavy in the stare- down between Charlie and Cameron.

"Everything all right in here?" Her uncle Jack's voice broke through the tension and Charlie and Cameron both stepped back from each other.

Charlie glanced at her uncle and gave him her best smile. "Everything's fine Uncle Jack. I'm just finishing up setting the table. Jason, why don't you and Cameron go back into the living room? Supper will be ready in a little bit."

"Come on," Jason said gruffly, directing Cameron toward the living room. Jason gave her uncle a quick nod of respect as he passed.

Once they were alone, Jack put one hand on his hip and scrubbed his beard with the other one. "You sure you're all right? That Cameron doesn't seem to like you much."

"No sir, he doesn't. But it's nothing I can't handle." Charlie moved closer to her uncle and patted him on the arm. It shocked her when he captured her hand in his and gave it a gentle squeeze.

"You know you're as much my daughter as Jen or Lisa. All you girls are. So I'm gonna give you a little unsolicited advice," Jack said softly.

Charlie met his intense gaze. A fierceness sparkled in his blue eyes that she'd only seen a few times. The last time she'd seen it, Jen told him she was pregnant and that she wasn't going to marry the father. "It doesn't matter what anybody else thinks of you. Not me. Or Jen. Or Lisa. Or Daphne. And especially not some friend of a friend."

Charlie opened her mouth to protest. Jack made a flat warning sound and held up one finger to stop her. "There's only one opinion that matters about who you are, and what you're capable of, and that's yours. You understand me?"

"Yes, sir," Charlie said, her lips tugging into an appreciative smile.

"Good. Family is where they love you, no matter what," Jack said.

"Thank you," Charlie's heart swelled with adoration. She leaned in and kissed his cheek. "For the record, I love you, too. Now I better get this table set before Evangeline has my hide."

"Can't have that, now can we?" he said and let her go. They went their separate ways but she looked back over her shoulder and watched him disappear around the corner toward the living room. He was right. It didn't matter what anybody else thought. Not Cameron. Not Jason. Not even her Tom.

Still, being called a liar stung, and no amount of shaking it off soothed the wound. Only time and distance could do that. With the case pretty much solved, she was ready to put as much distance between her, Jason and Cameron as she could get.

CHAPTER 22

"Sounds like you're having a devil of a time with the boys," Evangeline commented from her place at the stove.

"It's fine." Charlie opened the silverware drawer and pulled out another set of cutlery. Then reached into the cabinet above her and grabbed another place setting. "I can take care of myself."

"I have no doubt about that, sweetie," Evangeline said and scooped up the last batch of shrimp onto a large platter. "But you can be stubborn. The whole lot of you can."

Charlie grinned, and rolled her eyes. "Now I wonder where we get that from?"

"I have no idea," Evangeline quipped.

"You know I have a spell for that," Jen said softly.

Charlie turned and looked her cousin squarely in the eye. "For what? Stubbornness?"

"No. For opening a jackass's eyes. Well, his third eye. And only for long enough to get a little perspective," Jen said.

Charlie chuckled. "Now that's a spell I could get behind."

"Shush you two," Evangeline scolded in a harsh whisper, her eye toward the door.

Charlie and Jen exchanged a knowing glance. Their aunt didn't like it when they spoke of using spells in what she sometimes referred to as a 'frivolous manner,' especially in the kitchen where Jack might overhear them.

Charlie reached for the drawer next to the cutlery, where the napkins were kept. She listened to her aunt and cousin discuss the logistics of moving the food into the dining room. Then their voices suddenly seemed far away. She pressed her finger against her ear and a faint buzzing sound filled her head. The world swam in gray and Charlie reached for the counter to steady herself. She closed her eyes tight. The vision filled her mind, transporting her somewhere else for a moment.

When she looked around, she saw Ben holding up a cross. Which was a strange thing, because he was a witch, and there were no crosses in the practice of witchcraft. She heard him speaking Latin.

"*Revelare nomen tuum...*"

The growling sound echoed through Charlie's head. Her eyes were drawn to the young woman standing across from him. There was something tiger-like and fierce about her face, but there was no mistaking those eyes. They were solid black. Nausea washed over her. A demon.

The demon raised her arms and suddenly it was as if Ben were weightless. He lifted eight feet into the air just before he sailed across the room, slamming into the wall, denting the drywall. A cloud of dust and broken plaster rained down on him. He lay motionless. Was he breathing? Charlie couldn't tell.

A strangled sound ushered from Charlie's chest and she blinked, aware of the wetness on her eyelashes and cheeks. When her eyesight cleared she found Jen and Evangeline kneeling next to her. Somehow she had lowered herself to the floor. She looked around, reassuring herself. She was in her uncle's kitchen. Sitting up against the counter, squeezing a linen napkin in her sweaty palm. The fabric felt oddly rough and soft at the same time. She pinched the napkin between her thumb and forefinger, grounding herself in this place.

Worried looks marred the faces of her aunt and cousin.

"Charlie?" Jen said, her voice quiet but strained.

"I'm okay," she said.

"What happened?" Evangeline asked.

"Just a vision," Charlie said. "I'm sorry if I scared you." She gave Jen a weak smile. "Help me to my feet?"

"Of course," Jen said hopping up. Evangeline took Charlie's elbow and Charlie put her hand into Jen's and pulled herself up to standing. Dizziness swirled through her brain for a second and she held tight.

"You sure you're all right?" Jen said. "Maybe I should get daddy."

"No," Charlie said. "I'm fine. I don't want to worry him. It'll pass."

Jen nodded and swallowed hard. Her large blue eyes searched Charlie's face. "You called Ben's name."

Charlie sighed. She was caught. There would be no way to evade questions now.

"That's because I saw him. And I'll tell you all about it, but first, I need to call him. To make sure, he's okay." Charlie gave Jen's hand a squeeze and returned Jen's smile.

Charlie blew out a breath and headed to the back porch. She pulled her phone from her back pocket and quickly thumbed through her contacts. When she found Ben Sutton she didn't hesitate calling. Her visions could be wrong. They had been in the past. She closed her eyes and said a quick prayer.

Mother goddess hear my prayer, Keep Ben safe and free from harm.

Her heart thudded in her throat and part of her

wanted to hang up. But another part of her knew this call was too important. She had to make sure he was all right. If only for Jen's sake.

*　*　*

BEN SAT ON THE EDGE OF HIS MOTEL ROOM BED AND LEANED forward with his elbow on his knee, propping his head up with a makeshift ice pack. How had it come to this? How had he let this happen? He'd gotten his ass handed to him. He should have *known* better.

Facing off with a demon was probably one of the most dangerous things he ever did in his job. And if today was any indication, he was woefully underprepared and lacked the experience to do what was necessary to bring this demon to heel.

He scrubbed his fingers through his hair and lay back on the bed. The cold, wet washcloth wrapped around ice felt good against the hot throbbing of his cheek. He stared at the dingy ceiling, wishing he were somewhere else, anywhere else. Well, maybe not just anywhere. Jen's adorable face drifted through his brain. The way she smiled. The way she made him feel. He had it bad, and now, he had totally screwed it up.

The phone in his pocket began to buzz and he dug it out. He looked at the screen and pressed the green talk button.

"Hey, Charlie? I didn't expect to hear from you," he said trying to keep his voice light.

"Are you okay?" Charlie asked.

"Yeah, I'm great. Why do you ask?" He hoped she was buying his ruse. The last thing he wanted was for Jen to get word of this conversation. She might be mad at him and hurt, but he knew in his empathic heart that she cared about him. Of that he had no doubt.

"Did you hit your head?" she asked. "I'm sure it's nothing, but I just had this flash of pain in my head and face."

"A flash, huh?" He sighed. Damn her and her psychic abilities. If the DOL knew about her they'd be at her door tomorrow. Her gifts were some of the most honed he'd ever encountered and he'd met some pretty talented psychics in his line of work.

"Well," he started, his voice rising half an octave. "Now that you mention it."

"What happened?" Charlie asked, her voice full of concern.

"I met her," he said.

"Who?" Charlie said.

"The demon. Although I'm just assuming it's a female because of the form she took."

"Dammit," Charlie muttered.

"What?"

"I was hoping I was wrong. It's possessing the witch that summoned it, right?" Charlie said.

He pinched the bridge of his nose. "Yep. You saw it?"

"I had a vision."

"Great. Thank you, goddess. I love it when you share my fuck ups," he called to the ceiling.

"How bad is it?" Charlie asked.

"It's been a while since I've done this. I'm rusty, I guess," he said.

"I saw you sailing across the room and being knocked out when you hit the wall," Charlie said.

"Wow. I bet Evan can't get anything over on you, can he?" He joked but it was only halfhearted.

"You need our help." It wasn't a question. It was a firm statement. Ben closed his eyes and grimaced. He was torn between wanting to say yes and wanting to say no. He'd grown rather fond of Charlie Payne and the women in her family.

"No. It's too dangerous." His voice cracked.

"That's it, we're coming," Charlie said. "What's your address?"

"Charlie, I just said it's too dangerous. I don't want any of you to get hurt."

"We'd all be heartbroken if something happened to you."

Damn her. She wielded guilt like a pro. *No, like a mom.* Not that he really knew what that felt like, but he could imagine it. She thrust the dagger in deeper and twisted. "Especially if we could've stopped it."

Ben couldn't stop the smile stretching his lips. It felt strange (and wonderful) to be cared about in this way. He wished he could bottle up this feeling and pull it out on those days when it felt like no one gave a shit about him.

"Stop being hardheaded. Let us help you," Charlie finished.

"Charlie, no . . ." he started but his protest was lackluster at this point. "She almost killed us. Her aunt, the witch helping me, is at the hospital right now in a coma."

"What kind of shape are you in?" Charlie's tone grew concerned.

"I'm okay. A little banged up. I figure I'll try again in the morning."

"No. You can't face her alone again," she said.

"I don't have a choice, Charlie," he said.

"Of course you do! Why on earth do you think I'm calling? We're gonna finish supper and then we're coming to you. No more arguing."

"You think the reaper would come?"

"Sure. If I ask him," she said.

"A reaper would be good," Ben muttered. "Is there any way you can just send him?"

"No way. You need all of us," Charlie said.

Ben scowled, but it made his face hurt and he gave up. "Fine. I surrender. Just make sure you bring the reaper too. Okay?"

"Okay. Now tell me where you are," Charlie said.

"I'm at the Lazy Dog Motel just on the outskirts of Acadia Georgia. Off I-85," he said. It felt good to just give it over. His heart felt a little lighter.

"You hang tight. We'll be there in a jiffy," she said.

The line clicked and she was gone before he could respond. He put the phone on the bed next to him and closed his eyes. A smile tugged at his lips. The cavalry was on the way.

CHAPTER 23

A fearful energy rolled off Jen. It prickled against Charlie's bare arms and left her stomach roiling with nausea. Being an empath definitely had its downside. Charlie's dinner went mostly untouched and after her call to Ben she focused on just getting through the rest of the evening. Maybe she would have Evangeline pack it up so she could eat it later. She hated to let fried shrimp go to waste.

Jen's vacant stare and the tapping of her heel against her chair leg seemed to put everyone on edge — empath or not. Everyone except Cameron. He was too focused on Charlie to notice the heavy cloud hanging over the table. Charlie glanced at the antique banjo clock hanging above the buffet. If she hadn't known better she'd have sworn the pendulum swinging inside the glass box stopped for a long pause before swinging back and stopping again. Why did time always seem to slow down like this when she needed it to hurry up? Charlie exchanged a concerned glance with Lisa across the table.

"So," Jack cleared his throat. Charlie braced herself for him to ask what the hell was going on. His gaze shifted from one side of the table to the other. He pressed his lips together and they disappeared into his thick grizzly beard. A heavy breath with an undertone of a growl resonated from his nose. He settled his gaze on Jason. "Charlie said you boys solved your case."

"Yes sir. We made an arrest yesterday afternoon. There was an ... um ... unfortunate incident and he's in the hospital, but as soon as he's well enough, there will be an arraignment," Jason said.

"And Charlie helped you boys out?" Jack said.

Jason shifted in his chair. "Uh, yeah," Jason said, sounding a little taken aback. He threw Charlie a what-the-hell look.

She shrugged her shoulders and mouthed. "I didn't say anything."

Jack's shrewd stare bounced from his niece back to Jason. He made a judgmental sound in the back of his throat.

"It's too bad that you had to give up your vacation. I'm sure it was disappointing you didn't get to spend more time with my daughter."

"Yes sir," Jason offered a half-hearted smile. His fork scraped against the porcelain as he pierced his green beans. He gave Lisa a sideways glance but she didn't seem to notice him. She was too busy watching her sister.

"This food is delicious ma'am," Cameron said.

"I'm glad you're enjoying it, Cameron." Evangeline smiled but Charlie noted that her aunt's tone lacked its usual warmth.

Cameron didn't seem to notice, though, as he speared a fork-full of crispy squash and a shrimp. He shoveled it into his mouth and chomped his food. Charlie cringed as he spoke with his mouth full.

"I love the squash."

"Jen cooked them," Evangeline said.

"They're delicious, Jen. You did a great job. I don't think I've ever had squash so crispy before."

Jen didn't seem to notice his compliment. Charlie tapped her lightly on the arm with her elbow.

"What?" Jen asked.

"Cameron said he likes the way that you made the squash." Charlie said.

"Oh," Jen said, then directed her comments to Cameron. "Thank you. I'm glad you're enjoying it."

"Is everything all right?" Cameron asked. He picked up his napkin and wiped his mouth. Charlie watched him shift his focus to her cousin. She couldn't deny that, despite his jackass behavior toward her, Cameron seemed to like dealing with people, especially those in distress. She wondered if he had a superhero complex. Jason could be the same. It was a trait Charlie used to admire about Jason. Maybe she was being too hard on Cameron.

"Yes, thank you," Jen said. She took a bite of her food, as if to prove it.

"It's just you seem a little distracted," Cameron said offhandedly. "When I was a kid, we always talked about whatever was bothering us at the dinner table."

Jason turned and stared at Cameron. His dark brows tugged together and his top lip twisted upward in disapproval. Lisa's eyes widened and her mouth formed a perfect little 'o' as in *here we go*. Daphne leaned forward, a curious half-grin on her lips, her gaze circled the table. Tom bit his lips together, as if he was trying not to smile.

"Really?" Charlie began, unable to stop herself from picking. Maybe that would shut him up. "Did you talk about what happened to Kyle at dinner?"

Cameron shifted his gaze from Jen to Charlie. The concerned expression he'd worn just a second ago morphed into absolute disdain. "No. We didn't. It made my mother cry to talk about my dead brother. But thanks for asking."

Charlie's cheeks heated with shame and her desire to put him in his place evaporated. Why had she said that? She knew the boy in her vision was dead. Knew it the way she always knew such things. But she just had to pick at it, like a scab that wouldn't heal. "I knew that. I shouldn't have said anything. I'm sorry."

"Well you are the psychic, right?" Cameron said, his voice dripping with sarcasm. He wiped his mouth with the napkin and folded it across the plate. "Ma'am, that really was delicious. If you'll excuse me, I'd like to get some air."

"Of course," Evangeline said, her voice sounding strangled.

"Cameron?" Jen turned her big blue eyes on him. "Thank you."

"For what?"

"For being concerned about me. I truly do appreciate it." A smile crossed her lips. Charlie had seen it too many times to count. The smile that could melt the iciest heart. She'd always had that ability and it was one of the things that Charlie loved best about her.

A thousand emotions passed over Cameron's strong features from anger to confusion to uncertainty before finally landing on acceptance. He tipped his head in a slight nod and smiled back at her then disappeared through the door into the kitchen. The screen door's hinges squealed and then closed with a slam.

"Well that wasn't awkward at all," Daphne said.

Charlie squeezed her eyes shut and put her hands over her face. "I know; I feel terrible. I shouldn't have baited him. Oh gosh," Charlie looked up. Cameron had outed her to her uncle. "Uncle Jack, what Cameron said about me I ... " She struggled to find the right words. "I don't know what he meant by that exactly."

Jack cleared his throat loudly. Every eye in the room turned to him. A latent anger bubbled just under the surface of his red leathery face. It shined in his sharp blue eyes, and Charlie could feel it swirling around him, could almost hear the roar of the wind of his thoughts. She braced for the impact of his anger when it finally reached down and ripped through them like a tornado.

"Do y'all think I'm stupid?" Jack snapped.

"What?" Charlie met his fiery stare. "No sir, of course not." Charlie's gaze darted to Lisa across from her and then to Evangeline at the end of the table. Both looked stricken by Jack's words.

"Do you think for one minute I don't know what goes on in my own house?" Jack said.

Charlie swallowed hard. "I ... uh ... no sir. I don't think that."

Jack released Charlie from the weight of his stare and his gaze flitted between the other women around the table. His nostrils flared as he spoke. "Thirty-six years I've heard voices lower to whispers as soon as I left a room, or stop altogether when I walked in. As if it was some sort of secret. As if your mama didn't share that part of herself with me. I never interfered, at first because I was humoring her. But you can only see and hear and feel so much before the reality of it sets in and you admit that you're surrounded by magic and ghosts and psychics and whatever else is out there. And your well-trained scientific brain has no other choice than to accept it and love it. Because to deny it would be to deny my heart."

"Daddy," Lisa said.

"No, don't," Jen said. "Just don't."

"So I know you're not a witch . . ." Jack said to Jason. Jason straightened up in his chair and opened his mouth to answer him, but Lisa touched his hand with hers and he stopped. Jack shifted his gaze to Tom and narrowed his eyes. "But I have no idea what you are."

"Me?" Tom touched his hand to his chest. All eyes widened and turned on Tom. "I'm a mortician, sir. Charlie likes to joke that I'm a death dealer."

"I guess that's one way to look at it," Daphne muttered.

"Daphne," Lisa and Jen snapped at the same time.

"What? It's true," Daphne whisper-yelled.

"Uh huh," Jack said. His lips twisted with disbelief. "Fine. We'll go with that for now. My point about all of this is that it can take a long time to admit that there is a whole other world out there. One you can't see directly without some sort of faith. So why don't you give old Cameron a break? All right?"

A chorus of yes sirs went around the table.

"Now Jennifer Elizabeth what is going on with you?"

Jack asked, not dropping the stern tone in his voice just yet.

"Ben's in trouble, Daddy," Jen's bottom lip quivered as she spoke.

"Can you help him?" Jack asked.

"I hope so," Jen said.

"Yes, she can," Evangeline said, sitting up straight and looking Jack directly in the eye. "We all can. But it means we need to take a trip to Georgia to do it."

"All right then. Let's get it done. I'll take care of Ruby while you're gone. Vange, who can run the cafe?"

Jen got up from her chair. She swiped tears from her cheeks and sniffed just before she threw her arms around Jack's neck. "Thank you, Daddy."

"Manuel and Dottie can handle the cafe for us. We won't be gone long," Evangeline said.

"Good," Jack said. "Now can we at least cut that cake before you leave?"

Jen laughed and stood up straight. "Of course we can."

* * *

LISA WALKED INTO HER CONDO WITHOUT SAYING A WORD. Jason and Cameron trailed after her. Her fluffy, cream, flame-point cat headed toward her with his tail raised. She bent down and gave him a quick scratch behind the ears. The cat purred loudly, pressing his head into his mistress's hand.

"Good boy, Butterbean," Lisa cooed. "Keep an eye on them for me." Butterbean sat down and curled his tail around himself, nonplussed. His sharp blue eyes watched as Jason directed Cameron into the living room.

"I won't be long," Lisa said and dashed off toward her bedroom. She wasn't sure why they had come. They could've said their goodbyes at her father's house, but Jason had insisted and since Cameron was his guest there, they came as a package deal.

Lisa stepped into her walk-in closet and pulled the leather weekender bag from the top shelf. She wasn't even sure they would spend the night. At least she hoped they wouldn't. It was hard to know how long these things would take. She'd had very little dealings with demons but if she had to get her hands dirty, so be it. All she wanted was to bring Ben back to Palmetto Point so her sister would be happy again. It broke her heart to see Jen so miserable since he left.

Lisa laid the weekender on the bed and unzipped it. Butterbean sauntered into the room and promptly jumped inside the open bag. He looked up at her and gave her a low pitiful meow. She scratched him under his chin. "Don't worry. I'll be home tomorrow. Probably." She frowned. It felt almost like a lie. "Till then Jason's gonna take care of you. Okay?"

The cat opened his eyes and stared at his mistress. He meowed as if in agreement. Lisa smiled and picked up the heavy cat and hugged him close. She placed him on the floor. "I have to pack. Go entertain our guests."

Butterbean gave her one last soulful look before he strolled out of the bedroom, swishing his tail.

Through the open door Lisa could hear Cameron and Jason talking. She heard Jason stoop down to Butterbean's level, talking to the cat in baby talk. Lisa snickered. Jason didn't realize Butterbean was actually her familiar and her guardian. That he understood more than just any old normal house cat.

One day she would tell Jason there was no reason to talk to the cat as if it were a baby. Butterbean fully understood. She went to her bureau and pulled enough clothes for two nights. Just in case. Then rushed into the bathroom and grabbed her toothbrush, cleanser and face cream. There didn't seem to be much point in worrying about makeup. She shoved the toiletries into a zippered bag she found under the sink along with a hairbrush and a couple of ponytail holders.

"Hey," Jason said, moving into the bathroom behind her. She glanced up at the mirror and met his gaze.

"I'm almost done," she said.

"No rush," he said. The corners of his mouth turned down slightly.

"What?" Lisa said trying not to let defensiveness creep

into her voice.

"Are you sure you need to go?"

"Yes. This is going to take all of us," she said.

"Are you going to take your wand?" he asked softly.

"Maybe. Why?"

"I would feel better if at least one of you had a weapon."

"What makes you think we're not the weapon?" Lisa asked dryly. "I'm sure Jen is taking an arsenal of crystals and herbs."

"Right." There was just a hint of sarcasm in his tone and it made her bristle.

"Since when don't you trust those things? How many times has a stone and a pendant or a pound of salt protected you?" she asked. Her cheeks reddened and blotchy patches crept from her chest to her neck. "I think maybe Charlie's right. Cameron is a bad influence on you."

"That's what you think?" he said, his defenses up. "Well you know what I think? I think you're picking a fight so you don't have to feel bad when you leave."

"That is the stupidest thing I think I've ever heard," she snapped.

Jason's phone rang. The ringtone was familiar. One he'd assigned specifically to his partner. Jason slid his phone out of his pocket and held up his hand. "What's up Beck?"

Lisa gritted her teeth and shoved the tube of toothpaste into her bag. She moved from the bathroom into the bedroom and finished folding up her clothes. The sound of Jason's voice made her stop the angry diatribe going through her head. She zipped up the weekender and turned to watch Jason talk to his partner.

Jason held his forehead with his freehand and all the color had drained from his cheeks. "Holy fuck," he muttered. "You're sure?"

Jason's jaw tightened. "That is just fucking great," he said, but there was nothing great about the seething in his tone. Lisa folded her arms across her chest and hugged herself tight.

Jason closed his eyes and blew a breath through his teeth. He shoved the phone back into his pocket.

"What's wrong?" Lisa asked.

"Gabriel Curtis escaped custody," Jason said.

"What? Are you kidding me?" Lisa asked.

"Nope. He killed a deputy and a nurse and vanished into thin air." Jason shook his head, his expression incredulous.

"Babe, I'm so sorry," Lisa said. "What are you going to do?"

"SLED is putting together a manhunt. We'll join in," Jason said. "Man, this storm is bad timing."

"Yeah," Lisa said.

"So you still want to pick a fight with me?" he asked.

"No," she said in a small voice.

"Well, you may just change your mind about that," Jason said. "Especially because of what I'm going to ask you."

"What?" Lisa said.

He stepped closer and lowered his voice. "You can't tell Charlie."

"What? Why not?" Lisa asked.

"I don't want her to get all riled up again with this demon idea," Jason said.

"Maybe Charlie was right though, did you ever think about that?"

"Please, not you too," Jason said.

"He was shot, right? Curtis?" Lisa said.

"Yeah," Jason said. "So?"

"So how did he manage to kill a nurse and a deputy? And escape completely undetected?" Lisa asked.

"I don't know," Jason huffed. "We're looking into it."

"Right," Lisa said scowling. She slung the strap of the leather bag over her shoulder. "I have to go."

"Fine." He grabbed her by the hand and stopped her before she could walk through the door. "I need you to promise me that you won't tell Charlie anything."

"Jason, I . . ." she started.

"Promise me. I don't want her obsessing over this, especially when there isn't anything she can do about it," he said.

Lisa's lips twisted with disgust. "Fine."

"Thank you," he said and gave her a peck on the lips.

They emerged from the bedroom together and Lisa put her bag on the floor by the breakfast bar. On the wall was a keyholder with four hooks. They'd been dating for two months but still hadn't exchanged keys. She took her ring of extra keys with the house key and her car key on it and handed it to Jason.

"This will get you in the door."

"Okay." He put the keys in his front pocket. "How long do you think you'll be gone?"

"Shouldn't be more than a couple of days," she said. "But if we are gone longer there's extra food for Butterbean in the pantry on the floor. He gets a can a day. And make sure that you scoop his litter and give him fresh water daily. He hates it when it sits for too long."

Jason cracked a smile. "You do know I have a cat, right? I know how they work."

It was just enough to make her smile back and break the tension between them. She touched his arm. "I know."

His eyes flitted sideways at Cameron. He sighed, then closed the gap between them. He put his hand over hers and squeezed gently. "I really wish you didn't have to go. And not because you aren't capable."

He paused and took a deep breath as if he were searching for the right words. His gaze flashed to

Cameron again, then steadied on her face. He whispered, "I feel like I should give you my vest or something."

Warmth bloomed inside her chest and she couldn't help but smile. In that moment, she knew for certain what she'd suspected for a few weeks now. She loved him and he loved her. But she wasn't quite brave enough to say it yet.

"I appreciate that. But I've got everything I need to protect me and you're gonna need it." She kissed him quickly on the lips. "We'll all be fine. I promise."

A soft, shaky breath escaped his lips and he nodded. "Okay. Text me as soon as you get there. All right?"

"I will. Y'all go catch that guy. And keep an eye on that storm for me. Text me if they figure out where they think it's headed," she said.

"I will," Jason said.

"And Cameron? You take care of him, okay? This guy you're after is pretty dangerous."

"I will." Cameron gave her a solemn nod. "And you be careful too. Whatever it is you all are doing."

"We will." Lisa locked her gaze on Cameron's face for a moment and something quiet passed between them. An acknowledgement that each was important in Jason's life. That each had a place. A role to play. And that they would both do what it took to keep Jason safe. A knock on the front door broke their brief connection and Lisa let out a nervous laugh.

"That's Daphne." Lisa looked down at Butterbean, who was now sitting next to Jason's feet, watching her. "And you. You be good. Don't give Jason a hard time, all right?" The cat meowed as if to say *I will.*

Daphne opened the front door, knocking against the hollow steel. She walked into the foyer. "You ready?"

"Yeah." Lisa grabbed her overnight bag and slung it over her shoulder. "Let's go."

As she followed Daphne out, dread coiled in the pit of her stomach like an icy, hissing snake. She fought the urge to look back at the men standing in her living room and pulled the door shut behind her. But for one split second a sharp cold spike of intuition pierced her heart and the thought she might never see Jason again filled her head. It was a silly stupid thought and she dismissed it quickly. After all, she wasn't the psychic in the family.

* * *

BEN SAT ON THE EDGE OF THE UNCOMFORTABLE HOSPITAL chair and held Arista's hand. The sharp, silvery black Shungite crystal he had placed in her palm, pressed against his fingers. He bowed his head and closed his eyes. Sweat traced from his scalp down the side of his face, leaving a hot, itchy trail. Healing could be exhausting, strenuous work and so far none of his usual spells had worked. He hated to admit it, but he needed help.

Needed more energy. Charlie had said they were coming. Extra bodies, especially bodies as powerful as Jen and Evangeline, who were mature in their practice, would be a welcome boost.

"So mote it be," he whispered and opened his eyes. Arista lay so still that if it weren't for the slight rise of her chest every few seconds he would have thought her dead. He squeezed her hand then folded her fingers around the stone and stood up. His whole body ached, even after he'd gone back to his motel, taken a hot shower, and slept a few hours. The sky was finally starting to lighten. Dawn would be here soon and he would have to decide what to do. To find Megan and stop her, he needed Arista. She was his best chance for exorcising the demon and keeping Megan alive.

"Come on Arista," he whispered. "Open your eyes." He scrutinized her face for any little twitch. Any sign at all that she'd heard him. But only the hum of the machines monitoring her I.V. and blood oxygen levels, and the occasional whir of the blood pressure machine, answered him. His front pocket vibrated; he retrieved his phone, and walked over to the small window overlooking the parking lot.

A text from Charlie stared back at him.

We're here, was all it said.

A surge of relief spread through his chest. He was no longer alone.

I'm at the hospital with Arista. Do you need directions?

Nope. We're downstairs near your car. Have you eaten breakfast?

How did you find me?

Psychic, remember?

He chuckled.

Be right down.

He shoved the phone back into his pocket and shifted his gaze to Arista.

"I'm going downstairs for a little while," he said to Arista's motionless body. "Once I get a few things taken care of, I'll come back and we'll try again. Okay?"

Arista's chest rose and fell but she made no noise to acknowledge that she'd heard him. He touched the top of her feet and grabbed his bag off the floor then headed out the door to meet Charlie.

* * *

EVERY STEP HE TOOK ACROSS THE PARKING LOT PUMPED anxiety into his chest like sour breath into a balloon. Jen would be with Charlie, and as much as he wanted to see her, he also feared seeing her. What if she only came because Charlie asked? What if ... what if she was mean to him? It was a stupid and irrational thought. Jen Holloway didn't have a mean bone in her body. Still, he couldn't shake the ridiculous feeling that she might be here out of some sense of obligation, because a fellow witch needed help.

He spotted Charlie standing next to his car. Her long blond hair was pulled into a messy bun and she had her back to him. As he drew closer the others came into view. Lisa stood in front of Charlie, and she pointed over Charlie's shoulder. Charlie turned to face him. Daphne and Evangeline exited the front of the black SUV parked next to his car. When Jen emerged from the back door of the SUV, Ben's heart dropped into his belly like an icy rock and he stopped in his tracks. Her lovely elfin face and wide blue eyes regarded him with a wary expression. He wanted more than anything to scoop her up into his arms and hold her close to him, but instead he approached with caution.

"Where's the reaper?" The words rushed out of his mouth.

Charlie scowled. "Good to see you too."

"You're right. I'm sorry." He tapped his forehead. What a stupid way to start this conversation. "It's very good to see you. It's been a long night."

"Don't you worry about it, Ben. From what Charlie says, you've been through quite an ordeal." Evangeline stepped forward and moved in close. "How is your friend?" She patted him on the arm and a sense of calm spread through him. How did she do that? He would have to ask her about it sometime.

"She's still unconscious," he said. "I've tried every healing spell I know, but without her to set an intention for herself to be healed ..." He blew out a frustrated breath.

"Yes, that is tricky," Evangeline said. A reassuring smile crossed her face and she steadied her wise gaze on his. "But it's not an impossible situation. And we're here to help."

"Normally I wouldn't expose you to this danger, but honestly I'm glad you're here," Ben admitted. He scanned their faces, landing on Jen last. He gave her a weary smile and it lightened his heart when she returned the smile.

"Tom is coming by the way. All I have to do is call to him and he'll be here," Charlie said.

"That's good news," Ben said.

"You look like hell," Jen said softly, stepping closer. "Are you sure you're all right?"

"I'm okay. I promise." He softened his tone. "I'm just worried that we won't be able to heal Arista and without her, there's not much hope of saving Megan."

"Who's Megan?" Charlie asked.

"She's the witch that summoned the demon," Ben said.

"The one I saw in my vision? The one being possessed?" Charlie asked.

Ben nodded. "You know, I've only been in on a few exorcisms. And each time, the host died. I was really trying to avoid that."

"And there's a child missing, too, right?" Charlie asked.

Ben opened his mouth to ask how she knew that, but stopped himself. Psychic, right? echoed through his head as he remembered her text. Ben nodded. "Yes, Megan evidently killed a couple and took a baby. I'm just not sure if she did it to please the demon or the demon was already possessing her when it happened."

"Does it make a difference?" Lisa asked.

"It does according to the law," Ben said. "Witch law, that is."

Lisa pursed her lips and nodded.

"We'll find her," Charlie said. "With or without Arista."

Ben wished he had Charlie's confidence, but maybe she knew something he didn't. Maybe those psychic gifts of hers would be the key. Ben's stomach growled. He patted his hand to his flat belly.

Jen perked up. "Sounds like the first thing we need to do is get some breakfast. We're all gonna need our strength for this."

"Jen's right," Evangeline said. "We can eat and make a plan of attack."

"I saw a Waffle Hut on our way in. Have you eaten

there?" Charlie asked.

"Yes I have. But don't expect greatness."

"Is a witch running it?" Charlie asked.

"No, of course not," Ben said.

"Then why on goddesses green earth would I expect greatness?" Charlie gave him a wry grin. Ben chuckled and the anxiety he'd been holding onto dissipated in their warmth.

"Waffle Hut it is. Jen," he said softly. "Would you like to ride with me?"

Her wide blue eyes glittered and she nodded. "I would like that very much."

"Now that's settled," Charlie grinned. "We'll meet you there.

* * *

CHARLIE SPIED THE BIG CORNER BOOTH AND CLAIMED IT before anyone else could in the seat-yourself-style restaurant. The circular table was large enough to accommodate all of them and Charlie scooted in first, following the rounded booth to the middle. Daphne sat on one side of her and Lisa on the other with Evangeline sliding in next to her daughter. They left open space next to Lisa for Ben and Jen when they arrived.

A waitress in a faded yellow uniform with a mustard colored pocket square and a nametag that read Gina approached the table. She pulled an order pad from her right hip pocket and a pencil from behind her ear.

"What can I get y'all," she said.

Evangeline glanced up at her and smiled. "We're gonna need just a few minutes. We haven't even had a chance to look at the menu."

"What's to look at?" The waitress said. "The best thing we have on the menu is waffles."

"Yes," Evangeline "I'm sure they are. But we'd still like to look. If that's all right."

"Suit yourself." The waitress shrugged and tucked her pencil behind her ear again. She walked away, grabbed a coffee carafe from the nearby machine and began filling the cups for the folks in the booths along the wide front window. Charlie grabbed the laminated menus from the holder in the center of the table and passed them around.

"This table is sticky," Daphne grimaced. Her large purse sat on the seat next to her and she unzipped the leather bag and plucked out a travel-size package of baby wipes. With the flick of her thumb, the top on the refillable container flipped open and she counted out wipes.

"Here," she handed one to Charlie, Lisa and her mother and the four of them wiped down the table until no trace of syrup or other stickiness could be felt.

Charlie surveyed the narrow menu. There were twenty different types of waffles and a build your own omelet that looked promising.

Evangeline glanced over her shoulder at the griddle and muttered, "It's not as clean as I would like."

Charlie followed her aunt's line of sight and watched as the short order cook scooped out an egg mixture and poured it onto the griddle. Next to the griddle was the waffle-making station with four different waffle irons all going at the same time. Another cook manned that station, churning them out as quickly as he possibly could.

"Looks like they at least have the process down," Charlie noted.

"Come on mama, let's just decide what we're going to eat and not worry about how other people conduct their business."

Daphne didn't look up from the menu in her hand as she spoke. Evangeline clucked her tongue but didn't give her daughter a response.

Charlie perused the waffle choices and quickly chose the pecan waffles. "I wonder if the syrup is real maple syrup."

"Oh, you can bet it's not real," Evangeline mumbled. She took a napkin from the chrome holder in the center of the table and polished her fork. "Not for the prices they're charging."

"I wonder what's keeping Jen and Ben?" Lisa said.

"Do you know what you want?" Charlie asked.

"Of course I do," Lisa said matter-of-factly. "I just want to eat, help Ben and get out here."

"Yeah, you got a hot date?" Daphne asked.

"No," Lisa said her voice full of irritation. "I've been getting weather alerts on my phone and it looks like Charleston may take a direct hit by this storm."

"Great," Charlie said. The storm was the last thing they needed to deal with.

"Are they thinking it's going to be a hurricane that when it hits or a tropical storm?" Evangeline asked.

"It strengthened to a cat one hurricane overnight. Hopefully it won't get any stronger."

"Well that's not too bad." Evangeline said. "We've certainly been through worse."

"Yeah, I know." Lisa squirmed.

"What's really bothering you?" Charlie asked. "You've been fidgety since before we even got here."

"Nothing's wrong," Lisa said.

The little bell that went off in Charlie's head when she detected a lie sounded off, loud and clear. "Nope. Try again."

Lisa rolled her eyes and sighed. "I left my cat with Jason and he'll probably be put on patrol with the other deputies. I'm just not sure what's going to happen to him, that's all."

"You're worried about your cat or Jason?" Daphne said her voice full of disapproval.

"My cat. Jason can take care of himself. I love that cat," Lisa said. Charlie regarded her cousin's admission. Lisa did love her cat and her apprehension about the storm seemed real enough, but something felt off.

"He's more than just a cat and you know it, Daphne," Evangeline scolded.

The bell over the door jingled, drawing their attention. Jen and Ben walked in and headed to the booth. Charlie did not like the solemn expression on Jen's face. Jen squeezed in next to Lisa and Ben next to her.

"Sorry we're late," Jen said, a little breathless. Her cheeks were flushed and Charlie figured it wasn't because of the heat.

"Everything okay?" Charlie asked.

Jen met her gaze and painted a smile across her face. "Of course. So what's good?" Jen picked up the laminated menu and perused it.

"The waffles," Ben said.

"Alrighty then." Jen laid the menu flat on the table. Her cousin's strained energy vibrated like a guitar string strung too tightly. One too many plucks and it would break. "Waffles it is."

Jen folded her hands in her lap and looked anywhere but at Ben. Whatever he had said to Jen on the way over had definitely done a number on her cousin. Charlie frowned and tried to get a read on Ben but as usual his stone wall was firmly in place.

Evangeline straightened her back and rested one arm on the table. Charlie could see her aunt assessing the situation and the energy between them. Her sharp blue eyes went from face to face, narrowing once she rested her gaze on Ben.

The waitress came and took their orders, but still Evangeline's heavy stare went back to Ben. Finally he looked up at her from beneath his brow.

"If there's something you want to say Evangeline, I'd really appreciate if you went ahead and said it," Ben said.

"I don't really have much to say, Ben," Evangeline said. "It seems whatever is going unsaid at this table is more between you and Jen than you and me."

Evangeline looked down her long straight nose. "I don't know what's going on with you two. And I don't mean to be harsh, but honestly, y'all need to work it out." Evangeline leaned forward and lowered her voice. "We are about to go into battle and that means focus. So whatever is chewing on y'all, you need to set it aside for now. Do you understand me?"

Jen's whole demeanor changed and she sat up straight. The sullen melancholy expression that had marred her face disappeared.

"Yes ma'am," Jen said. Ben glared across the table at Evangeline. The line between his brows deepened as he seemed to ponder her words. Charlie knew Ben wasn't used to being part of a coven but in the greater scheme of things, Evangeline was the elder at the table and her position demanded respect, even from someone who wasn't used to giving it, like Ben. Charlie and her cousins stared at Ben. Charlie could feel his recalcitrance beneath the surface. His nostrils flared and his lips pressed into a straight line. Jen nudged him in the ribs with her elbow.

Ben's face softened. "Yes ma'am."

Jen's body relaxed when the waitress put waffles down in front of her. Her lips curved up slightly and she ate with gusto. Charlie dug into her waffles too, and didn't complain that they didn't serve real maple syrup.

Evangeline was right. They had serious work ahead of them. Dangerous work and it would take all of them working together to win the battle ahead.

* * *

WHEN THEY RETURNED TO THE HOSPITAL, BEN DISTRACTED the nurse at the nurses' station just long enough for the five of them to slip into Arista's room unnoticed. Evangeline went first, followed by Daphne, Lisa, and a few minutes later, Jen and Charlie.

Ben stood at the counter, blocking the nurse's view, leaning over, flirting with her. Ben could be charming, that was for sure.

Once in the room, Jen quietly closed the door and drew the curtain around Arista's bed

"Charlie help me," Jen said as she plopped her messenger bag onto the tray table and began to unpack the necessary items for their ritual. Jen put a tiny bottle of dark amber-colored oil along with a sage smudge and smudging feather, some dried herbs, some dried clove buds, and various crystals on the table Charlie picked up a creamy white crystal and felt its weight.

"What is this?" Charlie asked fascinated.

"Selenite. For healing."

"And this one?" Charlie asked, picking up the green, sparkling stone.

"It's Fuchsite." Jen said.

"And this?" Charlie lifted the oil to her nose, uncorked it and sniffed. A deep piney scent filled her senses. Jen frowned and took it from her.

"That's myrrh and it's expensive." Jen replaced the cork and put it back on the tray table. After retrieving a package of blank index cards and a pen from her bottomless bag, Jen quickly wrote down the three lines of the spell they were to chant. Charlie admired her cousin's pretty cursive writing. Her own handwriting was little more than chicken scratch.

"Okay I think we're ready," Jen said.

"Good," Evangeline said. "Let's begin then. Jen I need you to smudge her body first."

The door opened and they all stood still, holding their breath, their eyes wide and listening.

"Just me," Ben whispered. He closed the door behind him tightly and he walked around the edge of the curtain. "Okay, what can I do?"

"Ben why don't you get on the opposite side of the bed from me." Ben nodded and scooted behind Daphne and Lisa taking his place at the head of the bed next to Arista. Evangeline moved into place directly across from Ben and motioned for Charlie to come stand next to her.

Jen pulled her lighter from her purse, flicked it into life and lit the end of the sage bundle. The flame chewed through the tip of the smudge a little before Jen blew it out. White smoke curled up from the smoldering smudge and Jen took the white feather and brushed the smoke over Arista from head to toe. Ben waived some of the sage smoke toward himself breathing it in. Evangeline and the others did the same.

When she was done smudging, Jen positioned herself at the foot of the bed next to the tray table and tamped out the sage smudge in the stone bowl she brought. She took the small vial and uncorked it, then carefully measured out seven drops of myrrh oil into her palm. Jen squeezed in between Ben and Lisa and dotted Arista's forehead with the oil then dotted her chest. Gently Jen turned over Arista's hands and anointed her pulse points. The stone Ben had put into Arista's left hand was curled between her palm and fingers and Jen slipped the selenite into Arista's other hand. Then put the sparkly green fuchsite on the center of Arista's chest.

The last part of the ritual called for a bag of herbs and salt. Jen took a pinch of rosemary, cloves and Angelica and dropped them inside the small linen bag, along with a pinch of salt. She placed the bag in the center of Arista's belly and finally took her place at the end of the bed.

"Ben take her hand and keep the tourmaline tight between your two palms," Evangeline said. She picked up Arista's other hand and held the crystal between their palms. Ben did as she asked. "All right, the rest of y'all join hands."

When circle was complete Evangeline took a deep breath and opened her mouth to start.

"Wait," Jen said too loudly. She dropped her sister's and Charlie's hand and grabbed the notecards. "The spell."

She handed the note cards to Charlie. "This is what we need to say."

Each of them took a turn reading over the cards before handing them back to Jen. They each took a moment to whisper the words before joining hands again. As soon as they began practicing the official ritual, the energy in the room changed. The machine feeding into Arista's arm began to beep erratically. Ben reached over and pressed a button, to keep from drawing the attention of the nurse.

"Sorry, Evangeline. We're ready now," Jen said.

"Let's begin." Evangeline's gaze circled the group. "We thank the goddess above for all her blessings. May she guide us now to heal her our sister witch. So mote it be."

"So mote it be," the group repeated.

Evangeline closed her eyes. "Angelica, sage and selenite, use our love to restore her light. Rosemary, cloves and tourmaline, wash her soul and make it clean. Stones protect. Herbs restore. Goddess above, heal her very core." They joined Evangeline, chanting the words of Jen's spell over and over. The air around them crackled and snapped with electricity. The lights flickered. The energy pulsed through their hands, connecting them, forming a circle. Charlie's fingers vibrated almost to the point of discomfort. After a moment the lights went out completely. There was a commotion outside in the hallway, nurses moving up and down the corridor, talking to each other about the darkness.

The lights came back on. Evangeline was the first to stop chanting. The rest of the group stopped too as soon as they realized what was happening.

Arista sat up straight in her bed, still holding Ben and Evangeline's hands.

Evangeline grinned. "So mote it be." The other witches echoed the end of their prayer. "Hello Arista."

Arista blinked, her gaze circled the group. Panic

shined in her dark eyes. "Where am I? What happened to Megan?"

"You're in the hospital," Ben said. "You were hurt. Do you remember?"

"Yes. Sort of. It's all a bit hazy," Arista said. She pulled her hands onto her lap. "Who are these people?"

Ben looked up, his gaze settling on Jen. "These are my ... friends. They healed you."

"We," Jen said gently.

Ben smiled. "We."

"How are you feeling?" Evangeline asked.

"Little out of it but otherwise I think I'm all right," Arista said. "How long have I been here?"

"Not even twenty-four hours," Ben said.

Arista glanced down at the flimsy hospital nightgown. She picked up the fuchsite crystal in her lap and squeezed it. "Where are my clothes?"

"In the closet," Ben said.

"Can you please get them? I have to get dressed and get out of here," she said. "We have to find Megan."

Ben opened the laminated wardrobe door and retrieved the clear plastic bag the emergency room nurse had used to put Arista's clothes in. He set it down on the end of the bed. "One thing at a time. Okay? Let's get you out of here first."

"Agreed," Arista said and shooed them out of the room.

CHAPTER 24

Charlie sat in the backseat of Ben's old Toyota FJ50 watching the little town blur by her window, Lisa and Jen crammed into the front next to Ben. Arista sat next to her, holding a long slender wand in her hands. She kept spinning it between her delicate fingers. Charlie could feel the fear rolling off the woman, washing over and through Charlie. She took a deep breath and looked away, trying to fight the nausea. Ben turned into a planned neighborhood and small, uniform houses lined street.

"Do you really think she'll be there?" Charlie asked.

"Yes," Arista said. "If I know my niece she'll go somewhere she feels safe, and she feels safe in her house."

Ben glanced into the rearview mirror and Charlie met his gaze. Charlie heard the click of the blinker and the truck slowed down and turned right. Charlie's butt ached from the small, not well-padded backseat. She shifted and held onto the strap hanging near the window.

The house at the end of the street looked just like all the others. Cookie-cutter boxes with plank siding and covered front porches just wide enough for a couple of rocking chairs or a porch swing. Probably built in the 90's, Charlie thought. Only one stood out to her, and she felt it before she saw it. Just like Gabriel Curtis's house, Megan's house pulsed. A steady rhythm of Bomp Bomp Bomp pounded against the inside of her skull.

"Charlie?" Ben asked. "Are you all right?" You look a little green."

Jen turned in the front passenger seat and reached her hand back. "You okay?"

Charlie swallowed back the taste of bile coating the back of her throat. "Yeah, I'm fine."

"What's going on?" Jen wiggled her fingers, a sign that she wasn't about to let Charlie tuck herself into her shell like a turtle. Charlie grabbed onto her cousin's hand and held it. A calm spread through her and the pounding in her head quieted and her heartbeat slowed to a more normal pace. "Can't you feel it?"

"I can," Arista said and tightened her grip around her wand. "That thing is growing stronger."

"What do you think that means?" Charlie asked."

"I don't know," Arista said. She stared out of the window, a faraway look on her face.

The brakes squealed a little when Ben stopped in front of a cute little suburban house. It didn't look much different from the ones on either side of it; they were all painted either cream or white. Only their front doors set them apart. Megan's door was painted a dark purple and a dark energy oozed from beneath it and over the windowsills of the two windows facing the street. This demon was strong. Stronger than the one in Gabriel Curtis from the feel of it.

"So what's the plan here?" Charlie asked.

"I have everything we need behind your seat in a duffle bag. Can you hand it to me?"

"Sure," Charlie reached into the sparse space and grabbed an army green canvas bag. She took it and shifted it to Ben. "Charlie I think you and I should be the ones to exorcise this thing. You're ... uh, friend is coming, right?"

"Yes, he'll come when I call him," Charlie said.

"Great. The others should form a circle and cast a protection spell around us," Ben said.

Charlie and Jen piped up in protest at the same time. "No way."

Anger flashed through Jen's blue eyes. "You're are not going in there without me." She leaned into his face. "I'm not gonna stand outside in a safe circle while you're in there risking your life."

Ben's head bent forward and he gave Jen a side-eyed glance. Charlie could see the smile playing on his lips, as he secretly gazed at her cousin. Maybe she'd had it wrong. Maybe they didn't fight on the way to breakfast. She would be sure to ask Jen after this was done.

"I agree with Jen," Charlie said. "If nothing else, Jen and Lisa should come inside with us." Charlie glanced at Arista. The woman's shaky hand had drifted to her throat and held onto it as if to support her head. Charlie let go of Jen's hand and touched Arista's arm.

"I don't want to go in there," Arista whispered.

"I know," Charlie said.

"I thought I could do this but I can't," Arista said guilt creeping into her voice.

"It's all right," Jen said. "I think I'd feel the exact same way if I'd been through what you have. In fact I do." She shifted her gaze from Arista to Ben and the two exchanged a glance. "What if we did this? What if Charlie, Lisa and I go in with you, Ben, and Daphne Evangeline and Arista form the circle?"

"That could work," Ben said. He glanced in the rearview mirror again. "What do you think Charlie?"

"I think that's a great idea. I don't particularly want to go in there with just two of us. I know I'm not strong enough of a witch to back you up like you need to be," she said.

"Okay," he said relenting. "That's the plan. Let's get set up."

*　*　*

Ben, Jen and Arista got out of the car, but Charlie stayed behind. Jen stuck her head back in sighed. "Everything okay?"

"Yep, fine. I'm gonna call Tom." She said.

Jen gave her a quick nod and closed the door to give her some privacy. Charlie closed her eyes and concentrated. She called up the image of Tom's face. Every line, every wrinkle, the sparkle of his warm golden-brown eyes.

"Tom. I need you," she said softly.

The chill started on her left side and spread up to her neck until all the hair at the nape stood up. The air in the back seat stirred. From the corners of her eyes, Charlie could see his robes fluttering then becoming very still as he transformed. She'd never watched him directly before and still didn't quite have the guts to do it now.

Her stomach flip-flopped when she felt the warmth of his hand on hers and the fear to look at him dissipated. He brought her hand to his lips and gave the back of it a soft kiss. "Hello, Charlie."

"I'm so glad you're here," she said. She leaned over quickly gave him a peck on the cheek.

Tom glanced around toward the back window of the truck. "Looks like we have a crowd."

"Yep, a crowd and a plan," she said.

"I'm all for a plan. Are you ready?"

"I think so," she said. "You're gonna have to go in there as a reaper aren't you?"

His amber-colored eyes locked on to her face and he nodded. "If I'm to be of any help, I am. Are you okay with that?"

"Of course," Charlie said.

"You know I could just go in and take care of all this. You wouldn't have to risk your lives." He squeezed her hand.

"What do you mean?" she said.

"I could kill her and retrieve the demon, then cart him off to where he belongs."

"But ..." A cold cloud of fear swirled through her chest and she gently pulled her hand out of his. "You don't kill people remember? How many told times have you told me, you're not death?"

"Too many to count, I suppose," he said. "But there are cases where I can take life as collateral damage. Unfortunately when you separate the demon from her, she will most likely never function again as a whole human being.

She may not live. Demons tend to be very hard on their host bodies."

Charlie glanced through the back window at Arista. "Her aunt is determined to save her. I don't think killing her is the right thing to do. No matter how damaged she may be when she's separated from it."

"I will do as you wish," Tom said.

"We should go join the others," she said.

The two of them emerged from the truck. Charlie and Tom sidled up next to Daphne.

"Hi, Tom," Daphne said, her voice a little too chipper but Charlie didn't expect anything else. Her cousin's bottomless well of perkiness overflowed from her on to the others. It sometimes made Daphne seem dimwitted or ditzy, but maybe that's the way she wanted it. Maybe she wanted people to underestimate her. Daphne was no nitwit. She had a keen, observant eye and a sense of people that Charlie didn't have, despite her empathic abilities. Sometimes Charlie thought her ability to sense people's feelings and thoughts and actually impeded her judgment of them. One of the things she loved best about Daphne was her ability to cut through all the bullshit and see to the heart of a person or situation. Maybe that's why Daphne and Lisa butted heads so much. They were a lot alike in that regard.

Daphne looked Tom up and down. "You're looking good today." He wore a pair of tan cargo pants and tight black t-shirt that showed off the muscles of his chest. "I like your outfit."

Tom grinned, his eyes cutting over to Charlie for a second. "Thank you Daphne. This is one of Charlie's favorites or so she says."

"Stop it," Charlie whispered. Her cheeks and chest filled with heat. "We've got business to attend to."

"I just want to start this by saying thank you," Ben said. "You have no idea how relieved I am not to have to do this alone." Jen placed her hand on Ben's arm and looked up at him with adoring eyes.

"Evangeline, if you wouldn't mind?"

"Of course not, Ben," Evangeline said. "Y'all join hands." She waited a beat while the group did as she said, then closed her eyes and lifted her face skyward. "Mother goddess, this we ask, protect us in this difficult task. Keep us safe from those who wish to do us harm and bring our sister Megan back into this coven's arms. As above, so below. So mote it be."

"So mote it be," echoed through the circle.

"You four are with me," Ben said. "Arista?"

She didn't seem to hear him. Instead her gaze was centered on Tom.

"How did you get here? I don't know of any witches who can teleport."

"I'm not a witch." Tom held out his hand. "I'm Tom Sharon by the way. Good to meet you."

Arista took his hand and shook it. Charlie saw her visibly shudder at the connection, then pull her hand away quickly, wiggling her fingers as if she'd been shocked.

"Tom is a reaper, Arista," Charlie explained. "He wears a glamour. He's a friend of ours, so he's agreed to help."

"A reaper?" Alarm colored Arista's voice. "I told you Ben, I want to save Megan's life."

"I'm not here to kill your niece, ma'am," Tom said. "I am here to help capture the demon once he's been exorcised. I promise I will not harm her."

Arista let out a ragged breath but still regarded him with wariness. "How do I know you're telling the truth?"

"I have no reason to lie. I'm in another reaper's territory at the moment. And I have not said hello yet. Let's just hope that he doesn't show up."

"Yes," Ben said. "That's the goal. Get in, get out and not draw attention from anyone. Especially not the local reaper. Nobody needs to die today."

"Except the demon," Daphne said. "Demons can die right, Tom?"

"Well, nothing really dies," Tom said. "But I will collect him and take him back to where he belongs."

"Sounds good to me," Ben said. "Everyone has their protection bags and wands ready?" A chorus of "yes" spread across the group. "Good. Let's do this."

The four of them headed toward the house while

Arista, Evangeline and Daphne stood on the front lawn, close to the cars. Charlie glanced over her shoulder and watched as the three women joined hands and began their invocation. She said a quick prayer to the goddess and hurried her pace to keep up with the others.

CHAPTER 25

Ben led them around to the back door. Megan had placed a ward on the lock but with some help from the other witches, he was able to break it. Once inside the house, the sharp stink of brimstone coated his throat. Jen pinched her nose together and tried to breathe through her mouth. The only one unaffected by the smell was Tom and Ben thought it might've been a limitation of his glamour. Maybe he was unaffected because he just couldn't smell it. Or maybe being a mortician and inhaling the fumes from embalming had burned out any sense of smell he had. If he got a chance, he would ask the reaper.

A low growl rumbled through the house. Ben stopped and raised his eyes to the second floor. She was upstairs and that thing squatting inside her was not going to let her go. Maybe he should just let the reaper go upstairs and put Megan out of her misery. Jen touched his arm. "What do you want to do?"

"It's upstairs," he said.

"Lead the way," Jen said.

Ben continued through the house from memory. When they got to her bedroom the door was closed and Ben expected it to have a ward on it to stop them, just as the back door had. But as they approached, the knob turned and the door creaked open.

Ben didn't like to resort to wand work. He liked his magic to be more organic but even he couldn't deny the wand made an excellent weapon, allowing the user to focus his or her energy in a precise, almost surgical way. Charlie moved in close to him, holding her wand in front of her. Ben held his wand, a long slender piece of ebony with a silver handle encrusted with clear quartz. He squeezed and the cool metal warmed at his touch. As they approached the room, he heard cooing. A baby. Ben's pulse sped up. The baby that Megan had kidnapped was still alive. Ben stepped through the doorway and his heart lurched into his throat.

Megan sat in a rocking chair near one of the windows holding the ten-month-old infant in her arms. The child suckled at her breast. She had no children, had no milk offer this child. Then he saw it, a green mist emanating from her breast coating the child's lips.

"Put the baby down," Ben commanded. He pointed his wand at her. Megan didn't look up. She continued feeding the child, stroking the boy's fine blonde hair. Ben's stomach churned. What the hell was she feeding that child? "Stop what you're doing, right now."

Megan laughed, but it wasn't her voice. It was the demon's, deep and gravelly, full of contemptuous mocking. The sound skittered over Ben's arms like fingernails tapping on glass. "There's nothing more natural than breast-feeding Ben," the demon said.

Ben hated that it wore Megan's face. "Whatever it is you think you're giving that kid, it's certainly not the milk of human kindness. You need to stop now."

The demon looked up. Its eyes were completely black with no sign of Megan's green irises. "Who's gonna stop me? You? Or maybe you, Charlie?"

Charlie bristled but held fast her wand. "Get out of my head."

The demon chuckled. "Or what about you, little cute elfin girl, what's your name? Oh right, Jen. Jen and Ben. Ben and Jen. How fucking adorable." The demon taunted. "Do they call you Bennifer behind your back?"

"Shut the hell up," Ben said. He knew better than to let this thing get under his skin, but still he couldn't stop it.

"I'm glad to see your lover's quarrel is over. Did you enjoy your quick little fuck in the back of Ben's truck,

Jen?" Jen blanched. "There's no way you had the big 'O' though. That's assuming that old Ben here even knows how to touch a woman."

"Shut your mouth," Jen said. The tip of her wand glowed blue.

"And you Lisa. Keeping secrets. Keeping secrets," the demon said in a singsong voice that made Ben's skin crawl.

"That's enough. It's time for you to leave now," Lisa said.

"And you…I don't know about you," the demon shifted his gaze to Tom. "You are all darkness and fog." It stared at at Tom. "And you have no wand. What kind of witch doesn't carry a wand?"

"Charlie," Jen said.

"Yep," Charlie took the protection bag in her hand and flung the contents toward the demon. The large grains of salt struck the demon and it cried out, tossing the baby away from it, so that it could swipe at its face.

A stream of blue energy emerged from the tip of Lisa's wand, wrapping around the child and cradling it before it could hit the ground. Lisa pulled back on her wand almost as if it were a fishing rod and the energy grew shorter pulling the child toward her.

"You fucking cunt," the demon growled.

"You have a nasty mouth," Charlie said. "I think it needs to be washed out with some soap."

"I have a nasty mouth," the demon mocked. "What about little Bennifer? Why don't you ask her about her nasty mouth?"

"On my mark," Jen said.

"On my mark," the demon continued to taunt her. "How did it feel to have that tight little vagina wrapped around your cock, this morning Ben?"

"Shut your fucking mouth," Ben growled and slipped the pendant from around his neck and held it in his hands.

"Do it Jen," he said.

Jen began to chant.

DEMON HEAD, DEMON HEART,
I command you.
I cast you out of this body.
Leave this realm. Go home.
To the netherworld where you belong.
Demon head, demon heart,
Leave this realm. Go home.
To the netherworld where you belong.

LISA GRABBED THE BABY AND PUT IT BEHIND HER, STANDING firmly in front of it him. She joined the chant. All four of their wands emitted streams of light that joined together into one bright yellow beam. It wrapped around Megan's body, encircling her, trapping her. Her arms rose into the air and all the dresser drawers opened. Megan's clothing began to fly around the room striking the three witches.

Tom stood perfectly still, the clothing not coming close to him. The demon raised its hand and the mattress lifted into the air. It thrust its arms forward and the mattress flew toward them. Ben dove to the floor, tackling Jen to the ground. Lisa grabbed the baby and jumped out of the way and Tom stepped in front of Charlie and put his hands out. The mattress stopped as if it had hit a wall and fell backward onto the floor. The demon let out a guttural cry. "What are you?"

"You know. Deep inside. You know what I am and what I'm here to do," Tom said.

A strangled scream ushered from Megan's mouth. And she charged forward at Tom. Tom metamorphosed, his glamour melting away, revealing his true identity. The demon stopped in its tracks.

"Now," Ben said. The witches recovered. Pointing their wands at the demon, joining their energy together again. The bright cleansing yellow like the sun wrapped around Megan's body. Binding her in place.

"Demon head demon heart –" the witches began to chant. The demon struggled against the magic but the witches held fast. "I cast you out of this body..."

Tom raised his scythe into the air and plunged it into Megan's heart.

"No!" Ben screamed. Megan fell onto the ground and what was left clinging to the end of Tom's scythe was the pale gray creature with purple veins and black eyes. Tom didn't say another word before he disappeared dragging the demon with him.

Ben scrambled over to Megan's still body and touched his finger to her throat. Her pulse, weak and thready, beat through her skin.

"Call 911," Ben said. "She still alive."

CHAPTER 26

Charlie picked up Evan early on Sunday morning. It had been a crazy forty-eight hours and she was glad to be back to some sort of normalcy. Well if you could call getting ready for a hurricane normal. Scott seemed glad she was taking Evan with her for a change. He was going to be on call at the hospital because two of his patients were due to go into labor. Once the storm got close enough, it would be too hard to make it to the hospital, so he was going to sleep there until the storm passed and help out where he could. She had to admit that at his core, Scott Carver was a good man. A hard man. A controlling man sometimes. But a good man.

As for the demon encounter, she was glad to have it behind her. They had taken Megan to the hospital and she was holding on by a thread, but the doctors didn't seem hopeful that she was going to come out of her coma.

The most exciting thing was that Ben had come home with them. And Jen had not stopped glowing since he'd gotten home. They had all gotten up bright and early this morning. Evangeline, Daphne, Ben, and Jen and had gone to board up their businesses.

The storm was set to hit in earnest overnight. Dark grey clouds had already moved in and there had been sprinkles of rain, reminders of what was to come.

Charlie wondered about Vanessa. Was she still standing on that beach waiting for her lover to return? Some part of her felt that they had escaped the ghost's curse and she was glad for it. Maybe when it was all said and done she would take Tom down to the beach and they would find Vanessa and give her the option to be reunited with her lover on the other side.

Charlie pulled a loaf of bread from the pantry and took out eight slices of bread, a package of sliced ham, a jar of mayonnaise, the small bottle of mustard and a jar of pickles. She slathered mustard on each slice of the bread, adding mustard for Evan to one of them, then layered on the ham. When she finished, she cut the sandwiches into triangles and placed them on a platter with several pickles.

It was nearly 1:30 in the afternoon. Since Evan arrived,

Jack had had the boy and Ruby out following him around helping him prepare for the storm to come. They took all the furniture off of the back porch and carried it down to Jack's storage shed. Jack had showed the children how to secure the chicken coop, making sure the girls could get into the small run beneath the roost but not into the larger yard. The last thing they wanted was for the girls to escape and be lost in the wind. Charlie didn't need any more ghost chickens, thank you very much. One was enough.

She'd watched from the back porch as Jack and Evan closed the shutters on Charlie's little cottage and locked them into place to protect the windows. It was one of the features that she loved about the place.

Charlie's phone buzzed on the counter and she picked it up and quickly read the text from her cousin, Lisa.

Jason has to work. He's gonna drop Cameron off to stay with us during the storm. Then he's on duty until the storm is over, I guess.

Charlie let out a little growl. Why wasn't Cameron going home? Their case was closed. Charlie jotted off her reply.

Fine.

I'm gonna pack some clothes, get Butterbean in his carrier and I should be over there shortly. Jason is going to drop off Watson (his cat).

Charlie chuckled. She knew who Watson was.

Okay. I'll be here.

Jack's was the place to be during a storm. He had a gasoline generator already set up in case the power went out and he had plenty of fuel, and of course there was food for days. There were also boardgames and decks of cards and books for those who didn't want to play games. And plenty of liquor for the adults if things got too boring.

Charlie glanced at the platter of sandwiches. She sighed.

Do you think they'll need lunch?

Lisa didn't have a chance to answer. Jason's black Dodge Charger rambled up the gravel driveway and parked behind Jack's shiny new red Chevy Silverado.

Jason wore the uniform — tan pants and brown shirt — and Charlie could tell by the thickness of his chest that he had his vest on beneath. Well they all had their talismans. Cameron was unhooking his seatbelt as she took four more slices of bread and quickly made two more sandwiches. She wrapped one of them up in some wax paper. She didn't bother cutting it into triangles. She took a deep breath and headed out onto the back porch. It was time to bury the hatchet. Jason wasn't going anywhere. And although she enjoyed being called on for help by him, not working with him wasn't going to kill her. He was practically family and she had a sneaking suspicion that at some point in the future he would be as much a part of the family as she was.

She raised her hand to wave. Then walked down the steep steps to take him the sandwich.

"Here," she said without acknowledging Cameron. "I made you something. Case you get hungry later."

Jason looked her in the eye for the first time in days and smiled. He took the sandwich and put it on the front seat next to him. "Thank you."

A minute later, he opened the back door and wrangled the cat carrier holding Watson. Charlie heard a low growl. "Don't mind her. She growls at everybody when she's in this carrier. I swear to God she won't bite."

"Do we need to let her out of the carrier?" Charlie asked.

"Lisa said you can just stick her in a bedroom," Jason said. "She said she would set up a litter box. And make sure she gets fed."

"You can stick her in my bedroom," Cameron said, coming in behind Jason.

"Okay," Charlie said. Why was Cameron getting a bedroom?

"Hey," Jack said as he approached. Ruby skipped behind him and Evan came over and wrapped his arm around his mother's waist nestling in close to her. Charlie wrapped her arm around his shoulders.

"Jason, Cameron. How are y'all doing today," Jack said.

"Very good sir," Jason said. "I hear this is the place to be when there's a storm. Wish I could hang around."

"Well you got a job to do. I spent many a night in the hospital with patients when there were storms. Duty call sometimes and you can't ignore it."

"No, sir you can't," Jason said. He handed Watson's carrier to Cameron along with a bag of her food and some litter. "I hate to run off like this but I need to get down to the station."

Jason jumped into his Charger, backed up and turned around.

"Come on Cameron, I'll show you where you can put her," Charlie said. "Uncle Jack, there's sandwiches in the kitchen for y'all."

"Thank you Charlie girl," he said.

Charlie took Cameron upstairs to the yellow book bedroom. "Here you go. You can let her out in here."

"Thanks," he said.

"You know I thought you would've gone back to Columbia by now." She folded her arms across her chest. "Not that I'm complaining. I'm not I promise."

"It's fine. I figured I would stick around for a few days. You know, help out with the manhunt where I could."

"What manhunt?" Charlie asked.

"I thought Lisa would've told you," Cameron said.

"Told me what?" Charlie asked. A sick feeling started

in the base of her belly and wound its way up into her chest.

"Curtis escaped. He killed the deputy and a nurse." Cameron said.

"Oh," Charlie said. He may as well of slapped her. "No, Lisa didn't mention it. I'll let you get settled." Charlie backed out of the room and closed the door behind her.

She was going to give Lisa Holloway a piece of her mind when she finally showed up. She headed back downstairs and made sure everyone had a sandwich. They all sat around the dining table crunching on pickles and drinking iced cold Coke. A special treat because it was a storm day. A few minutes later Cameron came downstairs and joined them. Charlie glanced at the clock.

"What was taken Lisa so long?" she said.

"Could be that cat of hers," Jack said. "He hates to be put the carrier."

"Maybe so," Charlie said. "When y'all are finished Evan and Ruby, take your plates to the kitchen please."

"Yes ma'am," Evan said. "Is there any dessert?"

"I don't know honey, we will have to wait for Jen to get back," Charlie said.

Evan scowled and picked up his plate and took it into the kitchen with Ruby trailing after him.

Charlie's phone buzzed her pocket. "Speak of the devil," she said as she retrieved it and saw Lisa's phone number on the screen. It crossed her mind that it was a strange thing that Lisa was calling instead of texting. But she swiped her thumb across the screen and answered the phone.

"Hey, we were just talking about you," Charlie said. "Where your ears burning?"

"My ears are always burning for you Charlie." The sound of his voice drove a cold stake through her heart.

"Who is this?" Charlie said that, although she already knew. She could picture him. Those ice blue eyes. Maybe Jason was right; maybe he wasn't possessed by a demon. Maybe Gabriel Curtis was every bit a devil.

"We never did finish registering me to vote," he said.

"And we never will," Charlie said. "Because they're going to find you and they're gonna lock you up and their gonna throw away the key."

"Maybe they will. But not before I kill Lisa."

Charlie's ears began to ring. Why had it not occurred to her before? He was calling from Lisa's phone. How would he have that?

"If you touch one hair on her head," Charlie started.

"She's going to make such a beautiful demon," he said. "I can't wait to devour her soul."

Charlie felt Cameron's eyes on her. Watching her face. Watching her body. He shifted from the friendly, almost likable guy sitting at her uncle's table eating lunch with them into FBI mode with the flip of a switch. She met his gaze. Surely her fear was written all over her face.

"Why don't you tell me where you are," she said. "It's not Lisa you want. Not really. It's me."

"That's where you're wrong. I want you both," he said.

"Tell me where you are," she said. "I'll come to you."

He laughed. "I somehow doubt that. I'll tell you what. You find me all by yourself before I kill your cousin and then I'll tell you where I am."

Charlie turned away from the table so she didn't have to look at Cameron and her uncle studying her, listening to her. "I swear to the goddess above if you touch her I will make you wish that you had stayed in hell."

The line went dead. Charlie jumped up from the table and ran to the small half-bath down the hall and regurgitated her lunch. Cameron stood in the door, a panicked look on his face.

"What happened?" he said.

Charlie spit into the toilet closed the cover and flushed. "That was Curtis. He has Lisa."

"What the flock? Are you sure?" he said.

"Yep. He called from her phone. How else would he have that?" she asked.

"I need to call Jason."

"No, don't do that," she said. A heavy downpour of rain drummed on the roof. "He's got enough on his plate with the storm."

"Charlie, don't be ridiculous." Cameron said.

"It's going to have to be you and me," she said. "Do you have your gun with you?"

"What are you talking about?" Cameron asked.

"I am talking about you having a weapon that you can use," she snapped. "Now do you have your gun or not?"

"Of course I do," he snapped.

"Good," she said. "You're going to need it."

Down the hall Charlie heard the back door open and shut and the commotion that came with several people. Jen called to the house. "We're back."

"Oh thank goddess," Charlie said. "Come on, we need to gather everyone together and tell them what's going on."

CHAPTER 27

"Jason will never forgive me if something happens her," Cameron said.

"He'll never forget any of us," Charlie said.

She sped through the rain holding steady to the steering wheel, fighting against the wind.

"Well, I'm sure Jack will never forgive you if you ruin his new truck, Charlie," Ben said from the cushy-looking backseat of the Silverado.

"Believe me, if we don't save his daughter Jack won't give a crap about his truck," Daphne said. Her usual positivity seemed to have taken a vacation. Charlie glanced in the rearview mirror. Jen sat between Daphne and Ben, her face wan and pinched. She didn't say a word.

"It's okay, Jen," Charlie said. "We're going to get her back."

"I know," Jen said, but it sounded rote to Charlie's ears.

"I don't get why you think he's going back to that house," Cameron said. "It's sealed up."

"Yes, I'm sure that yellow tape and that sticker across the door will hold out." Charlie didn't hold back her sarcasm. "He said something to me about registering him to vote, which is the ruse we used to get inside his house. That's why I think he's going there. That and my intuition," Charlie said. "Haven't you ever trusted your gut Cameron?"

"Well, your intuition also said that he was a demon," Cameron muttered and rolled his eyes. He turned his head to look out the window.

"He is a demon," Charlie said. "No matter what you and Jason think." She remembered Curtis's words. He was going to turn her into a demon and eat her soul.

"Just stop. Please," Jen said in a small voice.

Charlie pursed her lips. Why was she doing that? Why was she fighting with Cameron? She knew it would just upset Jen and Jen was upset enough. "I'm sorry Jen."

"Let's just get there and see if he's there," Jen said. Charlie turned her attention back to the road. She had to slow down several times because the rain fell in sheets so thick she couldn't see two feet ahead of her. It made the urgency swell into a balloon, robbing the air around them.

"Did you call Tom?" Ben asked.

"He's gonna meet us there," Charlie said.

"Why are you bringing your boyfriend?" Cameron asked. "He's a mortician, right?"

"Yep," Charlie said, biting back the smart-ass remark she wanted to make. "Among other things." She would not fight with him for Jen's sake.

Finally Charlie saw the orange reflector and turned onto the gravel drive that led to Gabriel Curtis's house. This time she pulled all the way up into the yard, ripping up what little grass there was in the yard. She reached into her messenger bag and pulled out her wand. It'd gotten more use in the last week than it had in months. She was seriously considering making a holster and strapping it to her belt.

"Okay, Harry Potter, what is that going to do?" Cameron asked.

Charlie glared at him. "Well, it can help us take down the demon that's inside Gabriel Curtis and then if Curtis is still alive, it will be up to you to arrest his ass," Charlie said.

"We ready?" Ben tapped her back seat three times.

"Yep, let's do this." Charlie said.

They all filed out of the truck and ran to the front porch, but couldn't avoid being drenched by the sideways-blowing rain. The wind whipped around them fiercely. Debris of paper and pieces of tree branches sailed through the air. The old tire that had leaned against the tree now lay on its side.

The front door was wide open when they stepped under the cover of the porch.

"Told you," Charlie said. "He's waiting for us."

"He's probably prepared, too," Ben said. "Wands up."

Jen stepped forward and handed a small linen bag strung on a long piece of jute to Cameron. "Put this on."

"Why?" Cameron said.

"Just humor me," Jen said.

Cameron's lips twisted with a grimace but he didn't argue. He slipped it over his head and unholstered his weapon. "Okay, I'm going to clear the house. Why don't you wait here until I tell you to come in?"

"Screw that," Daphne said.

"Get behind us, Cameron," Charlie said.

Charlie and Jen took the lead into the house.

The air felt heavy and oppressive, making it hard to breathe. Even Cameron noticed. He gulped in air.

"Okay," Charlie said, calling to the house. "You wanted me here. So here I am. Show yourself."

She heard footsteps shuffle across the floor upstairs. Charlie was on the steps taking them two at a time before anyone could stop her. When she got to the second floor landing Gabriel Curtis was waiting across the long hallway in the doorway of a bedroom.

"Charlie, no!" Lisa screamed. "Get out of here!"

All the doors in the hall opened and slammed shut several times. Gabriel stepped back, slamming the door behind him. Jen let out a growl of frustration and charged at the door. She jiggled the handle and beat her fist against the wood.

"It's locked!" she screamed. "Lisa! Lisa!"

A bloodcurdling scream echoed behind the door, and Jen became very still for just a moment.

"Ben?" Charlie said.

He pointed his wand at the door. A white electric energy zapped it, and Charlie jiggled the handle again it. Still locked.

Cameron sighed. "Stand back," he said. He lifted his foot and kicked the door in. The frame splintered, and the door flew back, hitting the wall with a loud bang. He held his gun up and entered the room.

"Gabriel Curtis, put your hands on your head."

Curtis turned around. A leer smeared across his lips. His eyes were completely black.

Cameron took a step back, visibly shaken. "What the hell?"

"Witches, three, two, one." Ben held his wand up and took aim, but Jen fired first. Her hand shook a little as she did, making the stream of energy unsteady. Curtis jumped behind Lisa, who was strapped down to a chair in the center of the room. A pair of metal wings hung on the back of the chair, making Lisa look almost like Bethany McCabe.

Jen took aim again, this time more confident in her stance. The other witches fired as well, joining their streams together until they merged into a yellow beam of light that encircled Gabriel's body, holding him captive.

"Demon heart, demon head..." Daphne began the chant. The witches joined in. "I cast you out of this body. Leave this realm. Go home. To the netherworld where you belong."

Gabriel began to scream. Thunder boomed overhead. The light flickered and the power went off.

"Hold him steady," Ben said.

"Where's Tom?" Jen asked.

"I don't know," Charlie said.

"Demon heart, demon head ..." Daphne continued chanting.

Curtis and the demon start to separate. His head shook in all directions. The skin of his face stretched in unnatural ways and his head looked as if it might explode.

For just a brief second, Curtis fought off the energy of the witches holding him captive. He broke free and raised the knife above Lisa's head. Charlie did not hesitate. She charged him, grabbing his wrist, fighting with him to keep it from stabbing her cousin. He shook her off and plunged the knife into her upper arm. A shot rang out, and the world around her fell into muffled chaos.

Tom appeared, and cut his scythe into Gabriel's chest. He plucked the demon from its human shell and Gabriel Curtis crumpled to the ground.

Charlie's legs went out from under her. An icy cold breeze overwhelmed her whole body and her teeth chattered. The voices sounded far away. The last face she saw was Cameron's. Telling her to hold on. Why did he seem so mad?

The world began to gray at the edges and Charlie closed her eyes, succumbing to the feeling of falling.

"Charlie girl?" Bunny said.

Charlie felt herself get up from her body and go over to her grandmother who was standing on the sidelines watching the commotion.

"Bunny what are you doing here?"

"I told you I was going to hang around a little bit."

Charlie looked down at her body. It was the strangest thing to see herself lying there so still. Cameron was tying his belt around her arm trying to stop the bleeding.

"It's not your time, honey," Bunny said.

Charlie felt a warm light at her back. All she wanted to do was sink into that warmth.

"I don't want to go back, Bunny. It's cold there." Charlie said.

"I know honey. But it's not your time. There's still too

much for you to do. And Evan needs you."

Of course he did. Evan needed her. What was she thinking?

"What do I do?" Charlie asked.

"Well the first thing, you gotta get back in your body. It's sort of like falling off a wall. You can do that. Can't you?"

Charlie nodded her head and walked around to her feet and fell forward. Her eyes flew open.

"I'm okay," she said.

"No, you're not," Cameron said. "You idiot. What the hell were you thinking?"

"Cameron, just stop it," Jen snapped. "We need to get you to the hospital, honey."

"No," Ben said. Let's take her back to your dad's. Evangeline and I will heal her."

"You all are the craziest bunch of people I have ever met in my life," Cameron said throwing his hands up in the air. "I should arrest you all for negligence."

"Yeah, whatever floats your boat, buddy," Ben said. "Charlie can you walk?"

"I don't know," she said.

"Okay." Ben scooped her up in his arms and carried her downstairs. Charlie looked over his shoulder and saw Jen and Daphne untying Lisa from the chair. Once they freed her, she threw her arms around them and sank into them with Gabriel Curtis' dead stare fixed on them.

CHAPTER 28

Charlie sat on her couch with her feet propped up on the trunk she used as a coffee table. Ben had done a good job healing her arm but it had gotten her out of the after-storm cleanup of her uncle's property, and she was enjoying the attention that Tom was giving her. He walked in to her tiny living room and handed her a cup of tea.

"Thank you," she said. She brought the warm drink up to her nose and inhaled the scent of peppermint.

Tom, I've been thinking about something," Charlie said.

Tom took a seat next to her on the couch. "All right, tell me."

"I think we should make a trip to the beach."

"Why?" Tom asked. "To look for her?"

"I feel like we should. I'm thinking she would come to me if I stood there long enough," she said.

"She's really William's catch," Tom said. "And do you really want to court another storm so soon?"

"So you don't want to go?" Charlie said.

"It's not that I don't want to catch her. But she's been a legend for so long. Taking her now would be almost like taking a piece of history away from the place," Tom said.

"Yes, but if we take her then she can't curse anyone else," Charlie said.

"Do you really feel that she cursed you?" Tom asked.

Charlie thought over the events of the last couple of weeks. She wasn't sure exactly what she thought. But cursed did keep popping up in her head.

"Maybe," Charlie said.

"You know what I think?" Tom said.

"What?" she said, taking a sip of her tea.

"I don't think a ghost can cast a curse. A very wise witch told me that once," Tom said.

"Did she now?" Charlie said, a grin spreading across her face.

"Uh huh," Tom said as he leaned in and brushed his lips across hers. "You taste like peppermint. My favorite."

"Mine too," she said.

The End

AUTHOR NOTES

Thank you for reading. If you loved this book you can order the next in series, or get information on the release here by joining my readers list: http://eepurl.com/czMPg1

By signing up you'll get a free deleted scene from this book and you'll be the first to know about major updates and new releases.

If you enjoyed this book, please give it a rating on Amazon. Your kind words and encouragement can make an author's day (ask me how I know – smile). Of course, I'll keep writing whether you give me an Outstanding review or not, but it might get done faster with your cheerleading (smile).

Want to comment on your favorite scene? Or make suggestions for a funny ghostly encounter for Charlie? Or

AUTHOR NOTES

tell me what sort of magic you'd like to see Jen, Daphne and Lisa perform? Or take part in naming the killers/ghosts for my future books? Come tell me on Facebook.

Facebook: https://www.facebook.com/wendywangauthor or let's talk about our favorite books in my readers group on Facebook;

Readers Group: https://www.facebook.com/groups/1287348628022940/ ; or you can always drop me an email,

Email: http://www.wendywangbooks.com/contact.html

Thank you again for reading!

Check out my other books:

Witches of Palmetto Point Series (Supernatural Suspense)
    Book 1: Haunting Charlie
    Book 2: Wayward Spirits
    Book 3: Devil's Snare
    Book 4: The Witch's Ladder

The Book of Kaels Series (Fantasy)
    Book 1: The Last Queen

AUTHOR NOTES

Book 2: The Wood Kael
Book 3: The Metal Kael
Book 4: The Fire Kael
Book of Kaels Box Set: Books 1-4
Short Stories: Love Lacey